Haunting Magic

by

Neely Powell

The Witches of New Mourne Series

Haunting Magic

Cover Art by *Debbie Taylor*

The Wild Rose Press, Inc.
PO Box 708
Adams Basin, NY 14410-0708
Visit us at www.thewildrosepress.com

Publishing History
First Black Rose Edition, 2017
Print ISBN 978-1-5092-1669-7
Digital ISBN 978-1-5092-1670-3

The Witches of New Mourne Series
Published in the United States of America

Overgrown weeds covered the back of cemetery. In the deepening gloom, Fiona stumbled over a stump.

Bailey grabbed her arm, pulling her up before she hit the ground. "Are you sure we should go on?"

The baby's screams filled Fiona's head. She had to help this child. She plunged forward.

The grave markers in the back of the cemetery were the oldest ones. Some of them were so weathered it was impossible to read the names and dates on them. When they reached the back corner, Celia stopped and pointed to a pile of stones, moss, and snarling weeds.

Fiona knelt. All she could hear was the baby's cry.

She dug through the weeds and scruff in front of her, ignoring the sting of thorns on her hands. Bailey dug with her, and soon she touched the cool stone of a broken grave marker. They pushed the weeds, dirt and twisted vine away, and letters became legible on the marker.

Fiona scrubbed off the dirt. "Baby MacCuindliss" was carved in uneven letters deep in the stone.

"It's her baby," Celia said.

"Are you sure?"

The spirit nodded.

Bailey drew in a deep breath beside her. "What does this mean?"

"This is the Woman in White's baby." Fiona dropped to her knees and traced the name on the marker with tender fingers. "Please don't cry," she whispered. "I'll try to find your mother, I promise."

The baby's cry faded to a whimper. Celia disappeared. The mist blew away, leaving Fiona and Bailey under a canopy of threatening clouds.

Praise for Neely Powell

"The power of magic, the strength of family and the battle of good versus evil—Neely Powell's fast-paced stories satisfy on every level."

~Erica Spindler, New York Times bestselling author of
The Lightkeepers series

~*~

"Neely Powell never fails to thrill readers with nonstop supernatural excitement and dark romance."

~Greg Wilkey, award-winning YA author of the
Mortimer Drake and Edgar Flax supernatural series

~*~

"The writing team of Neely Powell has the perfect magical touch in blending paranormal seamlessly with adventure."

~Terrie Farley Moran, multi-nominated, award winning author of the Read 'Em and Eat mystery series

Dedications

For our unexpected but much-loved blessing,
Natalie Grace Blankenship.
~Jan Hamilton Powell

~*~

With love and appreciation to my dear friends
in the New York/Tri-State Chapter
of Sisters in Crime.
Special thanks to two great New Jersey friends,
Candice May and the late Joan Tuohy.
Your encouragement and friendship
will never be forgotten.
~Leigh Neely

Chapter 1

Fiona Burns crested the final hill on Devil's Creek Road, ready for the last leg of her morning run. Then she slid to a halt and almost fell. *What the—*?

Beech Chapel cemetery had live guests on this muggy morning. One black crow sat atop each tombstone. Other crows blanketed the graves. Feathers ruffled and heads turned, but no caw sounded in the sea of black.

The land around the graveyard stood just as it always did—a barren, silent gash in the world. No birds or other animals ever gathered here. Always ominous, these surroundings now emanated evil. What wicked portent was this?

She waited for the rotten egg scent of sulfur or a geyser of fire from the ground—the calling cards of the demon who plagued her family coven. Nothing happened.

No spirits spoke to her, either, a great relief. Despite popular notions, ghosts don't hang around graveyards often, preferring to haunt the places where they had lived or died. This cemetery was an oasis on her daily three-mile run, a dead zone that was a rare place of peace from the spirits that continuously looked to her for help.

A disturbance overhead drew her attention. The graveyard's one tall, gnarled tree, its branches spread like the hands of time, was also filled with crows.

A murder of crows.

All of them staring at her with eyes black as evil.

"Holy Alfred Hitchcock."

Fiona jumped and turned. An unfamiliar man stood a few yards away. She hadn't heard him or his black, late-model Mustang. Not even the birds had signaled his approach. The crows still stood at attention upon the graves and the tree limbs, though their movements increased.

The man lifted his cell phone. "I wish I had a better camera, but this will have to do. Wow."

Fiona knew his camera would be useless. Her coven's blanketing Remember-Not spell zapped the memories and destroyed the recordings of outsiders who witnessed supernatural events in New Mourne. The protective wards should take care of anything this handsome young man's phone captured, but just in case, she silently chanted a blocking spell.

He frowned, his fingers working the buttons on his phone. "What's wrong with this thing?"

"It's the mountains," she lied, looking back at the birds that had suddenly gone still.

"Huh?"

"The mountains tend to interfere with technology."

"Maybe that's why my car died, too."

"Maybe." She suppressed a grin. The coven's spells were working well. No outsiders were allowed farther along Devil's Creek Road.

He stepped forward, ocean-blue eyes studying the birds. Fiona noted his even features and close-cropped, tawny hair. Crisp khaki shorts and a white shirt clung on his tall, muscular build in a way that only expensive clothes fit. His broad gold wristwatch and leather sandals would probably pay her rent for a year. Only the jagged edge of a tattoo peeking out from under his sleeve seemed out of place.

And that imperfection intrigued her most of all.

"This is the most amazing thing I've ever seen." His voice was low as he nodded again to the birds. "Are you controlling them?"

Why would he think she had that kind of power?

"You are Fiona Burns, aren't you?"

Her wariness intensified. When the demon came to town a few weeks ago, he had knocked on her cousin Maggie's door and presented himself as a handsome, articulate man. Was he in a new guise this time, complete with designer shades on top of his head?

"How do you know my name?"

"You do a webcast."

Fiona made her living as a medium and supplemented that income with an internet show about her discussions with the dead called "Spirit Talks."

"I've been trying to find you for more than a week," he continued.

Fiona had a vague memory of some messages from someone she didn't know. But she and her sister witches had been busy dealing with a demon and the family curse that could soon claim one of their lives. She hadn't bothered to return the calls.

A crow squawked. Fiona and the stranger turned as chaos erupted and the crows took off in a whirl of wings and caws that echoed through the valley.

The black-feathered bodies shot through the gray morning air. They flew toward the mist at the top of the mountains, a place that Cherokee legend claimed was guarded by a dragon.

Were the birds sending a message? A shiver chased down Fiona's spine.

"That was impressive," her visitor said. "If we'd caught that with cameras, it would make an amazing opening for your show."

Now Fiona felt very uncomfortable. Maybe he wasn't the demon, but this was not just some fan of her webcast who had tracked her down.

He held out his hand. "I'm Bailey Powers, from Powers That Be, a TV production company. We'd like to make you a star." The flashing white smile made no apology for the trite line.

She ignored his hand, aware she was being rude but not really caring. He reminded Fiona of the snakeoil salesmen she'd seen in the classic movies she loved.

"How about I take you out to breakfast at the diner and we discuss some business?" He flashed his megawatt smile at her again.

"How did you find me?"

"A very nice waitress at the diner named Misty told me you run out here every morning."

Fiona knew Misty, and she probably also gave him an invitation to get better acquainted.

"I have other things I need to do right now." Fiona turned back down the road. She didn't want any part of this man.

"What could be more important than making you one of the top mediums in the country?"

"I don't need—or want—that, either." *She didn't, did she?*

"You're kidding," he said as he followed her. "Everybody wants to be famous."

Fiona stopped and studied him, surprised at what she saw now. Her dead zone had been breached.

He stopped, smile dimming. "What is it? What's wrong?"

"I don't want to be famous, and I'm not interested in your offer, but I'll talk to you because I'm interested in your ghost."

"My what?"

"Your ghost. She's right behind you."

Chapter 2

Bailey watched Fiona jog away, intrigued in a way that was out of character for his skeptical nature. He had just asked to talk with her about a TV show, and she wasn't jumping for joy. She said she wanted to finish her run and would meet him at her office in about forty-five minutes. She was calling all the shots.

What was wrong with that picture?

He looked at the now-empty graveyard, gloomy under the day's gray clouds. No sign of the birds. Were they controlled by some kind of radio frequency? But why? Had the feisty Ms. Burns known he was coming and done that to impress him?

It wouldn't be the first time someone used tricks to be considered for a show. Even her reluctance could be part of the ruse.

Despite her protests, he imagined she knew who he was. He had left numerous messages for her, stopped by her locked office and left a note, and asked around town for her. She could be playing hard to get.

He watched her run up the hill. She looked good in her shorts and tank top, slim but muscular. She didn't look back.

He wasn't used to indifference. To his surprise, he found it sexy.

Suddenly impatient, he turned and only then remembered his car had stopped. "Wait a minute," he called after Fiona.

She kept running. Behind him, his car roared to life.

"What the hell?" He hurried to the Mustang. The remote starter was on the seat where he had left it. Maybe Fiona was right about the mountains' effect on technology. "I'm getting outta here."

At the top of hill he expected to see Fiona running on the road ahead. But she had vanished.

He was being played. Even her comment about his ghost was part of it. Fiona said "she" was right behind him. The back of his neck prickled, and he glanced in the rearview mirror. No one was there, of course. If Fiona was like any of the mediums he knew, this was just part of her act. She probably told everyone there was a ghost following them.

"But she made me look. I wonder how that will play to the camera." From what he had seen of ghost hunters on television, getting viewers to believe they might see something was half the battle.

He drove back to New Mourne, Georgia, and studied the small roads that trailed off into the woods. Fiona was nowhere to be seen. What in the hell was he doing here? Everyone but him thought his family's production company needed a paranormal show in their lineup. So why was he the one out on the backroads of Georgia looking for a supposed medium who did an obscure webcast that caught his mother's eye?

He'd seen her little program. She had definite appeal. In person, she was a combination of innocence and earthiness—very appealing. It had been a long time since he'd felt such attraction so quickly. Maybe Fiona had a love spell going, too. He should have laughed, but he didn't find the thought funny.

His mother or father should be here. They knew he wanted no part of this nonsense. What his family had been through since his sister Anna died should have made them all skeptics. Bailey would never understand how his parents retained their belief and interest in those who said they could talk to the dead.

In town, Bailey parked in front of the tiny storefront with "F. Burns, Paranormal Investigations" on a placard by the door. Down the street was the diner, a small boutique, a hardware store with toilets displayed out front, and a shop called Siren's Call. Britta's Bakery was in the other direction, and its heavenly aromas drew him forward.

He walked out with a Cafe Cubano, a black coffee and a box of pastries.

The door to Fiona's office opened, and she stepped out. She wore jeans and a vintage T-shirt. Her face was free of makeup, but her green eyes sparkled under dark, spiky lashes. Her straight hair was cut in an angle toward her chin, and Bailey saw streaks of auburn among the dark strands. She smelled like a field of wildflowers—sweet and clean. He could get lost in that scent. And thinking about that wasn't how he should start a meeting.

Fiona took the white box and held the door open and welcomed him inside. "I see you found our famous bakery."

Bailey looked around as he set the coffees on a desk. The office was utilitarian with a couple of chairs and a love seat—some photographs of the mountains on the white walls, and the same aroma of flowers that clung to Fiona.

Through an open door he spied computer equipment. Perhaps that was a studio where Fiona generated the special effects he had seen on her webcast. He knew all about the tricks that could be created with computers and green screens.

He put creamers and sugar packets on the desk. "I wasn't sure how you took your coffee. Or what pastry you might prefer." He frowned at the array of goodies revealed as Fiona opened the box. "I didn't realize I bought so many."

"Bitta is pure magic in the kitchen. You just can't help yourself."

Fiona sat behind the desk, used three of the creamers in her coffee, and selected a cinnamon roll from the bag.

Bailey sat in the chair beside the desk and took a cheese Danish. He closed his eyes in bliss when he bit in, then grinned sheepishly when he looked up and into Fiona's knowing gaze.

"Told you," she said. "Magic food. It's a New Mourne specialty."

He waited for her to say something about his ghost again. When his sister Anna was murdered fifteen years ago, Bailey was told by several so-called mediums that her spirit was trying to contact him. She never had.

But as always, thinking about it made the lightning bolt tattoo on his arm prickle.

He was relieved when Fiona didn't mention the ghost again. It was clever of her not to lay the supernatural crap on too thick.

Before they could begin their discussion, the cell phone on the desk chirped. "This is my cousin," Fiona said. "I need to take it." She pressed a button and answered, "Hey, Eva Grace."

She waited, concern knotting her features. "She's not back yet? Okay, I'll come by tonight and see if I can connect with her."

"Something wrong?" he asked when she hung up.

Fiona leaned back in her chair. "So you know what I do, right?"

"I told you I've seen your webcast. My parents are big fans."

"Parents?"

"Dean and Beth Powers." He was sure she was only pretending not to know all of this, but Bailey explained that his parents had started the production company where he was now a partner. The Powers had initial success with a couple of sitcoms that hit big in the 1990s, but in the past ten years they had produced a string of popular reality shows. Bailey was in charge of scouting new shows.

"As I said in the messages I've left you, that's why I'm here."

"I haven't been keeping up with my messages too well. There have been some family concerns."

"Something to do with that phone call?"

"Sort of." She hesitated, and then seemed to make up her mind. "I'm going to be ghost hunting tonight. A spirit has disappeared from my cousin's shop, and we need to find her. Do you want to come along?"

He suppressed a grin. She was finally revealing her interest in what he had to offer.

"No cameras," she added.

He frowned. "But you'll no doubt tape it."

"That's different."

Because she could control it, Bailey thought. And

make it look exactly as she pleased in the editing process. He wasn't sure why he was disappointed. Mediums, psychics and the like were just tricksters, strictly for profit. If Fiona was clever enough, however, he might be able to turn it into a convincing show. Maybe that's what she intended to show him tonight.

The door opened just as Bailey asked for details about the evening's activities. A young man came in, and Fiona quickly got up to help him bring in some tripods and a couple of metal cases. Bailey went over to help as well, and watched as the two embraced. He wondered about their relationship. And wondered even more why it bothered him.

With her arm still around the guy's waist, Fiona said, "This is my videographer, Ryan Lynch. He's been in Atlanta working on a documentary about Atlanta's ground-breaking mayors."

Recognition sparked in Ryan's gaze. "You're a TV producer." He held out his hand. "Man, I really like some of the work your company does. The camera work on 'Viper Wars' is incredible."

Fiona gave Ryan a questioning look.

"I've told you about that show," Ryan told her. "Snake wranglers in Texas." He turned back to Bailey. "I'm so happy to meet you. What brings you to our magic hamlet?"

Bailey sensed an ally. "I'm interested in Fiona's webcast. How long have you been working with her?"

"Since the beginning. She knew I was interested in videography, and I knew she had an idea worth pursuing." Ryan warmed to the topic. "We celebrate our third year in a couple of months. What I like is that it's more than a ghost hunt. We help people understand the haunting. Sometimes we connect the living with the dead and get resolution." He looked sheepish. "Of course you know all that if you've seen what we do, but I'm proud of it."

"As you should be," Bailey said. He gestured toward the other chair in front of the desk. "Why don't you join us for the discussion?"

Ryan smiled at Fiona, who glared at him. Silent communication passed between the two. Fiona obviously won, as Ryan backed off. "Sorry, I haven't even been home yet. I'll leave the details to you and Fi, and get an update this afternoon." He gave Fiona a peck on the cheek and left.

Fiona turned to glare at Bailey. "Don't do that."

"What?" he asked in surprise.

"Don't go all slick and smiley and try to get me to do what you want. Don't try to get Ryan to go along with you. We're not gullible local yokels, suckers for the big-time producer."

"If you're not interested, why did you invite me to join you tonight?" Bailey asked as he wiped his hands with a napkin.

"To tell you the truth, I'm not sure why I'm even talking to you."

"Don't give me that. Why would you put yourself out on the web if you didn't want attention for what you do? I'm just offering you the possibility of a bigger audience."

The muscles in her throat worked. "You need to understand. My family…" Her voice trailed off.

"What?" Bailey prompted. "Does your family not like what you do?"

"They don't like the attention."

Bailey smelled family drama, which in reality TV could only mean ratings and revenue. "I'd like to meet them."

She glared at him again. "You can't charm my family, or me. Don't even try."

Bailey bit back a glib retort. He was curious about why she needed to pretend to be noble and conflicted about his interest, but he would see how this played out.

He held out his hand. "I'm sorry if I've offended you. Can I sit down and talk straight with you?"

She stood by the door for a few seconds, then closed it and returned to her desk. Very businesslike, she sat down and folded her hands in front of her. "Tell me how things work with your company. What could you do for me?"

Bailey took his chair again and began to explain.

Chapter 3

"Sarah will do something awful when she finds out about this producer." The green eyes of Fiona's sister, Brenna, flashed in anger.

Their cousin, Eva Grace Connelly, made a soft sound of agreement. "This could be serious."

The three of them were in the back of Siren's Call, Eva Grace's shop. Slender, with long red hair and the green eyes of all the Connelly witches, Eva Grace practiced the art of healing as well witchcraft. Voluptuous and auburn-haired, Brenna was an elemental powerhouse, able to command the forces of nature for magical purposes.

While the three witches talked, Ryan was doing a walk-through, setting up tape recorders and cameras in preparation for Fiona's attempt to contact the shop's missing ghost. Ghost hunting ate up calories, and Fiona was fueling for this session with chocolate truffles.

She knew her sister and cousin were right to be concerned about Bailey Powers joining them. Their grandmother, Sarah, was the coven leader, and she tolerated Fiona's webcast only because it focused on Fiona's abilities as a medium, not a witch. Fiona helped people in New Mourne with hauntings and ghosts, but the webcast featured only her cases elsewhere.

Brenna reached into the bag for a truffle. "Inviting him here is like telling him about the curse and the demon."

Fiona protested. "Even if he hears about the curse, what human is going to believe our ancestors bargained for survival with a spirit called the Woman in White when they arrived here from Ireland?"

"Think how appealing the Woman in White's story would be on a ghost hunting show," Brenna pointed out. "Imagine the reenactment. More than two hundred years ago, a young missionary's daughter falls in love with a Cherokee brave and has his child. The brave and the child disappear, and the young woman leaps to her death over Mulligan Falls. She becomes the Woman in White."

"And for some reason she decides to torture our family," Eva Grace added. "She and her demon."

"We've made payment to her every generation," Brenna said. "One young witch has died every twenty to thirty years. Many here in New Mourne know these deaths were tributes, not natural deaths. They know that Eva Grace's mother was taken." She reached for her cousin's hand, then turned back to Fiona. "Our neighbors have dealt with the havoc the demon causes when she's coming for one of us."

Fiona laughed. "Do you think anyone's going to get that story out of Willow, the head of our fae? Or the alpha of the local werewolves? The Druid who sits on the commission? Even if anyone talks, the Remember-Not Spell protects us."

"This is still a terrible idea," Brenna grumbled, reaching for another truffle.

Eva Grace gently pushed her hand away from the candy. There were only a few left, and she knew Fiona needed them more than Brenna did. "How do we explain why we're looking for Minnie tonight? Her disappearance is tied to the demon."

Minnie was the shop's ghost and had been part of this house in life and in death for nearly one hundred and fifty years. She hadn't been seen for weeks, not since the demon killed an employee and almost did away with one of the elder coven members on the premises.

"We don't need that producer here tonight," Brenna reiterated.

Eva Grace agreed. "Don't we have enough trouble without introducing outside interest?"

The steady witch inside Fiona agreed. She had been trained by Sarah to be cautious, to think carefully. More and more often, however, she wanted to follow the part of her descended from ancient Irish witches who had fought to defend their homes and families against the blackest magic.

"You're right that everything is very unsettled," she agreed. She took a deep breath and told them about her encounter with the crows this morning.

"By the Goddess," Eva Grace murmured, looking horrified. "You should have told us sooner. This could be signal that the Woman's pursuit of us is beginning again."

"And the producer saw all this?" Brenna demanded. "That's even more reason why he shouldn't be here tonight."

"Of course he recorded nothing, and he'll not remember it when he leaves," Fiona said. "Anyone he tells about events here will also forget them."

Anger crackled the air around Brenna. "You'll endanger us if he sees anything more."

"I don't care." Fiona was surprised to realize how much she meant those words. "I know that we're still in danger. But I can't sit around waiting to be tortured by the demon and taken as tribute by the Woman.

"Aren't you moving ahead with your life?" she demanded of Brenna. "What about your plans with Jake?" Jake was the county sheriff and Brenna's fiancé. "You've stood up to Sarah so often. Why are you trying to hold me back?"

Brenna looked uncomfortable.

Eva Grace's expression was thoughtful. "What's this producer like?"

Fiona shrugged. "California. Designer clothes, perfectly groomed hair."

Her sister studied her for a long moment. "You like him," Brenna said.

Fiona rolled her eyes. "Don't be stupid. We're not in grade school."

"You've never done foolish things over a man," Eva Grace said.

"He's not a man. I mean, he's a man, not a supernatural, but that's not why I'm interested. I just want to think about what he's offering. The reality show would be an extension of my webcast."

Brenna visibly struggled with her temper. "It wouldn't be that simple."

Frustrated, Fiona blew out a breath. "Brenna, you brought Jake in on the family secrets."

"Jake is part of the community and a shape shifter," Brenna pointed out. "We all have friends who know, like Ryan knows everything."

"Garth told Jake we were witches." Sadness deepened Eva Grace's voice. Garth had been her fiancé, also a shifter. He brought Jake to New Mourne after they served together in the military. Garth had been killed by the demon just a month ago, the day before the wedding that never happened.

It wasn't fair, Fiona thought. First the Woman in White took Eva Grace's mother, and then the love of her life. "Okay, I know Jake had to know about the curse because of the way Garth died and the trouble the demon brought to the town."

"I'm glad you can see how that's different from a television producer," Brenna muttered.

"How would a TV show be any different than the books about witchcraft and legends that our parents have written?" Fiona asked her.

Brenna made a dismissive gesture. "Academic studies are very different from reality TV. Our father was a well-known scholar of magic before he ever married Mother. It's not as if they travel the world doing a magic act."

"But what about this shop?" Fiona asked Eva Grace. "You sell potions and crystals and all things magical, and you do business all over the world through the website. If Sarah is okay with that, why can't I expand my horizons a little?"

"Because no one aside from the locals takes the magical aspect of the shop seriously," Eva Grace replied. "Tourists see it as fun."

"But some of them come here because they've heard about New Mourne's reputation for the supernatural," Fiona protested.

"And there'll be more of that sort of thing if you go on television. We'll be overrun." Brenna shook her head.

"Overrun with what?" Jake walked across the shop from the back door, tall and lean in his khaki uniform. He stepped up behind Brenna and laid his hands on her shoulders.

"Fiona's talking to a producer about doing a reality TV show," Brenna told him. "He's coming here tonight."

Jake looked concerned. "Shouldn't I check him out first?"

Fiona gave him a hard look. "I'm not careless. I checked him out myself this afternoon. He's exactly who he says he is."

Jake began, "Sarah will—"

"I know that, thank you very much," Fiona said. "That's why no one should tell her."

The bell over the front door jangled. "Hello?" a female voice called. "Where is everybody?"

Fiona wheeled on Brenna and Eva Grace and whispered, "What in the hell is Mother doing here?" The guilty look on her cousin's face revealed who had tattled about tonight's session.

"Hello?" a male voice asked.

Fiona groaned and rolled her eyes. Her father was here as well.

"Hi, everybody," said Delia Connelly Burns as she came around a display and toward the counter. She looked beautiful, as always, impeccably dressed in tailored slacks and a soft peach blouse, every fiery red hair in place. Twin to Eva Grace's mother, Delia resembled her niece more than her daughters. Eva Grace even had Delia's sense of style, always decked out in smart outfits. Brenna and Fiona preferred jeans.

Their father, Aiden Burns, appeared behind his

wife. "Is it okay if we stay in the shadows and watch, Fiona?"

Wanting to scream, Fiona attempted a smile instead. Since before she'd been born, her parents had been traveling the globe, lecturing and writing books. Brenna, Fiona, and Eva Grace had been raised by Sarah.

Delia and Aiden came home to New Mourne after the demon killed Garth, and it became clear the Woman in White was getting ready to take her next Connelly tribute. So far, the Burns showed no signs of leaving. As much as she had missed her parents, Fiona was feeling a bit crowded by them now. They were contributing to her overall dissatisfaction and unease.

"I just hope Minnie's not going to be afraid to come back with this crowd here."

"It never scared her before," Eva Grace said. "We've had the shop full plenty of times when I've walked up the steps and right through an ice-cold patch. A dozen customers saw her the week before she left. I think she liked being with all the people."

"Then I need to get ready." Fiona glanced at the time on her cell phone. Perhaps Bailey had decided against attending tonight.

"Just a minute." Delia put a hand on both her daughters' shoulders and squeezed. "I've got wonderful news. Your father and I are going to be staying in New Mourne. We're ready to write the next book, and we're going to do it here."

Brenna looked stunned. Fiona sighed.

Aiden beamed at his wife and daughters.

"How long?" Brenna asked with a weak smile. She had never entirely forgiven their parents for leaving them…

Fiona didn't think she could endure her sister and parents squabbling. She turned toward the front of the store. "Excuse me. I need some peace before we begin."

She grabbed a bottle of calming spray off a shelf near the door. It was meant for babies, but what the hell. She sprayed it twice and walked through the mist.

The front door opened, and Bailey stepped in. He had changed into jeans and a crisp blue oxford shirt. He glanced around and smiled. "Wow, all sorts of magical stuff."

"Nothing's magical until it's in the right hands."

He cocked an eyebrow. "Have you started yet?"

"Ryan is finishing his walk-through. He always makes sure I can go where I need to unimpeded and removes anything he thinks might block my reach."

"Like what?"

She explained how she liked mirrors covered and lights dim during a session, and Bailey looked around with interest. The ghost Fiona had seen with him at the graveyard hadn't been with him this afternoon and wasn't with him now.

She nodded toward the back of the store. "You can sit back here. I need to focus right now and get my mind cleared."

At the rear of the store, Fiona performed the introductions, ignoring her parents' startled looks when she explained why Bailey was here. To their credit, they didn't question him or her. Brenna glared at him. Jake studied him as if he were suspected of a crime. At least Eva Grace made an attempt at hospitality.

Fiona turned her back on them as Ryan came down the steps. "We're all clear," he said. "Are you ready?"

He took a moment to check the computer monitors he had set up. Fiona sat down in a chair in the center of the shop. A purple candle burned on a shelf to her left. Additional candles glowed throughout the shop as Eva Grace dimmed the lights.

Fiona closed her eyes and took three deep breaths, letting them out slowly. Her mind was abuzz with all the people present. She continued her slow, steady breaths and carefully dismissed each person. When she reached Bailey, his smile flashed, and she felt warmth spread through her body.

Not now, she thought, *not now. Let Bailey go.*

When her mind cleared, she opened herself. As soon as spirits began speaking, she spoke calmly but with authority. "Get out. No visitors tonight."

After a moment, she felt empty. It was peaceful but a little eerie, too. She was seldom completely alone in her own head. Calming herself, she stood and spoke softly.

"Minnie. Minnie Doyle, are you about?"

The silence continued. All she heard was Ryan's quiet breathing as he taped nearby.

"Minnie, we've been missing you. Won't you come out and talk to me?"

As Fiona waited, quiet and patient, she recalled what she knew about Minnie. A portrait of Minnie hung on the wall in the area where Eva Grace kept crystal balls and gems. She'd always said Minnie liked shiny things and gravitated to that area most often.

The portrait was circa 1868. Minnie still wore her "widow's weeds," or mourning clothes, though her young husband was killed in the Battle of Chickamauga during the Civil War in 1863. According to town lore,

Minnie dressed as a mourner for ten years and never remarried. The house had been Minnie's wedding present from her beloved. She lived there until she died in 1899. She had never left.

"Minnie," Fiona said again. "You know this is your house, your place to be. Come and talk to me."

She waited again. Ryan moved closer to her. She didn't acknowledge him or look his way.

Fiona took another deep breath and pushed her awareness out. She opened her eyes when she felt a glimmer of responsiveness in a far corner. She moved her head only slightly and let her eyes drift open.

Minnie's image was translucent, but Fiona could see the outline of the mourning dress and the tightly coiled curls atop her head. Fiona said nothing, waiting for Minnie to grow stronger, appear denser.

When the spirit was no longer translucent, Fiona said, "Hello, it's good to see you."

Minnie sniffed and said, "I can't say the same."

"Where have you been?"

"You of all people know the value of hiding." Minnie moved toward the gems and ran her hands over a batch of smooth stones.

"Why are you hiding?"

"It's not safe here," Minnie said.

There was a soft pop and Minnie was gone. Fiona sat without moving for a moment. She heard Ryan turn off the camera. His hand touched her shoulder.

"All right?"

"I'll be fine in a minute."

"That was amazing." Bailey stepped from behind the computer monitors. He was staring at the spot where Minnie had been.

"Incredible special effects," he said. "I couldn't hear what you were responding to, but I actually saw some orbs. I saw the stones move. How did you do that?"

The room went still and silent.

"No special effects, Bailey. I told you I'm a medium." Fiona rose slowly, her knees a little weak.

Bailey stood by the gem table and waved his hands through the air. "I can't find any strings or wire."

"There aren't any." Fiona's words came out a little sharp. She had to remind herself that he didn't believe, that it was his job to question what he had seen. He squatted and tried to look under the bin holding the gems, but it was flush with the floor.

Suddenly Minnie appeared again. She was less than two feet from Bailey. He stood and looked around, shivering. He rubbed his left bicep, Fiona noted, where she had seen a tattoo earlier.

"Geez, I'm freezing all of a sudden. What's going on?"

"There's a ghost beside you," Fiona said.

Bailey jerked backward.

Minnie shook her finger at Fiona. "It's not safe in New Mourne, and I'm not coming back until it is."

Then she was gone.

Chapter 4

Still sitting in the center of the store, Fiona drank green tea and watched Bailey study a display of athames and other ritual supplies. He hadn't said much since Minnie left the second time. He was still skeptical, and Fiona was trying to decide how she felt about that. Everyone else's feelings were clear.

Ryan had stomped upstairs moments ago to collect equipment, darting venomous glances toward Bailey.

Her father and Jake had their heads together, though their focus was Bailey.

Brenna and Eva Grace were in deep discussion with Delia, none of them happy.

Trouble was brewing on all sides.

Fiona set down her tea and stood just as her father crossed to Bailey's side.

"It's time for you to leave," Aiden told the younger man. "We need to finish here, and there's nothing else for you to see."

Fiona found she didn't like her father giving orders. "Please don't—"

"It's time for Mr. Hollywood to leave," Aiden repeated. "He has seen all he's going to see."

"But I asked him to come here," Fiona pointed out.

Usually polite and courtly, Aiden was blunt. "I don't trust him, and I want him to leave."

Before Fiona could say anything further, Bailey put

down the spiral goddess wand he was examining, his expression mild. "It's okay, Fiona. I'll leave. We'll talk later."

"I think you should just leave her alone, period." Jake squared his shoulders, and the badge on his shirt glinted.

Brenna came across the room to stand beside her fiancé. She looked at Bailey. "Please leave."

Fiona turned to Eva Grace for support. "This is ridiculous. It's your shop."

Her cousin hesitated, and Fiona's disappointment grew. Eva Grace usually supported her.

Delia came toward Fiona, hand outstretched. "He needs to go, dear."

Fiona's back stiffened as she drew away from her mother. Why was everyone so intent on telling her what to do? Her gaze locked with Bailey's. "I'll talk to you tomorrow."

He gave her a slight grin before he headed out the door. A babble of voices sounded as soon as he was gone.

"Good riddance," Ryan said from the stairway. "What a jerk. After seeing his shows, I thought he was intelligent and open-minded." He sat a silver briefcase down. "That's disenchanting."

Delia put a hand on Fiona's shoulder. "You can get rid of him tomorrow. I don't think it's safe for him to stay in New Mourne."

"You act as if he's a government agent."

"He's worse than that," Brenna snapped.

"Don't you realize what he could do to this town?" Aiden asked, making the same argument as Brenna and Eva Grace had.

"The show would be about me. Not about New Mourne," Fiona said. "About me, as a medium, not about me as a witch or our family as a coven, or this town as a haven for the supernatural."

"I'm afraid you're being naïve," Delia said. "Once he gets a glimpse of our world, he may try to reveal everything."

"We would stop him before that happened," Fiona protested.

"But why put yourself through that?" Brenna frowned at her. "If there's a chance he could betray us, why risk it?"

Fiona clenched her jaw. Brenna had offered herself up to the Woman in White as a sacrifice in an attempt to save their family. She had resisted everyone's efforts to dissuade her. For that matter, she was in love with a shifter who could become a massive white tiger in the blink of an eye. *Why was* she *always told to play it safe when Brenna never did?*

With her usual diplomacy, Eva Grace stepped between the sisters. "Let's not do this tonight," she suggested. "I'm sure you're exhausted, Fiona. We're all on edge, waiting for the demon or the Woman to come again. Bailey's appearance in town has added a new layer of tension."

Brenna started to protest, but a warning glance from Eva Grace shut her down. "All right," she agreed with clear reluctance. She looked at Fiona. "Please stay away from him until we can talk again."

Fiona made no promises, but Brenna, Jake, and her parents left without further protest. Ryan finished packing equipment and loaded Fiona's van. She told him she wanted to walk home, and to his credit he didn't protest before leaving her in the shop with Eva Grace.

"What a night," she told her cousin as they made sure all candles were extinguished and the shop was ready for opening the next morning.

Eva Grace gave her a considering look. "I hope you'll think about what everyone said to you."

"I wish everyone would give me a little credit."

"We do, Fiona. It's the rest of the world we don't trust. The world Bailey comes from."

Fiona remained silent.

Eva Grace put some papers in her big purse and stood. "I'm just going to say one more thing. Don't put yourself into this show or get involved with this Bailey Powers just because everyone thinks you shouldn't."

"That makes me sound childish."

"No, just someone who has always done pretty much what was expected of her. I do understand the urge to rebel."

"But you're not a rebel. Not like Brenna."

Eva Grace glanced around the darkened shop. "No, I was doing what I've always wanted. Everything was just right until Garth was killed, and we realized that we truly had to face the family curse. That's what makes me run away now, because everything's changed. I can see why you're thinking of taking risks."

Her cousin's assessment of Fiona's thinking was dead on. She linked arms with Eva Grace. "Does every generation think they're going to beat it?"

"Of course they do."

"But we're going to, aren't we?"

Eva Grace's silence was not reassuring. "Let's go home," she said.

Fiona grabbed her backpack, cheered by the bright designer fabric. A new backpack every year was her one splurge.

They walked out the back door into the humid night air and found Bailey leaning against his car in the parking lot. He was relaxed and comfortable, his arms crossed on his chest. He looked so damn sexy waiting there in the halo from the security light.

He stepped back and opened the passenger door. "Thought you might need a lift, since Ryan left."

"I'm taking her home," Eva Grace said. "You agreed to leave."

"I left the shop."

Eva Grace flipped her hand, and Bailey's car door slammed so hard it triggered the alarm. The horn blasted and the lights blinked wildly.

"What the hell?" Bailey fumbled for the remote a minute before the noise stopped.

"Don't, Eva Grace," Fiona murmured when her cousin raised her hand again. "There's no need for this."

"Fiona, be careful."

"I believe all he did was offer me a ride," Fiona said evenly. "You go on home. I can take care of myself." She headed down the steps.

"Are you sure?"

Refusing to answer, Fiona crossed to Bailey's side.

He watched warily as Eva Grace walked to her car, got in, and drove away. His expression made Fiona laugh.

"How did she do that to my car?" he asked.

"Do what?" Fiona asked with feigned innocence. "Didn't your car act up earlier today?"

He looked doubtful. "This town is wonky."

"That's one word for it." Fiona changed the subject. "What are you doing out here? I know you weren't here earlier. My father and Jake would have escorted you to the county line."

"I watched until everyone else left. I just want to talk. How about a cup of coffee at the diner?"

Fiona slipped into the door he had opened again. "Let's go to my office. I've got some wonderful caramel-flavored coffee."

"Sounds good to me." Bailey backed the car out of the parking space and headed toward her storefront.

The town around them was quiet as he pulled in the space in front of her office. The only lights were at the Irish pub. Fiona heard the music drift out each time a patron opened the door.

Bailey said, "Where is everyone?"

"This isn't L.A." Fiona unlocked her office door. "Let's go back to the break room. There are some comfortable chairs back there."

Soon the small room filled with the aroma of caramel. Fiona poured two mugs, and she and Bailey took seats in a matching pair of old easy chairs.

Bailey said, "I really wasn't trying to insult you back at the shop."

"Even though I knew you wouldn't believe what you saw, it's still not easy when someone thinks you're a fake."

"If we go forward with a show, I have to know what I'm dealing with," Bailey said. "I have a responsibility to my company."

"Who says we're going forward?"

"Oh, come on, Fiona. You wouldn't have had me

there tonight if you weren't interested in working with me. You can stop pretending disinterest. I'm not sure what you're trying to gain by doing that."

"I'm not trying to gain anything." She pursed her lips. "I'm truly undecided. This may not be possible given how everyone else in my life thinks it's a bad idea."

"It's your life."

She wondered what he would say if she told him about the curse and the responsibility a Connelly witch had to her coven and to this town. It wasn't just her life. Someone like Bailey couldn't possibly understand the complicated ties she had to her family and New Mourne.

"Tell me again why you would want to do a show about something you don't believe in," she said.

"My parents have wanted a ghost series for a while," he continued. "They've sent me on a couple of real wild goose chases. Tonight's the first time I've thought it might be a good idea. Powers That Be likes to handle unique projects, so we need a new angle. What I saw tonight makes me think we can work with you. You're very natural in front of the camera."

"What did you see tonight, Bailey?" Fiona watched him, wondering if he would be honest.

"There were orbs on the computer monitor, and the box of rocks moved. It was kind of spooky. Viewers love that kind of stuff."

"You think so?" Fiona's gaze shifted to the young girl who appeared behind Bailey. The apparition was full-bodied—a young teen with long, tawny hair and blue eyes. She wore tan shorts, sandals, and a Spice Girls T-shirt that Fiona instantly coveted.

Bailey shifted in his seat. "Why are you looking at me like that?"

Fiona sighed. "Who is the girl?"

Bailey sat back in the chair, a disappointed look on his face. "I guess you're referring to my sister, Anna. You don't need to bring her into this."

"So you know I can see her?"

Instead of answering, he stood and set his coffee mug on the counter. "What I know is that you've done your research, the same as I've done the research on your family. I know your grandmother is a renowned artist who works in natural stone and gemstones found in this area. I know your parents are international experts on witchcraft. I know there's another paranormal expert, a Dr. Rodric McGuire, staying here in town and conferring with your family. And I know a number of people who were once skeptics now believe that you can talk to the dead. You've helped several families find closure about loved ones."

"So you know a lot," Fiona murmured. "Research is easy these days."

The figure of the young girl remained beside the chair, her gaze fastened on Bailey.

He turned to Fiona again. "I'm sure you found it easy to discover that my younger sister was kidnapped from an amusement park when she was fourteen years old. She was murdered. Her body was found the next day. They never caught the killer. When the normal channels were exhausted, my parents turned to psychics and mediums. They've been to dozens. They were very open and public about their search for answers in every possible venue. What you may not have discovered is all of those so-called psychics and mediums were fakes."

"I didn't know any of this." Fiona met Bailey's suspicious glare with clear-eyed honesty. "All I did was call your references and look your company up on the Internet. I didn't try to find out anything personal." She kept her voice even and quiet. "And how do you know the mediums were fake?"

"Those con artists never connected to Anna. I always found something that gave them away. Always."

Fiona glanced at the ghost who stood so still beside the chair. "She has tried to reach you."

He rubbed his left bicep, just as he had at the shop. "If so, none of the so-called experts in that area were able to make it happen. That's another thing that gave them away. If Anna had wanted to talk to me, surely they could have helped me respond."

"It's not always easy," Fiona protested. "Spirits trapped between our world and the next can't always communicate. Not every medium can reach them."

"So I've been told."

The weariness in his tone touched Fiona. "I'm sorry," she said. "I can understand how disappointing it is to have someone so close, yet so very far away. Do you want me to try to help?"

His short laugh was raw. "No, I don't want your help."

The ghost beside the chair disappeared, but Fiona could still feel her presence.

"Why do you think she stays near you?" Fiona asked Bailey.

"She doesn't," he said, shaking his head. "Anna is dead." He shrugged. "You need to understand. I don't believe. Nothing you can say will make me believe."

"All right. That's your prerogative," Fiona said. "I don't try to sway anyone. Obviously your parents still believe. Would they want my help?"

Anger snapped in Bailey's eyes. "Don't talk to my parents about Anna."

Fiona got to her feet. "I wouldn't unless they asked me. You mentioned that your mother found my webcast. I thought maybe—"

"Don't call her," Bailey said, his voice low. "Do you hear me? Do not call her."

An uneasy silence fell between them.

"What about your sister's murderer?" Fiona said. "Don't you wonder about that?"

He frowned. "The police kept the case active for years. They interviewed sex offenders and anybody that could remotely be called a suspect. There just wasn't any tangible evidence. No fingerprints and no DNA."

"I can see why your parents started looking elsewhere."

Bailey moved toward the break room doorway. "Listen, I just wanted you to know where I'm coming from. I think you have something a TV audience can connect with. But if you need me to believe you're in touch with the dead, that's not part of the deal. You don't have to keep trying to convince me."

A part of Fiona wanted to tell him to stop being dense, to open himself to possibilities. The wiser half knew he would have to discover that in his own time, if he did at all.

Meanwhile, she wasn't sure what she should do about his TV offer. "I need to think about all of this."

"Sure. How about I work on a solid pitch for the

show and we discuss it over dinner tomorrow night?"

Fiona led the way to the darkened outer office. "I'll call you tomorrow," she promised. They stepped out onto the sidewalk. The town was even more silent than before.

Bailey looked up. "Amazing...you can see all the stars. No smog."

Fiona smiled at him and their gazes locked. He gave a slow smile. She looked up. "I guess we take the stars for granted around here."

"You shouldn't. They're beautiful. Like you."

Her gaze lowered. He was looking at her, not the sky.

Fiona exhaled. Just as she hadn't traveled far from New Mourne in her twenty-two years, she was decidedly inexperienced with men. She'd had her share of dates and admirers, but walking around with a head full of voices from the grave tended to keep her preoccupied. There had been no one like Bailey Powers with his potent charm and easy confidence.

He was close enough that she felt the warmth of his skin and smelled the faint citrus of his shaving lotion. She leaned in, breathed him in. His lips touched hers. Fiona's eyes closed as he drew her closer. His lips were smooth and soft and when they opened, his tongue against hers was electric. Putting her hands on his elbows, she pressed against his hard chest.

The air around them crackled. A bright light snapped on. While Bailey jerked back, Fiona found herself face to face with her grandmother.

Sarah Connelly put a hand on Bailey's shoulder. "I'm sorry we didn't get to talk since you're leaving."

Bailey smiled. "I'm leaving. Goodbye, Fiona." He

crossed the sidewalk, got in his car, and drove away without looking back.

"What did you do to him?" Fiona asked Sarah.

"Get inside," Sarah said and reached around Fiona to open the door. "We have to talk."

They were silent until they reached the break room when Sarah demanded, "Why is that man still in New Mourne?"

"Last I heard it's a free country. He can be wherever he likes." Fiona felt like she'd been caught sneaking a kiss on her grandmother's front porch.

"I won't have this. Your mother told me what that man wants, and I demand that you tell him to leave and never come back." Sarah's face was set and unyielding. "Nothing good will come from any association with a man like that."

"A man like what?" Fiona asked. "Someone who's interested in me and not my family? Someone who recognizes my talent?"

"He doesn't even believe in your ability. He told you so," Sarah said with a triumphant smile.

"Were you spying on us?"

"I do what I have to do to protect the family and the coven. You know we can't let any news of what goes on here go into the outside world. How long do you think it will be before he makes it known you're a practicing witch? Our town will be overrun with crazy people. You know that."

Fiona thought about recent activities in New Mourne and decided her grandmother might be a little late with her predictions. "My parents said exactly the same thing. At least try to be original with your disapproval."

Sarah's eyebrows rose at Fiona's snide tone. She sat down at the table. She looked expectantly at Fiona who walked over to retrieve a cup and fill it with coffee.

"It may be strong. I made it a while ago," Fiona said as she sat down.

Sarah waved a hand over it, and the aroma of a mocha latte wafted up. "It's fine. We've had a rough time lately. We don't need a stranger prying into town secrets to add to everything else. Tell your Mr. Powers to head his convertible back to California."

"I don't think so. He wants to talk to me, and I'm ready to listen. With a show in a big cable network, I could develop a following and help people around the country. Maybe even around the world."

Sarah took a long sip of her coffee, then leaned close to Fiona's face. "All that pretty man will do is make you love him and then leave you with two babies in your belly. Trust me. This much I know."

Then she was gone, disappearing as fast as only a powerful witch can.

Chapter 5

Bailey sat on the side of the bed in his room at the Red Oak Inn, the only motel in the town proper of New Mourne. He looked around in a daze. How did he get here? He had been kissing Fiona and enjoying her body's quick response. He didn't remember leaving her or coming here.

"What the hell's going on?"

He closed his eyes to relax and concentrate. He remembered talking with Fiona at her office. He remembered telling her about Anna, something he never did, and something he had no idea why he did tonight. He found it all too easy to open up to Fiona Burns. What was that about?

He went to the window and looked down on the quiet street. Fiona's office was too far away to view from here. They had stood on the sidewalk talking. They looked up at the stars. Then he kissed her. Like the conversation about Anna, that kiss was uncharacteristic for Bailey. He was starting a business relationship with her. He shouldn't have kissed her.

Try as he might, he couldn't remember what happened after that or how he came to be sitting here now. His cell phone indicated it was nearly eleven-thirty. He knew they had left Siren's Call around ten. He and Fiona had not been together more than an hour. Where had he been?

The street below him was empty. No cars came through, and no people milled about. Even the pub was closed, and there was absolute silence outside. It was Wednesday night in July in the middle of nowhere.

"It's too damn quiet to think," he said aloud. "I need some traffic and sirens. How do people live like this?"

The words were no sooner out of his mouth than a coyote ambled down the street. The lean, tough-looking animal stopped on the sidewalk across from the inn and looked directly at Bailey with eyes that glowed silver-gray. Bailey resisted the urge to duck behind the curtains. Was he seeing things? He closed his eyes. When he opened them, the animal was gone.

Rubbing his face with both hands, Bailey mumbled, "You're in the country. There are animals in the country. Don't scream like a little girl."

The ring of his cell phone jolted him again. He was relieved to see his father's face onscreen.

"Hey, Dad."

"Any ghosts make an appearance?" Dean Powers asked.

Bailey had texted his parents earlier today and told them about Fiona's invitation for the ghost hunt at Siren's Call.

"Fiona Burns is very good," he summed it up to his father, omitting the details of his heart-to-heart about Anna and the kiss that had followed. "But she's not as open to the idea as we'd hoped, and her family pretty much wants to get the pitchforks and torches and run me out of town."

"I thought Southern people were known for their hospitality," Dean said. "You're usually able to work your charm. That's why you're the advance man. What's going on?"

Bailey looked out the window again, half expecting the coyote to have returned with friends. "There's a lot more to this town than Fiona being a medium." Bailey blinked, trying to clear more of the fuzziness from his head. "This place..."

"What?"

He found himself reluctant to tell his father about the crows, his car and phone not working or even the coyote. An ache started in the center of his forehead and spread outward.

"Fiona's family is very...unusual." That wasn't the word Bailey really wanted. He thought of the sheriff's order for him to leave, the ire in Aiden Burns' gaze, and the distrust of her cousin with the long red hair. "They're intense to say the least."

"Intense can make for great TV when it comes to families."

"Usually." Bailey had felt many undercurrents tonight at the shop. "There's something strange in the air. Something not quite...right."

Dean chuckled. "You're not sounding like yourself, Bailey. You don't believe in anything that's not quite right."

"You shouldn't either," Bailey muttered, thinking of the parade of psychics his parents had visited after Anna's death. One kook after another had taken their money and broken their hearts.

"But I do," his father replied in an even tone. He began a story familiar to Bailey. "It goes back to your grandmother and the séances she used to hold at the house with that friend of hers. Your mother was there the night Marilyn Monroe visited. Marilyn confirmed her death was murder, not suicide. I'll never forget it."

"I know, Dad. I know."

Bailey's paternal grandmother had been a secretary for a motion picture executive, and had an eclectic circle of friends. To this day, she participated in weekly séances. The only difference was she now held them at her retirement home instead of the stucco Southern California rancher where Dean was raised.

The girl next door, Bailey's mother, was intrigued by the shenanigans in the Powers household. Thirty-six years later, Dean and Beth were still in love and still believed they once chatted with Marilyn Monroe through a medium at the family dining table.

"Your mother decided to marry me the night of that séance," Dean continued, warming to his memories. "She said my family was so interesting that we'd surely have quite a life together."

Bailey sighed. "I hate reminding you of this, but that medium friend of Gran's turned out to be a fake like all the rest who promised to reach Anna."

"She just failed to contact your sister. It was nothing personal, Bailey."

He sounded a lot like Fiona, and Bailey didn't want to hear it. "We will always differ on those details."

Dean laughed. "Well, whatever's not right in that Georgia town, you're sure to figure it out. Finding logical answers is your specialty."

"Yes, it is." Bailey was beginning to feel more like himself. There was most likely a good reason why he had lost a half hour of time after kissing Fiona. He had probably come back to the room, fallen asleep, and awakened disoriented. The coyote was most likely a dog. He needed to get a grip.

"What if this Fiona Burns turns out to be a real medium?" his father asked.

"That's not likely."

"You might try opening your mind just a little bit." His father's tone was wry, as if he knew this was a lost cause.

"She's talented, all right. Some great effects showed up tonight when she said she was talking with a ghost."

"You could see she was using special effects?"

"I couldn't find any wire or air vents, but I saw things move, and there were definitely orbs showing up on the computer screen."

"Maybe they were real," his father suggested.

"Yeah, right, Dad. I'm going to give Fiona another day or so to come around, then I'm coming home." He looked around the comfortable but quaintly decorated room. Maybe it was the chintz bedspread and ruffled curtains that were playing with his head. "I've been on the road too long this time."

They discussed a few additional points of business about other shows before Bailey ended the call with "Give my love to Mom."

He set his phone down and returned to the window. The street was still empty, and though he watched for a few minutes, nothing else happened. He closed the blinds and grabbed his tablet to add to the notes he had made this afternoon.

He couldn't find the file. That was strange. He had written about the gathering of crows, the intelligent gazes of the birds and their absence of sound. But his notes were gone. Once again, technology had malfunctioned. This town was driving him crazy.

He glanced nervously at the fireplace and the windows. "The Birds" was one of his favorite movies, but he wasn't sure he'd want the crows hammering through the glass or down the chimney with their sharp beaks.

He shook his head and wrote up the details of Fiona's interaction with the ghost she called Minnie. Bailey was sure Ryan had rigged something during his "walk through." But the chill Bailey had felt when Fiona said a ghost was beside him had been instant and penetrating. This was in the middle of a store with other people standing around. No one else reacted. He felt out of sorts as he wrote the question: *Was a real ghost standing beside me?*

He deleted the question and saved his notes, to his tablet and to the cloud. They weren't going anywhere this time.

Instead of thinking about cold drafts and ghosts, he remembered the flesh and blood woman he had kissed. *Fiona Burns.* He could still taste the sweetness of her lips. He could feel her smooth skin beneath his fingers. He could smell her sweet floral scent. But why couldn't he remember anything about leaving her and coming to this room?

He met his own gaze in the dresser mirror across the room. He didn't have time for this. Not only could Fiona potentially be working for his company, she was the most dangerous sort of woman, the kind who made you talk about yourself and examine your feelings. He had spent the past fifteen years avoiding that.

In the course of an hour, he told Fiona more about Anna than he had shared with the last woman he dated.

Twenty-four hours ago, he had never spoken to Fiona, and tonight he had talked about his murdered sister with her.

"Goddamn it." He stood and walked toward the bathroom, unbuttoning his shirt and tossing it aside. He needed a shower to clear his head.

In the glare of an overhead light, he faced himself in the bathroom mirror. He looked tired, his usual tan faded, and his hair in need of a trim. The jagged lightning tattoo on his left bicep seemed more sharply etched than usual.

He traced a finger over the black and blue lines. He was seventeen when he'd gotten the tattoo, on the second anniversary of Anna's brutal murder. He had chosen the bolt of lightning because it had stormed the night she died, and he had wanted a reminder of the shock of losing her.

A lot of time had passed since then. He had accepted horrible events happen, and he would never have any answers about his sister's death.

The tattoo prickled. Bailey touched the mark. Usually, this was when he allowed himself to think of Anna and to ask if there was something he could have done to protect her, to change how her life ended.

Tonight, however, he thought of Fiona. He heard her voice asking, "Do you want me to try to help?"

The voice poured through Bailey like a surge of hope. He started to answer, and then realized how off this was.

Because Fiona's voice wasn't just in his head. The question echoed again and again, off the tiled walls of the shower behind him.

"Do you want me to help?"

In a sudden cold sweat, Bailey fell back from the mirror. "Stop it!" he ordered, to make himself feel better, and to shut out the question. He pressed his hands to his head.

The voice stopped. Silence reigned even weirder, darker, and more complete, like a bottomless cavern.

"This town and that woman are fucking with my brain."

Bailey staggered from the bathroom, wondering what Fiona had put in his coffee or what he had inhaled at her cousin's shop.

As he fell deep into sleep, he heard the beating of wings, like the dozens of crows lifting to the sky.

Chapter 6

Fiona arrived at her grandmother's house just after eight the next morning. She glanced at her face in the van's rearview mirror. Lack of sleep showed in her features, and that wasn't good.

Bailey was the source of her sleeplessness, and Fiona didn't want her grandmother to know. She hated how Sarah, as well as her mother and father, had inserted themselves into her business last night. She needed to be firm about it being time to live her own life, her own way. She would deal with the sexy Bailey Powers.

She chanted a quick glamour spell that brightened her eyes and reduced the puffiness below them before heading to the house.

Fiona, Brenna, and Eva Grave had grown up here, in what was known as the Connelly home place, a comfortable, three-story farmhouse built from the first cabin constructed by their family in the mid-1700s. Tall, ancient oak trees stood sentinel in the steamy July morning. Hand-hewn rocking chairs lined the broad front porch. Strong, protective magic emanated from within.

The house always passed to the coven leader, and Sarah and her husband, Marcus Hayes, had used the wealth from their art careers to expand and update the family home. Fiona supposed someday the house would pass to Brenna, the strongest witch of their generation and a natural candidate for the next leader. Would Brenna raise children with Jake here?

Or would the Woman in White's curse or the demon take Brenna?

Fiona shivered. Brenna was the demon's target just weeks ago, her extraordinary powers the lure for an entity the family still didn't quite understand. Did the demon work for the Woman or was he his own form of evil? Somehow, they had to find out.

Fiona let herself in the front door. Breakfast aromas and familiar voices led her to the dining room. At the long oak table, Delia and Aiden Burns were reading on their tablets and eating toast and jam while her grandmother studied a newspaper. All of them looked up to regard Fiona with frowns.

"And it's nice to see all of you, too," Fiona said as she paused in the doorway.

Sarah laid down the newspaper and took off her reading glasses. As usual, her long gray hair was braided, and she wore one of her simple, cotton tunics, this one a pale blue. "I'm glad you're here, Fiona. We need to talk."

"Yes," Delia added. "We must discuss what happened last night." Her green eyes were as icy as Sarah's.

Fiona's father rose to pull out a chair for her at the table. "I'm sorry if we seem cross," Aiden murmured but without the warmth his voice usually held when he saw one of his daughters. "We're worried about you."

Before Fiona could reply, Marcus appeared in the doorway from the kitchen with two plates heaped with eggs, toast, and ripe, red sliced tomatoes. At least he smiled. Marcus, who was nearly two decades younger than Sarah, had helped raise Fiona, her sister, and cousin. Fiona loved him very much and was sad to think he might be disgruntled with her, too.

He set a plate down in front of his wife and offered the other to Fiona. "The special of the house. Want some?"

"No thanks. I'll just have some toast and milk. I've already had three cups of coffee." Fiona motioned for him and her father to sit down. "Enjoy your food while it's hot. I'll get what I need."

Helping herself also put off the inevitable confrontation, and slicing the homemade oat bread in the kitchen made Fiona feel she'd come home. Sarah made breads every Wednesday, and several loaves were cooling on the counter. Fiona opted for the microwave instead the toaster and slathered the steaming bread with lots of butter and blackberry jam made by one of the coven's elder aunts. She poured a glass of milk, took a deep breath, and went back into the dining room. Even Marcus didn't smile at her now.

"Is he gone?" Sarah asked as Fiona took a bite of her warm bread.

Wiping jam off her mouth, Fiona didn't pretend not to understand Sarah was asking about Bailey. "I don't know."

"Don't play games with me." Sarah set her fork down on her plate. Temper brimmed in her gaze, and as usual, Sarah's anger translated into magical energy that rattled the timbers of the old house. Dust shifted and fell in the room's stone fireplace.

Marcus took his wife's hand. "Steady, girl."

The rumbles faded but Sarah still stared a hole

through Fiona. "I'm sure you've checked to see if he's left this morning."

"I have not spoken to him since he was sent away last night," Fiona replied. "Why didn't you fly over to the inn and check on him? You had no hesitation about taking to the air last night." She turned to her parents. "Did Sarah tell you about last night? She put some kind of spell on Bailey."

"As well she should have," Delia said, sitting back and folding her arms.

"We felt Sarah needed to intervene," Aiden added.

"All I did was encourage him to go home so I could talk to you," Sarah said to Fiona.

"You appeared out of thin air and interrupted a personal moment."

Delia's head whipped toward Sarah. "A personal moment? What was that?"

Fiona bit back her annoyance. Trust Sarah to surprise her by not telling Delia and Aiden everything about last night. She took a deep breath. She might as well get it out. "I kissed him, okay? It was just a kiss." Strictly speaking, that was a lie. Though Fiona's experience with kisses was limited, she thought that kiss qualified as special. She had certainly spent enough time between then and now replaying every delicious detail in her mind.

As had been the case for all of Fiona's life, her grandmother knew falsehoods from truths. Fiona could see it on Sarah's face. Beside her, Marcus's expression was thoughtful.

Aiden leaned forward, looking concerned. "People like this Bailey character will do most anything to get what they want. He could be trying to seduce you in order to talk you into this reality show he's proposing."

"As opposed to actually just wanting to kiss a hag like me," Fiona observed with a wry twist of her lips.

Delia protested, "Fiona, that's not what we're saying at all. Why wouldn't he want to seduce you, a young beautiful witch who might make him a lot of money?"

"He doesn't know about us being witches," Fiona retorted. "He wouldn't believe it if we told him. He doesn't believe I'm a medium, either. He doesn't believe in anything supernatural."

"And we should keep it that way," Sarah said.

"Then you need to keep your spells to yourself."

"Oh for goodness sake," her grandmother said. "He wasn't hurt, and he probably just went back to the inn and went to bed."

"He's human and skeptical," Fiona said. "He'll have a lot more questions now, I wager. You're so worried about me spilling the family secrets, but you're the one flying around. No telling what he's thinking today."

"Which is exactly why he needs to leave town, and you need to forget about doing a television show," Sarah said. "I think everyone will agree with me."

Delia and Aiden nodded. Marcus gave Fiona another one of his long, considering looks.

Her father tapped keys on his tablet. "I just looked Powers up. His family is well known in Hollywood. When Bailey joined the family production company, they went into the reality television business. Bailey is known for picking winners. He's also quite ruthless about making money off merchandising and such."

"I know all of that," Fiona said. "I've already

checked him out."

"What will you do when thousands of people begin showing up in New Mourne looking to buy 'I Brake for Witches' bumper stickers and Connelly bobbleheads?" Sarah threw her napkin on top of her unfinished eggs. "You can't be so selfish that you'd risk the rest of us for a little fame, especially now with the threats we face."

Finally, Marcus spoke up. "Sarah, you can't believe Fiona would endanger the family or the town the coven protects."

"I think she can be young and foolish," Sarah said. "I was once."

Fiona tried not to roll her eyes. "Are you going to start talking about Bailey planting two babies in my belly again? I'm not you. I won't make the same mistakes you did."

Sarah's gaze chilled even further. "I don't regard your mother or Eva Grace's mother as mistakes." Her twin daughters had been the result of a fleeting teenage encounter with a young man she largely refused to discuss, although Fiona had heard he was a gypsy.

"Now, now," Marcus soothed as sharp words broke out around the table. "I think what Fiona is asking for is a little respect for her judgment."

"Thank the Goddess that you, at least, understand," Fiona told him with relief. She turned back to her parents and grandmother. "Please let me worry about Bailey Powers. We have something far more serious to discuss. I came out here to talk about the Woman in White and the demon. We've got a problem."

There was a collective intake of breath. "What?" Sarah demanded.

"I was running on Devil's Creek Road yesterday,

out toward the old cemetery—"

"What were you doing out there?" Sarah demanded. "You were told as children to stay away from there. That still stands."

Fiona said, "That's why I've never told you that I run there every day. I don't have to deal with any ghosts there, and I can run in peace."

Marcus said, "Nothing has ever grown on that land."

Fiona frowned. "And it's right next to Uncle Van's dairy farm."

Delia nodded. "Your uncle and your cousin run the biggest dairy operation around here. The farm's been in the family from the beginning, just like this land, but those acres have always been barren as far as I know. The one time I asked, Uncle Van told me not to question the ways of nature."

"Does anyone know why?" Fiona pressed.

Aiden and Delia looked at Sarah, who avoided gazes by stacking dishes. When she rose to take them to the kitchen, however, her daughter stood to block her way.

"What's going on?" Delia asked and took the dishes out of Sarah's hand. "What do you know about that land?"

Sighing, Sarah took her chair again. "Something happened there before I was born. My grandmother mentioned it when she ordered all of us to stay away from there. She said it was something to do with black magic and shouldn't be discussed openly. That meant we never talked about it."

"More secrets," Delia murmured, sitting down again, as well. "Why have generations of this family tried to sweep events under the rug? It's as if everyone who came before us didn't want any of us to learn from their mistakes."

Sarah glared at her. "It's always been this way. To live with the present—"

"I know, I know." Delia waved her hands. "In order to live with the repercussions of the curse, no one wants to talk about the curse."

There had been numerous quarrels between the elders of Sarah's generation and the younger coven members about secrets the family held too tightly through the years, information that could possibly prevent another tribute being taken by the Woman.

"Don't you want to know what happened to me in the dead zone?" Fiona asked as tension simmered between her mother and grandmother.

"Tell us," Aiden said.

Fiona took a deep breath and told them about the crows. "Though they didn't threaten me, they seemed to be waiting for me. They definitely sent an ominous message."

Aiden said, "There are many legends and superstitions about crows and ravens. Most well-known is their association with death."

"An old English poem says one crow means sorrow," Delia added.

"This was many, many more than that," Fiona said. "There were dozens. Maybe hundreds."

"I've heard that crows protect the dead," Marcus said. "It certainly fits this situation. Could something in that area be threatening those resting peacefully in their graves?"

Sarah sighed. "I don't know. We just never talked

about it."

"What about *The Connelly Book of Magic*?" Fiona asked. "There could be something there."

No one said anything for a moment, though Marcus reached across and laid his hand on Sarah's. Fiona saw that her grandmother squeezed his fingers and smiled at him before she walked into the hallway where a bookcase stood near the stairs.

She came back with a hefty book, bound by fraying ribbons and with a cracked leather cover imprinted in gold. "I'll call a coven meeting for tonight," she said. "The silence has gone on long enough."

She laid *The Connelly Book of Magic* in the center of the dining table.

Fiona felt another vibration go through the old house, and the iron chandelier over the table swayed. This time, however, it felt as if their family home place were signaling approval.

Chapter 7

Last night's empty street was full of activity when Bailey emerged midmorning from the inn. No coyotes on the sidewalks, he noted. He had to laugh at himself. The sun broke through the clouds, making his evening adventures more unreal.

"What the hell happened last night, and why the hell can't I remember?"

He unclipped his sunglasses from the placket of his gray silk, camp shirt and put them on. The shirt was the last clean piece of clothing in his suitcase. The khakis he wore were looking downright scruffy. He'd been on the road too long and needed some new clothes.

It was a blue jeans kind of town, he thought as he ambled down the sidewalk. Flags from the recent July Fourth holiday hung from lampposts, and baskets of petunias bloomed everywhere.

Most of the people seemed to be tourists, intent on New Mourne's cluster of shops. There was a florist, an antique store, and a line of people outside Bitta's Bakery. The scent of bacon from Mary's Diner made Bailey's stomach rumble. He had slept through the inn's complimentary breakfast, so he headed there.

The morning rush was clearly over, and the "Seat Yourself" sign was up. Bailey headed toward a booth. The skinny waitress who had sent him to meet Fiona yesterday morning came bustling up.

"It's Misty, isn't it?" he recalled and grinned. It never hurt to have an ally.

Misty smiled flirtatiously before she said, "Miss Willow would like you to join her."

"Willow?"

Misty pointed in the other direction to an old woman seated at a table by the window. She was slowly stirring her coffee and smiling at him. Her white hair was neatly styled, and she wore a soft black dress and old-fashioned pearl earrings. Though her skin was wrinkled, she radiated energy and vitality. She also gave him a knowing look that was as intriguing as it was annoying.

Just as he knew befriending a diner waitress in a small town was smart, Bailey was aware grandmothers also came in handy. He was usually a hit with the senior crowd. If the woman was a local, he might be able to learn something more about Fiona and her family.

"Sure," he told Misty as he turned toward the woman. "I'll have bacon and scrambled eggs, orange juice, and coffee, please."

"Grits, gravy and biscuits?"

Though tempted, Bailey reminded himself he had not had time for a good workout in days. "Wheat toast?"

Misty's nose wrinkled. "Suit yourself, sweetie." She trotted off to put in the order.

He approached the older woman's booth and held out his hand. "I'm Bailey Powers."

"Willow Scanlan." The old woman's hand was soft and unexpectedly warm.

There was a buzz in Bailey's palm, and then a tingle moved up his arm to his shoulder. It took effort not to jerk his hand away.

Willow kept a firm grip on his hand. "I believe I have some information that will help you in your efforts with Fiona Burns."

A wave of dizziness pushed over Bailey.

"Won't you sit down?" his elderly companion said. "You look a little pale."

The feeling faded when she released his hand. Bailey sat down across from her and shook his head to clear it. "I guess I'm hungrier than I realized."

"Oh, yes. Hungry." A shaft of sunlight fell across Willow's face, and for a moment her small, sharp teeth flashed in a smile.

Bailey blinked, and the illusion of predatory glee was gone. Willow appeared once again a nice-looking older woman. Misty placed his drinks on the table, and he took a long sip of orange juice. Obviously, he needed some sugar in his system.

He asked Willow, "Did you say you could help me with Fiona? Fiona talked to you?"

"Good gracious no," she said with a chuckle. "But I've got my little spies all over town."

Bailey could have sworn her vivid blue eyes twinkled. Okay, he needed food and needed it now. His imagination was in overdrive.

"Can I get you something to eat?" he asked.

"Just finished," Willow replied. She was once more stirring her coffee and studying him. "You know you're not in New Mourne by chance, don't you?"

"I came here looking for Fiona. She has an Internet show—"

Willow cut him off with a gesture from one gnarled hand. "I know that. I know all about the Connellys."

"Fiona's family." He nodded. "I'd like to know more about them myself."

This time her laugh resembled a cackle. "Good gracious, you're eager. It's been a while since we had such an eager, young stranger around here asking about Connellys."

Bailey had the uneasy feeling he had stumbled into a Tennessee Williams play or an episode from the "Twilight Zone." He was an outsider in a small Southern town, and Willow was the matriarch who pretended to befriend him. In most of those stories, his character ended up dead or escaping in the nick of time.

"So you want to put Fiona on television, do you?" Willow asked, surprising him with her knowledge. Maybe she was right about her spies.

"What do you think about her?"

"What specifically?"

"Is she the real deal, a medium?"

"That's a riddle you have to solve on your own," Willow replied with another enigmatic look.

Misty arrived with his breakfast, and Bailey tucked into the food, eager to erase his unsteadiness.

"The reason you're here has very little to do with your business," Willow continued. "The time is right for you to meet your destiny. You have a role to play in Fiona's life."

Bailey set down his fork. This was one strange woman. "Why do you say that?"

"It's already set in motion," she said.

"I didn't even know Fiona until yesterday." Bailey gave Willow his full attention. "What's in motion?"

Willow smiled as she tapped the lid of one of the small jars on the table. "You should try the blackberry jam," she offered. "One of Fiona's relatives makes it for the diner. Most people find it irresistible, although I don't care much for sweets myself. Her people are so talented in so many ways. I've heard you met her sister, her parents, and her cousin, Eva Grace. They're all lovely girls, aren't they?"

"Yes," Bailey replied, though he refused to let her divert him. "Can we go back to what you said about me meeting my destiny?"

"I'm just telling you what to expect." She stirred her coffee again, and Bailey realized she had yet to take a sip. "Have you heard about the Connelly family curse?"

So the woman *was* nuts, he decided as he picked up his fork to finish his meal. She probably suffered from a little arterial flow problem or maybe dementia. He sat back, ready to indulge her. "There's a curse?"

"You met Fiona's grandmother, too. Sarah Connelly."

Bailey's head started to buzz. "No, I didn't—"

Willow's laughter whipped out again. "Oh, that's right. You don't remember Sarah, do you?"

"I've read about her," Bailey said, puzzled. "She's an artist who works in stone and metal."

"An artist? Yes, she's that, too." Willow's expression was gleeful now. "Her family has protected this town for centuries."

"Protected New Mourne? From what?"

"More coffee?" Misty interrupted, stopping beside their table.

"Thank you." Willow held up a cup that was suddenly empty. Bailey frowned. When did she drink the coffee? He was off his game in a big way this morning.

Misty refilled both cups. "Y'all look like you're having a nice visit," the waitress remarked, smiling at him. "Is Willow giving you all the details about our town?"

"She's telling me about Fiona Burns' family."

Misty clucked at Willow. "You should watch out, Miss Willow."

Expression hardening, Willow made a dismissive gesture. "Go on, Misty. This one's not for you."

"No he's not," Misty agreed with another smile at Bailey. "Such a shame."

The older woman rolled her eyes as the waitress walked away. "Silly girl to be warning me about what I say."

Bailey watched Misty stumble and almost lose her grip on the coffee pot. She glanced back at Willow and hurried toward the kitchen. He got the distinct impression the waitress was frightened.

Willow stirred her coffee again.

Bailey tore his gaze from the spinning dark liquid and back to hers. "What were you saying about Fiona's family?"

"The Connellys protect us."

Bailey glanced around the diner and outside at the people on the sunny street. There was no hint of anything that indicated an unusual morning or a need for guardians or protectors. He had to remind himself he was listening to the ramblings of someone who was at least eighty, maybe older.

"Why does an idyllic little town like this need protection?"

"Because there's evil here. It's come back."

Congratulating himself on showing no reaction to her words, Bailey cleared his throat. "What kind of evil?"

"The worst you can imagine," she said.

"But the Connellys can stop it?"

"You don't believe me," she observed with a huff. "But you will. The troubles are coming again, and what happens to Fiona will affect you."

"What could happen to her?"

"It's a pity, really, the sacrifice made for our town by all those lovely young Connelly witches."

"So they're witches?" he repeated. "I thought the Connellys were friends of yours. Sounds like you don't really like them."

"My kind knows what's necessary."

"Your kind?"

"Though I have good reason to dislike the Connellys, I've always been supportive. It's more difficult when it's time for their sacrifice, but I try to help them."

Bailey knew he should just pay for his meal and leave the town's resident loon to ramble on by herself, but he was fascinated. "Tell me about the sacrifice."

"The Connellys are magic-born, with gifts from the gods and goddesses. That's why the evil craves them and takes one as a sacrifice. The Connellys face it every generation, and this time it will be Fiona, her sister, or one of her cousins."

"Like a virgin-and-the-volcano sacrifice?"

"You're making fun of me." Her hand stilled on her coffee, and her blue eyes went cold and flat.

Bailey swallowed hard, once again thinking of every movie about the stranger in town who disappears.

He was genuinely disturbed by this little old granny, her odd manner and shifting moods.

"What are you saying about Connellys, Willow?"

Bailey turned to find Fiona standing behind him.

He got to his feet, relieved. He'd had just about enough of Willow's crazy talk.

"He has a right to know," Willow said to Fiona.

Fiona frowned. "He's not part of this."

Expression disapproving, Willow got to her feet and reached for her square, old-lady leather purse. "I see you're as determined as most Connellys to ignore my guidance. I was hoping you might be different."

"What guidance are you offering?"

Willow's gaze slipped from Bailey to Fiona, a thin eyebrow arching as she smiled. "You'll see."

She turned to Bailey with her hand outstretched. He really didn't want to touch her again, but he also wasn't rude by nature. This time her skin was cool, more what he expected from an elderly woman.

"It was so nice to meet you, Mr. Powers. I'm sure we'll talk again."

He hoped not, but he kept that observation to himself as Willow glided out the door. Outside, a large, dark sedan stopped at the curb, and a gaunt old man got out of the driver's side and came around to open the door for Willow.

"Does she live in a mildewing old mansion on the outskirts of town?" Bailey murmured to Fiona as they watched the car leave.

"Actually, she lives in a very nice house surrounded by lush gardens."

"But I bet she has chains in her basement."

There was a moment of silence, then a grin tugged

at the corner of Fiona's mouth. The mouth he had kissed last night, Bailey recalled. The pleasant memory dispelled the last bit of anxiety caused by the strange conversation with Willow.

"I guess she's what's known as a colorful, local character," Bailey observed.

"You have no idea."

"We could feature her on your show."

"The world is not ready for Willow in primetime," Fiona replied in a dry tone. "What was she telling you?"

"I'm sure it's the usual tale she has for the tourists. How your family members are witches, and you sacrifice yourself to some resident evil for the good of the town."

The color drained out of Fiona's face.

He laughed. "The thing is, I think she really believes all of it."

Her laughter was weak, but she touched his arm. "Let's get out of here. We need to talk."

Bailey paid his check and followed Fiona out to the still-bustling sidewalk.

Chapter 8

Out in the hot summer sunlight, Fiona fought to quell her panic.

Why had Willow, the area's fae leader, told Bailey about the Connelly curse? How was he a part of any of this?

All she knew was Willow, though ancient and crafty, was dangerous when crossed. The coven might protect New Mourne, but the fae were powerful residents with a stake in keeping the town a safe refuge for the supernatural. The fact Willow had connected with Bailey and told him so much was significant.

He frowned as he slipped on sunglasses. "Is something wrong? Surely you're not upset by one old woman's ramblings?"

Fiona wondered what he would say if she let him know, Willow was older than he could imagine. It would be better to avoid that. "I only heard part of what Willow told you."

He recounted the elderly woman's talk of his destiny and admitted, "She was unsettling. One minute she was friendly, then almost…threatening."

"Probably most towns have an eccentric like her."

"An eccentric crone, a medium, and a family of witches," Bailey mused. "This is an intriguing place."

Fiona forced out a laugh, trying to act as if this were all a joke. She had boasted to her family that

Bailey would not discover more about them than they wanted. She had to play this cool. "In the South, instead of locking our crazy folks up, we celebrate them. That's why Willow is running loose. You weren't the first person she disturbed."

Bailey looked ready to ask another question, so Fiona rushed on. "Can we walk to my office and talk? I need to make a stop on the way."

"Sure, but—"

She hooked a hand in his elbow and guided him to the right. "Dagen from the antique store called my grandmother this morning and said he had an armoire he wanted my family to check out."

"Dagen?"

Fiona laughed. "His name is actually George Dooley, but his family was part of the original Irish settlers of this town and named Dagen. Everyone calls him that."

"As I said before, an interesting town."

"He does an amazing business and puts on an auction every Friday night during the tourist season from Memorial Day through Thanksgiving."

They were almost to the store when a well-dressed couple stepped out of a small home décor store in front of them. Fiona stiffened and prepared for a confrontation.

"Hello, Fiona," Rev. Fred Williams said in his best pastor's tone. "How are you today?"

"I'm fine. Just heading to see Dagen about something. Bailey Powers, meet Reverend and Mrs. Williams." She desperately hoped Fred would keep Ginny moving so she wouldn't speak. But luck wasn't going her way.

"You must be that Hollywood producer everybody is talking about." Cold blue eyes gave Bailey a rude onceover. "I hope you don't think anybody here enjoys that awful stuff you call reality shows."

"So you must have watched a few to know you don't like them."

Bailey's mild tone made Fiona grin.

"I would never have anything to do with such filth." Face flushed, Ginny turned to Fred. "We need to get to church for the committee meeting."

"Of course," Fred said smoothly, taking Ginny's elbow. "Good to meet you, Mr. Powers."

The couple hurried down the street with Ginny muttering angrily to Fred, who patted his wife's arm.

"Are all the church people around here like that?" Bailey asked.

"No way," Fiona said. "This is actually a friendly community with an air of live-and-let-live most of the time. Fred's not so bad, but Ginny is very vocal in her distaste for anything she doesn't agree with."

They were in front of the antique store now.

"Why are you checking out the armoire? Is it haunted or something?" Bailey asked.

"Spirits do attach themselves to objects."

Bailey peered through the glass door at the old furniture and glassware. "See any ghosts there?" He pointed to an old spinning wheel.

The only ghost Fiona sensed was Bailey's own personal guardian. His young, tragically murdered sister shadowed him now as she had last night, fading in and out, and focused solely on Bailey. Fiona was open to communication with Anna, but had no link to the teenager. It was important to understand why his sister remained at his side before mentioning it to him again.

"No ghosts in the window," Fiona said truthfully and pulled the shop door open. A small bell tinkled overhead as they entered. "Dagen told me our family name is carved inside this armoire. He said he bought the piece at an estate sale just over the North Carolina border. More than likely a Connelly family member sold it years ago."

"Will you want it back?"

"Definitely. My grandmother told me to look it over, and she would come in to haggle with Dagen later this week."

Sarah was definitely in the mood for restoring Connelly possessions to the coven. This morning, Fiona had helped her grandmother and her parents search *The Connelly Book of Magic* for information about the barren land near the old cemetery. Many pages of the book were missing after so many years. The coven had restored some of the book recently. However, every time they turned to the book for answers about the curse, they found miscellaneous items, including recipes, photos, and faded greeting cards instead of information. Sarah was upset about the book, too. As coven leader, she should have been guarding it. Instead, it was a mess.

A young, female clerk interrupted Fiona's thoughts and greeted them from behind the antique shop's counter.

"Hi there," the attractive young woman said to Fiona, though her gaze was focused on Bailey.

Deliberately not introducing him, Fiona said, "Is Dagen around?"

The clerk batted her big, blue eyes, and Bailey

grinned at her. He really had a smile, Fiona admitted to herself, a bad-boy, all-knowing, and sexy smile. She didn't like the way it brightened for the young girl.

"Where is Dagen?" Fiona prompted again.

With obvious reluctance, the young woman glanced Fiona's way. "He's waiting for you. He's very excited about this armoire. You know the way to the dock, don't you? And maybe I can show your friend some antiques."

Taking Bailey's elbow again, Fiona led the way to the back.

"This place is larger than it looks from the front," he commented as they wound their way through the maze of furniture and boxes into a crowded storeroom.

"And almost always full to the bursting," Fiona said. "I don't know where Dagen finds everything. Or how he sells so much."

"Our production company produces a couple of shows about antiques." Bailey stopped to study a small, golden lamp. "People love digging up the past. I try to concentrate on the here and now."

Fiona thought that explained how hard he tried to run from his past. As if reading her mind, Anna's ghost materialized at his side and looked at Fiona.

Her figure disappeared, however, when a voice called from near the open garage doors at the back of the storeroom. "Fiona? Is that you? I've got something exciting to show you."

Fiona hurried forward to greet the fifty-ish, ruddy-cheeked antique storeowner. Sweating through his shorts and T-shirt in the humid morning air, Dagen was wiping down a large, dark wood cabinet with a white cotton cloth. "This is an amazing piece."

After introducing Bailey, Fiona stood back to admire the armoire that the elders in her coven would have called a wardrobe. The piece was at least six foot tall and maybe four feet wide. A beveled mirror, cloudy and silvering in spots, covered the center door. Twin wooden panels framed the door.

"It's quartersawn oak," Dagen said, running his hands lovingly over the wood. He touched the two carvings on the wooden panels. "I love the Celtic-knot design."

"It's repeated here," Fiona murmured, fingers tracing the carving that ran down the edges of the panels. "And here." Her fingers hovered over the door's ornate brass lock and key.

Red face gleaming with perspiration, Dagen regarded the cabinet the way some men might a beautiful woman. He couldn't keep his hands off it. "She has an oak crown." He gestured toward the top, where a leaf design decorated the wooden molding.

"Where did you find our name written?" Fiona asked.

Dagen swung the door open. In contrast to the beautiful carving on the front, "Connelly" was scratched in crude block letters on the back of the door.

Bailey stepped forward to look closely at the letters. "That's ugly. Wonder why someone would do that to a fine piece of furniture."

"It doesn't harm her too much." Dagen stood back, looking plump and pleased with himself. "I don't know if I can bear to let her go."

Fiona knew Dagen's home was as full as his shop and that if he brought another piece home his wife would protest. "Don't fall too deeply in love. She belongs at the home place with Sarah."

As she stroked the Celtic knot design, the oak warmed beneath Fiona's touch. Her senses sharpened. She hadn't been kidding when she told Bailey that spirits could attach to furniture. Was there something here, in this cabinet branded Connelly?

"I want to show you something else." Dagen leaned down and took hold of the twin brass pulls on the drawer. "I found it after we talked. There's a false bottom in the drawer, and I found some papers. I think they belong to your family."

He eased open the drawer. There was a rattle, a flash of brown, and then Dagen jumped back and clutched his leg.

Bailey leapt in front of Fiona, shouting, "Snake!"

Dagen stumbled across the floor grabbing his shin. "It bit me." He knocked over lamps and small tables before he fell to the floor, screaming. The clerk came running in from the store. Bailey yelled for her to stop.

The snake coiled just under the armoire, rattles shaking.

Fiona, feeling oddly calm, started forward again.

"Stop!" Bailey ordered her. "Don't move. I produce a show about rattlesnake wranglers in Texas. I don't think we should make any sudden movements."

"And let it bite him again?" Fiona shook her head. She called on her magic and spoke in a calm, quiet voice to the others.

"Dagen, hush," she said. "Calm down. You need to slow your heart rate." Dagen stopped screaming and writhing.

Fiona looked at the terrified clerk. "Call 911. Get help. Tell them it's a rattlesnake bite." Needing no further prompting, the young woman lifted her cell phone and vanished to the front of the store.

Once again, Fiona moved toward the snake.

Bailey held her back. "Shouldn't we wait for help?"

She infused her voice with more magic. "Use your belt as a tourniquet on Dagen's leg. Cut off the blood flow from the bite."

His movements slow and methodical, Bailey drew off his belt and moved to Dagen's side to comply with Fiona's command. While he was distracted, Fiona pulled her magic forward another notch. A huge hunting knife appeared in her hand.

In the distance, sirens screamed. Emergency help was on the way.

But Fiona wasn't going to wait. This was no ordinary snake. She stepped forward again, knife drawn. The rattler coiled tighter and hissed. Fiona lifted her weapon, and the snake rose like a cobra, mouth open wide. Fiona jumped back as a man's face appeared on the head of the snake. His hairless head glistened, his eyes glowed red, and his mouth gleamed with enormous fangs.

The snake body rose up farther, pushing from beneath the cabinet, and the man's eyes locked on Fiona's. She could feel the darkness tugging at her, inviting her to move closer. Only her power helped her wait, knife clutched in hand and prepared to attack. Then the man's face melted to a cloud of black smoke that shot to the ceiling and out the back door.

Fiona ran out on the loading dock, but saw nothing in the deserted alley behind the store. The only sign of life in the hot summer afternoon were the sirens spiraling ever closer. No snake. No smoke drifting away in the air.

Back inside she found the snake dead on the floor in front of the armoire. Bailey was struggling with a weeping, pleading Dagen. Fiona heard shouts from the store and pounding footsteps. Paramedics or the police were almost here.

Knowing she needed a believable story, Fiona quickly sliced off the snake's head.

Two paramedics raced to Dagen's side. Bailey stood and joined Fiona. He looked in surprise down at the dead snake. "You killed it."

"My grandfather trained me not to mess around with rattlers. I grew up doing a lot of hiking."

"But where did you get the knife?" Bailey took the weapon from her. Blood dripped off the sharp blade.

"It was right here," Fiona claimed, nodding to a stack of boxes nearby. "I saw it sticking up and grabbed it."

Bailey rubbed his forehead, looking dazed. "But—"

"We should check the cabinet," Fiona said, turning back to the armoire.

Bailey protested, but she swung the door wide. As she expected, the interior was empty. So was the drawer she eased the rest of the way open. At the bottom were the papers Dagen had mentioned.

They looked very familiar.

Fiona plucked the yellowing, handwritten pages from the drawer. These were from *The Book of Connelly Magic*. She recognized the ornate scroll pattern on the paper. There was a map. What were they doing here? And what information did they hold that the snake was guarding?

"Fiona?"

She looked up at Bailey.

He was regarding her with suspicion. "What's going on?"

"These are family papers," she explained. "Very old papers."

"And so—"

Bailey's question was cut off as firefighters arrived with a stretcher and helped the paramedics lift Dagen. A sheriff's deputy was close on their heels, and he had questions for Fiona, Bailey, and the clerk. Meanwhile, an ambulance backed up to the loading dock, an easier option than wheeling him through the crowded store.

After the ambulance raced off and the deputy took photos for his report and left, the store clerk stared down at the dead snake, shaking in fear. "I called Dagen's wife to meet them at the hospital, and I'm going to close the store. What if there are more snakes?"

Fiona patted her arm in reassurance. "I imagine the snake arrived with the armoire. Dagen said the delivery just came in this morning. The snake attacked when Dagen started checking it out. He told me earlier the armoire had been stored in an old house which is a perfect place for a snake to hide out."

Not convinced, Bailey rubbed his chin and studied the cabinet again. "But why didn't Dagen find the snake before, when he found the papers?"

"I'm glad we were here and could help." Fiona knew the snake came for her after she touched the armoire. A Connelly witch's touch had summoned an evil guardian, but to what end? She turned to the clerk.

"You go lock the doors. I'll clean up this mess."

The clerk hurried off, and Fiona looked down at the papers. Did they hold the secret to saving her family from a centuries-old curse?

Abruptly, Bailey said, "This is a weird place."

She rolled up the papers and slid them into the back pocket of her jeans. "You mean Dagen's store?"

"No, this town. Very weird."

"So I imagine you want to leave, huh?" The pang in her belly was dismaying. Things would be much easier if he just left, so why did she want him to stay?

He grinned. The killer smile betrayed his utter delight and sent an unusual flutter through her.

"Hell, no," he said. "I'm not leaving. I'm fascinated. Your show is going to be so much more than I thought it would be. This town is all Southern gothic strange with crows in the graveyards, snakes in cabinets, crazy old ladies in the diner, and you talking to ghosts. We will kill in the ratings."

She shrugged. "I need to talk to my family."

He cocked his head. "About the show?"

"Among other things."

"Okay. Can we have dinner tonight and discuss this? I've got a lot of ideas, but I'm going to need your help to get the whole town on board."

Not going to happen, Fiona started to protest. Then she stopped. If she just said no, he really would leave, and she didn't want that. She had never wanted anything less in her life. Was it the show she was interested in or was it Bailey? She wasn't sure.

Bailey turned. "I'm going to find something to clean up this snake carcass."

"I'll do that."

"I did the manly thing and let you have the kill. Let me clean it up."

"I'm going to take the snake home," she blurted out. "To my grandmother."

Bailey wheeled back to her, startled. "You're going to take a dead snake to your grandmother?"

"It's a family thing," she murmured, trying not to look like she was lying. The alternative was to explain that the snake was magic-possessed, and her family's coven needed to examine the remains.

Bailey shook his head, smiling again. "I wish this was all happening on camera. Could I come with you and have Ryan tape the presentation of the snake to your grandmother?"

She wondered how to explain to him that Sarah would be more likely to turn Ryan and Bailey to dust. She settled for, "Let's not do that just yet. Now get going, and let me clean up this snake."

Chapter 9

Fortunately for Fiona, the elder witches of her coven were already at the home place for lunch and some Irish crocheting. They held a session like this a few times a year, hoping to keep alive the lace-making practice passed down from their ancestors. As usual, they had pressed a few of the younger members into joining them, so Fiona only had to make a few calls from the antique store in order to summon a full coven meeting immediately instead of tonight as Sarah had planned.

They all needed to see the papers from the armoire as soon as possible.

Others were arriving as she pulled her van to a stop in the driveway. Fiona lifted a plastic garbage sack from the floorboard and grabbed the new pages from the family's book of magic.

Eva Grace stepped out of her smart sporty convertible.

Brenna, in paint-splattered T-shirt and jeans, stood on the front steps with her gray, feline familiar, Tasmin nearby. An illustrator working on a children's book, Brenna had been painting in her third-floor studio when Fiona called.

Cousin Maggie Mills, an avid lace-maker who had also been at the home place, stood by the front door. She clutched the hand of her daughter, three-year-old

Rose.

The other cousin of their generation, Lauren Mayfield, worked at Siren's Call. She appeared from Eva Grace's passenger seat, auburn hair gleaming and ripe figure barely contained in a cherry-red sundress.

"What have you found?" Maggie demanded as the young witches assembled on the front porch.

Fiona shot Maggie's red-haired little girl a concerned glance. "We should talk about it inside with the others."

"But we're the five in danger," Maggie protested.

Rose looked up at her with round, green eyes full of concern. "Mommy, what's wrong?"

Perhaps because she was the mother of a budding young witch of the next generation, Maggie was always borderline hysterical when the coven discovered a development in their quest to break their family curse. Just weeks ago, the demon talked Maggie into trading access to their family for immunity from the curse. As a consequence, the demon had almost killed Brenna in order to absorb her powerful magic. The coven learned the demon could not make promises on behalf of the Woman in White. They were still trying to figure out the relationship between the two beings.

Brenna knelt in front of Rose and summoned Tasmin. "Take the cat inside and play," she told the little girl. The gray tabby rubbed against the youngster's chubby legs. Giggling, Rose followed the cat into the house.

Brenna stood and gripped Maggie by both shoulders. "You need to calm down."

The young mother's auburn ponytail swung side to side as she shook her head. "I don't know how you can say that when the days are just clicking by, and we're waiting for the next awful thing to happen."

"We're not just waiting," Fiona said and quickly updated Maggie and Lauren about the crows at the cemetery and last evening's encounter with the ghost at Siren's Call. "Minnie warned me that she's hiding because it's not safe in New Mourne. That must mean the Woman in White or the demon will strike again soon."

Lauren's green eyes held faint accusation. "I heard you brought in a Hollywood producer for last night's séance."

Despite her own misgivings about Bailey, Brenna quickly jumped to Fiona's defense. "It wasn't a séance, and Fiona did nothing that she's not done on her webcast dozens of times."

Lauren and Maggie still looked disapproving.

"I hear the producer's hot." Lauren flipped her hair off her shoulder with a languid motion that Fiona suspected men would find sexy. Fiona wondered, as she often did, what it would be like to have such ease with her sexuality. Thinking of Bailey's lips on her own, she wondered how she had measured up to the other women he had probably kissed. She wasn't experienced enough to be sure of herself. Today, he hadn't seemed particularly interested in anything about her but the show he was proposing. Maybe she had failed.

Eva Grace interrupted her thoughts. "We're here to learn what Fiona found today. We can talk about Hollywood producers later. Let's go inside."

The others sat in the dining room to the left of the broad central hall where Rose was using a string to tantalize Tasmin. With their crochet supplies laid to the side, the witches sat at the long table where many generations of the Connelly coven had met, plotted, planned, and eaten. The ancient wood gleamed, complemented by new chairs that Marcus had designed last year. With arching backs and simple carving, the chairs displayed his extraordinary talent and harmonized new with old.

Fiona loved this room, the stone fireplace and the wall shared with the kitchen that was the old timber exterior of the first Connelly cabin built here. Most of all, she loved everyone gathered at the table.

Sarah, as coven leader, and her older twin sisters, Frances and Doris, known as the elder aunts, sat at the head of the table. Doris still had a small bandage on her neck from surgery she'd had to repair her carotid artery after an encounter with the demon. Both Doris and Frances had white hair teased into the helmets favored by many Southern matrons in their seventies, quite a contrast to Sarah's sleek, hippie-like braid. They all shared the Connelly green eyes.

The daughters of the three women—Delia, Estelle, and Diane—sat nearby. The younger witches took their customary places, with Brenna at the foot of the table, facing Sarah. Only Fiona remained standing.

"What's wrong?" Sarah asked her.

Fiona placed the papers found this morning on the table. "More pages from *The Connelly Book of Magic*."

A ripple of energy moved around the room, and Fiona saw one of the house's ghosts, an elderly woman she had always called Granny, peep out from the kitchen door. Granny looked alarmed.

Without a word, Delia got up and retrieved the family book from the sideboard where it was placed after this morning's discussion. She laid it on the table beside the new papers and looked at Sarah. "The pages look authentic."

"And what do they tell us?" Sarah asked Fiona. "I'm sure you've read them."

"First let me tell you how I found the pages." Fiona related what happened with the armoire, and told them about the scratched Connelly name inside, the papers Dagen had found, and finally, the snake.

"I brought the snake," Fiona said, gesturing toward the garbage bag she had placed on the hearth.

"We'll burn it in the clearing," Sarah said, referring a sacred place in the woods where the coven conducted rituals and celebrated holidays.

Doris said, "Is Dagen all right?"

Fiona nodded. "I talked to his wife on the way here. Because help came so soon, he will quickly recover."

"I can take him a poultice," Eva Grace murmured, ever the healer.

Frances, also an avid gardener, nodded. "Maybe a tea. Tulip poplar root, ground with dried sunflowers and starry campion."

Diane suggested a spell for the antique shop that would drive off any other snakes that had slithered in and burning sage to clear bad spirits. Aunt Doris disagreed on the exact wording of the spell.

Fiona could see the meeting dissolving into the chatty mess of so many others in the past. She tapped on the table, and everyone looked at her. "Dagen will be fine. What we need to focus on is the snake appeared when I touched the armoire." She told them about the snake with the man's head.

Doris's hand rose to the bandage on her neck.

The door to the kitchen opened and slammed shut. Fiona turned, expecting to see Granny race to the hall and the staircase. Instead, the apparition was a blur she didn't recognize. That was strange.

Rose ran in, crying for her mother. Tasmin streaked past her and jumped into Brenna's lap.

Maggie soothed her daughter and Brenna stroked her cat, but before the hubbub could diminish, *The Connelly Book of Magic*'s pages turned, and the new papers lifted and fluttered into place in the middle of the book.

No one moved for several seconds. Fiona reached for the loose papers, thinking she would see how they matched the surrounding pages. A light flashed, and the book incorporated them.

In the ensuing silence, Sarah cleared her throat. "I think that answers any doubt about where the pages belong."

"Can we be sure it's not the demon at work?" Maggie whispered, her arms tightening around Rose.

"There is no demon in this house," Sarah stated.

"But he burned down your studio," Brenna pointed out, referring to a devastating fire that had destroyed Sarah and Marcus's work area near the house just weeks ago.

Sarah stood. "There is no demon here." Thunder rumbled as she spoke.

Fiona felt the strong wills of her grandmother and Brenna ready to battle. The old generation continually resisted the power of the new.

Candles on the mantel lit and blew out and the lace curtains over the window seat billowed.

Little Rose's eyes were once more wide and frightened.

Again, Fiona tried to bring the meeting to order. "Do you want to hear what these pages reveal?"

There were nods all around, and Doris suggested Rose should leave.

Maggie's lips tightened. "This is her problem and her family, too."

Sarah agreed. "You young ones have said we hide too much from you about the curse. Let the child stay."

Fiona sat and pulled the magic book toward her. "The new pages are dated in the 1880s. They're about an ancestor of ours named Albert."

"Oh, my," Frances murmured.

Fiona continued, "Apparently Albert inherited a little magical ability, but was always jealous that the women in the family possessed the true gifts."

Frances turned to her twin sister. "Do you remember Grandmother telling us about him? He was a bad one who turned to black magic."

"I never knew the males in our family had magic." Fiona looked at Maggie, who was descended from a male relative. "Does Uncle Van have magic? Or your brother Sully?"

"Not unless you count their abilities to coax cows to give milk," Maggie retorted. She hugged Rose, who had fallen asleep on her lap. "You're not suggesting that Dad or Sully have something to do with—"

"No, Albert was a strange one, and had no children." Doris leaned forward, brow furrowing. "If I remember correctly, he made sacrifices of the family cats."

Tasmin hissed from Brenna's lap.

"Albert sounds like a serial killer in the making," Eva Grace commented, her face pale.

Sarah added, "He probably used the energy from the sacrifices for his evil spells. He must have known the magic worked better if the animal was beloved."

"According to these pages," Fiona said. "Albert made a deal with a demon so he could steal another's magic."

"Was it our demon?" Brenna demanded.

"Do you think there are two?" Fiona answered and looked back at the book. "It says here that Albert went after a faerie instead of a Connelly witch."

"That must have pissed off the demon," Brenna said with a faint smile, no doubt remembering when the demon came after her.

Sarah turned to her elder sisters. "Do you remember hearing that Albert messed with the fae? That's very bad business."

Frances shook her head. Doris looked stricken. "That would be terrible."

Fiona turned a page of the book. "He ended up killing the young faerie. Her sister retaliated."

"Willow," Sarah muttered in a hushed voice. "That must have been Willow's sister."

Everyone stared at her.

She continued, "Albert killed Shivon Scanlan, and Willow's magic easily defeated Albert and the demon that used him. Then Willow sealed Albert's spirit in a cave in The Valley of Shadows."

Fiona swallowed hard. Her grandmother had just recounted most of what was in the book. "How did you know that?"

Sarah rubbed her forehead, looking weary. "I think

it's the Remember-Not spell wearing off. Every time we find missing pages from this book, memories come back. I must have read or been told this story years ago. Then the coven used the spell to wipe it away." Her gaze went around the table. "As we've told you, that spell was used for generations to help the family cope with the curse."

"Just don't use it on us," Brenna gritted out, her cheeks growing hot. "Not remembering has not helped us at all."

Fiona turned the book around and slanted it so that everyone could see. "The last of the new pages has a map to The Valley of Shadows."

Delia traced the map's markings for New Mourne, the Connelly farm, and the old cemetery. "It's the land near Van's farm. We were talking about it this morning."

"Is this why the land there is so desolate?" Fiona asked.

"The cave was sealed by fae magic," Sarah said sharply. "And we were all told to stay away from that whole wretched stretch of land. We told all of you to do so as well."

"My brother and I went there anyway," Maggie admitted. "It was kind of like the neighborhood haunted house, you know; we couldn't resist. But we never saw a cave."

Lauren looked at her in surprise. She and Maggie had played together often as children. "You never took me there."

"Because you'd have said it was yucky," Maggie retorted.

"I can't believe Van didn't stop you," Frances said.

Maggie smiled. "Trust me, he did when he caught us, but it was just too tempting to stay away. We loved the silence. There were never any crickets or frogs, no birds or squirrels, just complete silence."

"I'm surprised at you, Maggie," Sarah said. "I never would have thought you'd so blatantly disobey coven orders." She glanced at Brenna. "I guess it's a good thing that Brenna didn't discover it. She might have built a bonfire at Samhain and loosed the hounds of Hell."

Brenna grinned and rolled her eyes. "Pity I didn't think of it."

"Kids are always braver than adults," Maggie said. "You don't truly understand fear until you're responsible for the life of another." She glanced at her daughter again. "If Rose ever sneaks down there, I'll lock her in her room."

"So what does this have to do with the curse?" Eva Grace asked, frowning at the map.

"Obviously, we have to find the cave," Fiona said.

Comments rang out around the table, but Sarah's commanding voice drowned everyone else out. "Absolutely not. We will not look for that cave. Those crows were warning you away, Fiona. And these pages are another warning to stay away from that place of death."

"But why?" Brenna asked. "Fiona's been running down there every morning for a long time, and nothing happened before the crows appeared. Perhaps they and the pages are signs that we should look in that direction in order to break the curse."

Before more bickering between Brenna and Sarah could break out, Fiona said, "I wonder why these pages were in an old armoire."

Doris said, "Our mother sold the furniture in our sister Rose's bedroom after the Woman in White killed her. I seem to remember a beautiful old wardrobe that had been in the family a long time."

Mention of their sister taken as tribute by the Woman in White caused all three elders to sag visibly. Without speaking, they linked hands.

"Getting rid of the furniture was part of Remember-Not," Sarah said. "It was the same when my own daughter was taken." Tears swam in her eyes as she looked at Eva Grace. "I couldn't bear to think of your dear mother, and I had to focus on raising you. It seemed imperative to forget. That's why I put all of Celia's things down in the barn."

"And in her belongings in the barn was where I found other pages of the family book," Brenna said. "That can't be a coincidence."

"We still don't know what Albert has to do with the curse," Fiona said.

"Obviously it was a time of tribute when he ran amuck," her mother said. "Let's look in the book and see when the next young Connelly witch died."

They found it was only months after Albert's misadventures that a young witch named Cornelia was taken. Official word was she was victim of a rattlesnake bite.

"Now that is strange, considering what happened today," Fiona said.

"And we all know it was no snake. Just the work of the Woman in White," Brenna added.

Eva Grace sighed. "So the demon was out ahead of the Woman, trolling for trouble in our family the same as he's been doing lately. Only he ran into Willow first."

A sob wrenched out of Maggie. "Then one of us died."

"Everything ties back to the Woman in White," Brenna said. "We've got to find out what happened to her and why she takes it out on our family."

"Maybe there are some answers in that cave," Fiona said.

Sarah stood again. "Didn't you just hear what we said? Please stay away from that place."

Even Delia looked doubtful. "I'm not sure it's the best decision to go taunting the demon. That's what Celia and I did, and the Woman took my sister right away." She reached out for Fiona's hand. "Please, promise me you'll let this one go. There have to be other clues to breaking the curse. This involves the fae, so it's especially dangerous."

Fiona protested, "I'm the one who found these pages. They practically came to me. I mean, why was I the one that Dagen called? He knows all of you. It seems like a sign to me, something that must be explored. We have to look at every avenue until we find the Woman in White's story."

"I agree," Brenna said. "All we know about her now is that she was probably the daughter of a missionary and fell in love with a Cherokee brave. She died near the waterfall where all the Connelly witches are taken."

Fiona tapped her chin in thought. "I wonder what it all has to do with the cave where Albert is sealed."

"You need to stay away from The Valley of Shadows," Sarah repeated. "Promise me, Fiona?"

As she was, always and forever, the good child, the obedient one, Fiona almost gave in. Then temper rose in her. Sick and tired of behaving herself, Fiona stood and faced her grandmother. "I won't promise. I'm not going to stay away from a place we might finally find our answers."

Without waiting to see the coven's reaction, Fiona left the house.

Though she heard Brenna and Eva Grace calling for her, she ran out to her van and turned around in the graveled driveway to hurry away in a cloud of dust. Horns blared as she pulled onto the highway without stopping.

"I don't think it will improve the situation or your temper if you hurt someone else by driving carelessly," a voice said from the passenger's seat.

Fiona glanced over to see her Aunt Celia in the seat beside her. It was disconcerting, seeing the person who looked so much like her own mother, a ghost that Fiona had been trying to reach for years. She swerved into a neighbor's driveway and parked the van.

Breathing hard, she turned to find her aunt still occupying the passenger's seat. "You were at the house," Fiona accused. "With Granny."

Celia nodded. "I was trying to keep her calm. The poor old thing worries about all of you."

"But why have I never seen you before?"

"Because the time wasn't right until now. I'm finally strong enough to help you."

"How?"

"By becoming your spirit guide."

"All these years of talking with ghosts and now I get a spirit guide?" Fiona sighed. "What can you do for me?"

"I can show you how to find the cave in The Valley of Shadows. We can start saving Connelly witches there."

Chapter 10

Bailey spent midday strolling around New Mourne feeling restless and wondering what he was going to do with himself until dinner tonight with Fiona.

He had the uneasy feeling he was being watched. The business people he encountered in the shops were friendly enough, but there was still the strange, prickly sensation he had associated with Anna ever since her death. It was the feeling he could turn around and she would be standing there. Right after she died, he'd always turn to find no one was there. He had proven to himself many times he would never see his sister again, no matter how strongly he felt her presence. He also knew no one existed who could make that happen, despite what Fiona claimed.

So why were the hairs on the back of his neck standing? Why was he contemplating asking Fiona more about Anna?

"Oh, God," Bailey moaned, scrubbing a hand through his hair. "I hate this shit."

He shrugged off his unease, bought an éclair from Britta's Bakery, and found a comfortable shaded seat in the town park midway between the inn and Fiona's office. After consuming the delicious pastry and resisting a zombie-like compulsion to buy another, he got a steady wireless connection on his phone and took care of some work emails.

His business world seemed oddly calm, perhaps because the old and new shows for this fall were already in production and going well. His main duty was lining up new programs for a January launch. The priority, at the moment, Fiona's show.

No, not just Fiona's, he decided as he once again glanced at the town's bustling main street. After this morning's adventures, he had to wonder what other unusual people and events were waiting for him in New Mourne.

"Hello."

Bailey turned at the greeting and stood as a red-haired man approached.

"Dr. Rodric McGuire." The man put out his hand, and Bailey shook it wondering why the name sounded familiar. He looked a bit older than Bailey, shorter and solidly built. Despite the warmth of the day, he wore a navy sports jacket over a button-down shirt and gray slacks—all of them wrinkled. His tone was courteous, but there was something not so friendly in the intelligent brown eyes behind his square-rimmed glasses.

"I have a feeling you know who I am," Bailey said.

"The producer who is interested in our Fiona's show."

"*Our* Fiona? Are you a relative?"

"A very good friend of Fiona's soon-to-be brother-in-law. You know him as Sheriff Tyler, I believe."

Yes, Bailey remembered the good sheriff's warnings last night. He also recognized Dr. McGuire's accent as Scottish. "You're a ghost hunter," he said, realizing why the man was familiar.

"A scholar who studies paranormal phenomena,"

the doctor corrected.

The very helpful diner waitress had told Bailey there were two world-famous paranormal experts in town. Fiona's father, whom Bailey had met last night, and another man she called "the Scottish dude." Bailey had looked him up on the Internet yesterday when he was pulling together notes on the day's events, and wondered why this little Georgia mountain town attracted the attention of someone like Rodric McGuire, PhD.

"Misty over at Mary's Diner told me you're a ghost buster," Bailey continued. "How's that different from what Fiona does?"

"Fiona's a medium, so she talks with the dead. I don't have that ability."

"But you see them, huh?"

"I study the effect the paranormal have on our environment," the doctor continued. "Depending on their form, they leave distinct imprints and sometimes cause unpleasant side effects."

"Can you get rid of the side effects?" Bailey's interest was piqued now.

"Once the phenomena are identified, I often work with those like Fiona who can help restless spirits cross over or at least stop interfering in the lives of the living. And sometimes, once I can prove that people are truly experiencing a haunting, they live harmoniously with the spirits."

Sounded a little like a ghost therapist, Bailey thought to himself, which wasn't nearly as cool as ghost buster. "So you don't zap ectoplasms and imprison them?"

The Scot's mouth quirked. "Though that sort of

activity made for several pleasant films from comedic geniuses, no, that's not how I work."

"Pity. With the right action, we could include you in the show I'm planning."

The brown-eyed gaze sharpened. "Fiona is doing the show?"

"I'm broadening the scope," Bailey replied with his normal confidence. "With Fiona's family and the interesting characters in this town, we don't have to keep the focus on Fiona's activities."

"And has Fiona's family agreed to that?"

"She's talking to them."

For some reason the doctor thought that was funny. He laughed aloud and clapped Bailey on the shoulder like they were old buddies sharing a private joke.

Bailey frowned. "I'm completely legit, you know. You can check me out."

"Jake and I have spent the better part of today looking into you," McGuire said. "You're quite good at what you do, Mr. Powers, but I doubt you're going to get anywhere in New Mourne."

"Fiona is very interested," Bailey replied.

"She's in no position to be doing this now."

"And who are you to be saying that?"

The doctor held up his hands. "There's no need to become contentious. I have no reason to stop Fiona from doing something she truly wants, but her family is involved in something very…" He stopped, as if searching for the right words. "I guess complex would be the best way to describe their situation."

"Next you'll be telling me they're cursed."

McGuire went slack-jawed. "What are you talking about?"

"An old lady in the diner——I think her name was Willow—told me the family members are witches and they're cursed."

The Scot fell back a step. "Willow Scanlan told you this?"

Bailey was confused. "Fiona led me to believe that Willow's the town loon, and she spreads tales like that all the time. I figured she had an old grudge against the Connellys and that's why she called them witches. It's a pretty general term, you know, not just a reference to old crones who fly around on broomsticks and stir up eye of newt and toe of frog in their cauldrons."

McGuire looked shocked. "You have some stereotypical views about the supernatural and some misconceptions—"

"And I have some pretty good reasons for them," Bailey retorted.

"There's no room for you here." The doctor stepped forward, and all trace of the absent-minded professor vanished. "Can I give you some advice?"

"I'm sure you will whether I want it or not," Bailey said affably.

"Leave Fiona alone."

For a moment, all Bailey could think of was kissing Fiona last night. Was the Scottish dude staking a claim? "If you and Fiona are involved, that—"

"What nonsense," the doctor cut in. "I simply know Fiona's family doesn't want you here."

"She didn't tell me that."

"You're just causing more problems for the Connellys. They don't need your interference or your disrespect for what Fiona is."

"I'm not disrespecting anyone, Dr. McGuire."

"Aren't you?" McGuire stepped forward. "Aren't you planning to exploit Fiona, her family, and this town?"

"Exploit is a strong word."

"I think it applies."

Bailey started to protest, and then sucked in a deep breath. Very little gain could come from a disagreement with a good friend of the Connellys. "Okay, I'll keep that in mind as I deal with Fiona and her family."

McGuire glowered at him, his fists clenched at his sides. "Sheriff Tyler and I will be watching you."

"So noted," Bailey said, although he didn't think the threat was necessary.

Simmering, he walked out of the park and along Main Street, heading toward Fiona's office without thinking. He wasn't going to exploit anyone. He produced entertainment. For God's sake, Fiona was already on the internet. Couldn't any of them see she wanted the exposure? Dr. McGuire and his lawman friend needed to relax.

His phone rang, and distracted by his anger, he answered tersely.

"My, but you sound angry," said his mother. "Am I interrupting something?"

"Sorry, Mom, I was preoccupied. Good to hear from you."

"Can we talk onscreen? You've been on the road so long, I've almost forgotten what you look like."

Bailey laughed. Once upon a time, his mother's need to see him often was annoying. With some maturity, he realized that losing one child in a sudden, horrific way might mean she needed some regular reassurances about her other child.

He had to turn his back on Main Street and press the app to get his mother's face on his phone. Her smile told him how pleased she was. "It's my same old mug. Nothing new here."

"I rather like that mug of yours," she retorted.

"It's a lot like yours."

With sun-streaked hair and blue eyes, Beth Powers still looked like the quintessential California beach girl. Both her children looked more like her than her husband.

Both children.

Bailey groaned and realized why his sister had been so in his thoughts today. "I forgot," he confessed to his mother. "Today's Anna's birthday."

His mother's smile was sad. "I'm actually glad you forgot."

"Mom—"

"No, honestly, your forgetting is normal and healthy."

"She'd have been twenty-nine."

He tried to visualize his gawky, younger sister all grown up. What would she have done with her life? "I'm sorry I didn't call you." Even fifteen years later, his mother had problems with the big occasions without Anna—the birthdays, holidays, and the anniversary of her murder.

"It's okay." Beth reassured him. "Tell me about this new show. Your dad filled me in last night."

"I think it's going to take a little longer than I expected to get buy-in from everyone involved."

"You think the medium is genuine?"

He lifted an eyebrow.

She laughed. "All right, I guess it would take more

than a day to convert you to a true believer."

"I'll tell you everything soon," he promised. "I want to get all of the details figured out before I present it. There's a lot going on here."

"I'm sure you'll do what's best," she said. "You always do."

"There was a time you wouldn't have said that," he replied, thinking of his wild years after Anna's murder. "You should go do something nice for yourself today. Like a spa or something, what you might have done with Anna for her birthday if she was here."

She looked pleased. "I'll do that. Love you, son."

"Love you, too," he said as he hung up.

He sat for moment in the sunshine, his head full of memories. Once more, a tickle of awareness ran up his spine. This time, he didn't resist the impulse to turn. What he saw was Fiona coming out of her office and loading something in her van.

Bailey hurried down the sidewalk and called out to her. She glanced up, her expression distracted and intense. As he walked toward her, he appreciated the way her worn jeans cupped her rounded behind and her snug black tank emphasized the firm swell of her breasts. Once more, he remembered the impulse that made him reach for her in the starlight last night.

"Was the snake duly delivered to your grandmother?" he said as he drew near.

"Yes." She hefted a loaded backpack into the van and slammed the door.

He glanced down at her ankle boots. "Going hiking?" he asked as he followed her around to the driver's door.

"No."

"Can I go along?"

"No." She finally turned to look at him. "I'm kind of busy right now. We're going to talk tonight."

"Sure, but—"

"See you about seven, back here." She got in the van, started the engine, and waved as she pulled away. She turned right at the traffic light, the same direction Bailey took yesterday when he tracked her down.

Not stopping to consider that he was pretty much stalking her, Bailey jogged to his car in the inn parking lot. He was on the road in minutes, and it wasn't long before he spotted the van up ahead in traffic.

He couldn't say why he knew exactly where she was going, but he did—back to the cemetery where they met.

Cars thinned out as they left the town proper, and Bailey hung back, not wanting her to see his car. At the crest of the hill before the road descended to the graveyard, he pulled off into the last patch of trees before the land turned barren. The van pulled in the cemetery, and Fiona got out and shrugged on her backpack. She gestured and pointed as if talking to someone invisible. Maybe she was on the phone. He glanced down at his own cell and remembered there was no service out here.

He eased out of his car when she struck off across the desolate landscape. She was looking down at a piece of paper in her hands, intent on the contents. He subtly followed, keeping her in sight and using the half-dead trees he encountered for cover. Thank God, there were no crows hovering today.

He paused beside a gnarled tree to give her some space and noticed his pants' legs were covered in tiny brown dots. Leaning against the tree, he pulled his leg up for a closer look and discovered they were not insects but some kind of plant. When he looked back, Fiona was out of sight. He got worried when he didn't find her right away and then almost got caught as he moved forward. He had to drop down behind a spindly bush.

Bailey realized there was no sound. There were no birds, no squirrels scurrying from tree to tree, no hum of bugs, or drone of bees. Just absolute silence. A chill ran through him, and he chided himself for acting like a dumb teenager in a B movie.

He shifted from his hiding place to sneak a look. Fiona was standing in front of the steep face of a rock cliff. She was chatting away, although there was still no one that he could see. He surveyed the area ahead, trying to find a place to be closer yet still hidden, but if he moved, she'd see him no matter which way he went.

Fiona removed her backpack and pulled several items out. Bright red fabric unfurled, a vibrant swath of crimson that came alive in the sunlight. A cape, he realized as it settled around her shoulders and she pulled the hood over her gleaming hair. The cape billowed around her as though a heavy breeze lifted it, though the air was still, heavy, and hot.

Next, she took out a long, curved knife. She drew a circle at her feet and crossing marks. She placed five candles around her—red, orange, purple, violet, and yellow. She stepped back and raised her hand. The candles flamed bright, and Bailey blinked. How had she done that?

Pulling her cape close, she took several deep breaths, dropped her head against her chest, and then turned her pretty face upward.

Bailey saw storm clouds gather in what had been a clear, blue sky.

Fiona lifted her arms. She looked like a beautiful red bird getting ready to rise to the sky. The wind roared, a sound amplified in the oppressive silence.

Bailey held his breath as Fiona began to chant. Her voice lifted, and he could hear every word.

"The hour has power, the power is mine. Where once was a door, open for me. Where once was a cave, please let me see."

Bailey drew in a sharp breath as the earth shook. Fiona's cape swirled in satin ripples around her outstretched arms. She shouted, "As I will, so mote it be."

The ground on the ridge in front of Fiona fell away in big chunks of rocks and earth. When the trembling stopped, a dark opening had been torn into the land.

Fiona dropped her arms the air calmed as once again silence fell like a numbing hum.

She blew out the candles, took off her cape, and repacked all the items in her backpack. She once again spoke to the emptiness beside her, shouldered the pack, and walked through the opening.

Bailey remained on his knees, stunned. His brain burned. Either the bakery had incorporated magic mushrooms into that éclair or Fiona had some kind of power. If he wasn't under the influence, then she had just moved a mountain.

Foreboding washed through him as he scrambled toward the cave's entrance. He had to stop Fiona or something terrible would happen.

Just inside the opening, he started to call out. Then

he heard a sound behind him and whirled.

Anna stood in front of him.

Anna.

Just as he remembered her from that last day of her life. After all these years of feeling her so frustratingly close, he saw Anna haloed by the sunlight, a smile on her lips. *Anna, here? Why? Had Fiona truly been able to summon his sister?*

Bailey stepped forward and pain shot through his head. His legs buckled, and the world went black.

Chapter 11

Fiona's steps faltered as she hurried down a dark, crumbling tunnel and deep into the forbidden cave.

"Hurry, Fiona!" Aunt Celia murmured, and Fiona jumped.

Her newly appointed spirit guide kept fading in and out. Moreover, the ghost's resemblance to Fiona's mother was unnerving. It was like having a twenty-year-old version of Delia at her side. Celia had died six years before Fiona was born, so they had never met until Celia came to Fiona at Siren's Call after an encounter with the demon.

Ignoring the swell of energy at the front of the cave, Fiona pulled a candy bar from her backpack and ate it in three quick bites. Casting the spell that opened the cave had sapped her energy, so she needed to fuel up.

"Keep going," Celia urged.

Fiona studied the flickering image of her aunt in the light of her small flashlight. "In the family photos, you and Mother didn't look so identical."

"Delia was always the pretty twin, so vibrant and alive." Celia flashed ahead of Fiona and peered around a jagged rock. "I was quiet and shy."

"But you're the one who came home pregnant from college and wouldn't tell anyone who Eva Grace's father was."

Celia faded again. Fiona knew Celia had been away for more than seven months and had told no one she was having a baby before she returned to New Mourne. She and Delia had delivered Eva Grace and Brenna at the exact moment on a stormy February night twenty-eight years ago, as the coven celebrated the festival of Brighid. Celia had died only weeks later, her generation's tribute to the Woman in White.

Fiona jumped again when Celia snapped back in front of her as a full-bodied entity. "Fiona, dear, you must concentrate on why we're here. We need to find out if this cave is related to the Woman; if there are clues here, they could help end the curse."

Digging out another candy bar, Fiona nodded. She chewed nougat and chocolate as she followed Celia, her feeble flashlight illuminating rough walls and a path littered with dirt and debris. The air was dank and damp with a hint of rot.

"I guess I thought we'd find something right away since this is a 'forbidden' place," she said as they rounded another curve. She yearned for her infrared camera, even though she'd decided it would be unwieldy on this search.

"A place that a ghost won't even inhabit is a bad place." Celia's form evaporated into the shadows once more, but her voice continued. "I understand why no spirits ever come here. It's very difficult to remain. I don't know that I could without your strength."

Fiona closed her eyes and opened herself, hoping to capture a glimmer of a spirit other than Celia. "The only other time I've felt a place so empty was during the height of the demon's visit." She paused, her arms out in front of her as energy pulsed through the air. She heard another sound behind them and turned, frowning. "Is someone there?" she called out.

A glimmer of light appeared, and then faded.

"What is it?" Celia's disembodied voice spoke from the darkness.

"I feel something behind us." At the same time, Fiona realized she was connecting to something ahead of them, too. A faint flicker.

While Celia remained invisible, Fiona walked into another tunnel that became smaller and smaller. There was that stink in the air again—like a dead animal. When it felt as if she were at a dead end, she crawled over a tumbled pile of rocks and into a larger cavern. A fire pit was in the middle of the room, and the top of the cave disappeared into darkness overhead. She could feel fresh air, so she imagined the chamber acted like a natural chimney when there was a fire.

She stepped toward the pit and a vision flashed, causing a sharp pain in her forehead.

"What was that?" Celia was an opaque shadow near the wall. "Did you see it?"

Fiona nodded. She'd seen a smoldering fire with glowing coals, a man standing over another man who was bound hand and foot, and two more men watching from the left side.

Hands at her temples, Fiona concentrated, and the scene became clearer. An older man stood over his captive and pressed a glowing brand into the bottom of the younger man's foot. The young man's screams echoed through the cavern and cut through Fiona's skull. She staggered under the weight of his agony. Then the vision was gone, and she stood once again in an empty cave.

"What is this place?" Celia murmured. "What happened here?"

"Could that have been Albert Connelly who was torturing that man?"

"He didn't look like a Connelly."

"No, but—" A whisper of sound drew Fiona across the room toward a small opening. She could sense something there, just beyond the wall, a spirit of some kind, almost blocked, but with the tiniest bit of energy coming through. She turned back to her aunt. "Should we go this way?"

Silence. Aunt Celia had disappeared again.

Taking a deep breath, Fiona entered the narrow space alone. After ten feet or so, she had to lower her head. A little farther in, she found it more comfortable to crawl. She looked behind her but found no sign of her spirit guide. Keeping her breath slow and steady, she moved forward until she reached another opening. Though she hesitated for a moment, she finally crawled through and cast the light around her as she stood.

Here, the rot was so bad she choked and put a hand to her mouth. This chamber was smaller than the last, with a table in the center. The table's marble top rested on a gilded frame with scalloped edges and curved but sturdy-looking legs. In the middle of the table sat a small blue vase.

"How odd." Fiona walked a circle around the table. She felt the same flicker she had on the other side of the wall.

She stepped closer to the table. On the vase, a blue floral pattern outlined a Japanese garden scene with a Geisha standing in the middle. Like the table, the vase looked antique. Fiona stepped away and took a photo with her cell phone. Dagen should be able to date the table and possibly the vase from her picture.

For a moment she considered taking the vase with her.

Though her instinct urged Fiona to pull back, she felt drawn to the vase. She could sense the magic. In the dead silence of the hidden cave, she could hear a voice.

Open me.

The purr made her reach out.

"What do you suppose is inside?"

Celia's voice made Fiona drop her flashlight, and it went out. She scrambled around on her knees until she finally touched the cool metal shaft and turned it back on.

"Where have you been?" she asked her aunt.

"It's not easy to stay here." Celia looked around, shuddering.

"Should we open it?" Fiona asked her, drawn back to the vase.

Celia hovered near the table and reached for the vase. Her arm fell back to her side. "I don't have the strength to move it."

"I'll do it," Fiona said, moving closer.

"Be careful. It could be a trap."

Fiona glanced at her. "You sound like Mother."

"Really?" Celia smiled. "That's nice."

"But I've explored enough places to know you can't find out what you need to know without opening a few doors and windows."

"Minnie said you've been opening too many doors."

Trying not to think of that warning, Fiona gently placed two fingers on the top of the vase. She lifted the lid and stepped back.

Nothing happened.

"That was anticlimactic," Celia said just as a voice roared throughout the cavern.

A gray mist spewed from the vase. Celia snapped out like a light. Fiona dropped the porcelain lid and backed up to the rough wall of the cave. The gray mist became drops that merged as they fell to the floor until the ghost of a man appeared.

"By the gods, I've been in there a long time," he said and his spirit brightened to light their surroundings. "Thank you for setting me free."

Shit, Fiona thought, staring at the red-haired, green-eyed entity. *It's Albert Connelly.*

Near the entrance to the room, a small whirlwind began and knocked her to the floor. Albert laughed like a mad man, and a red glow pulsed like a heart and grew larger with each beat.

The creature that appeared before them had white wings tipped with gold. Her dress was a regal, rich scarlet, heavy with ornamentation stitched in gold. Above her lovely, bare white shoulders, her face was long and oval, her eyes lined with tiny jewels, the lashes thick and long. A gold crown trimmed with rubies rested in long black hair with bountiful waves.

An old, important faerie, Fiona surmised. It could only be—

"Stupid witch! Do you have any idea what you have done?"

Fiona's stomach clenched with fear. She may not know this creature by sight, but she'd know that voice anywhere—Willow Scanlan.

Albert drew their attention with another round of

maniacal laughter. "Forever just ended, you crazy faerie! I'm free."

He raised his arms, closed his eyes, and yelled, "Take me now!"

A black, oily substance poured out of the walls. The smell of rot made Fiona gag. The demon she had hoped never to see again rose in a black cloud and melted into Albert's ghostly form, making him corporeal.

Willow's scream bounced off the walls like a banshee's wail. She threw a ball of fire straight at Albert, but fueled by the demon, he shot through the narrow passage and out of the room.

"Damn you stupid Connellys!" Willow yelled. "You've opened the wrong door now, and you'll pay the price." Her wings flapped. She rose off the floor and disappeared.

The faerie's screams echoed from the front of the cave, followed by Albert's laughter. The walls around Fiona began to shake.

Celia's voice whispered low and urgent in her ear. "Run, Fiona. Now!"

Fiona pulled herself up and out of the room, crawled through the passage, then dodged falling dirt and rocks in the larger cavern and raced down the corridor she and Celia had followed into the cave. Her flashlight was little help, and she fell, tearing her jeans. She chanted a shielding spell and wished for Brenna's power in her magic, power to keep the cave from collapsing around her.

When she tore around the first curve in the tunnel, Albert blocked her way. He raised his arms and lightning flashed from his fingertips. "Boom," he said, insanity gleaming in eyes that were now as red as fire.

The ceiling crumbled, and Fiona pushed back with magic. It held as she ran to the entrance. A movement to the side caught her eye. She watched in horror as the rocks tumbled down on Bailey, who lay just inside the entrance.

There was only one thing to do.

Fiona called on the magic that coursed through her veins, the ancient magic that had bound Connelly witches together since before time was measured. "Grandmother. Brenna. Help me."

Chapter 12

A heavy weight pushed down on Bailey. He fought his way up through darkness. He had to get free. He needed to get Fiona out of here. Together, they would find Anna and get away from this disintegrating hole in the earth.

His eyes flew open as he thought of his sister. Dirt fell in his eyes. He breathed it in, choked and coughed. His lungs felt like they could explode. He was buried, buried alive.

He pushed against rocks and dirt, clawing his way through the filthy rubble. *How had he gotten here?*

First, he had seen Anna. Then someone had decked him from behind. He must have passed out, and when he started to come around, the whole damn cave had fallen in.

He had to get out of here. He had to breathe.

Rocks began to fall away with more ease. He became aware of intense pain in his right leg. He couldn't move it. Still fighting to get the upper part of his body free, he rode the growing pain as he had ridden the waves off Malibu as a daredevil teen, knowing at any minute he could be crushed.

The pain curled over him just as Fiona's face came into view. She was working feverishly, pulling dirt and rocks away, and shouting in a strange language.

He pulled his head up out of the dirt and sucked in

a gasp of air.

"Thank the Goddess." Fiona's hand clasped his, and a charge moved through him.

Her skin was glowing in the faint light seeping into the cave. She seemed to have the strength of ten women as she pulled him up from the rubble. His right leg, however, remained pinned, and he fell back, gasping for air, spitting out the dirt he had inhaled.

"My leg is caught. I think it's broken."

He lifted his head and in the faint light, could see that a large boulder held him down.

Fiona moved to the side of the large rock, leaned on it, and agony radiated through Bailey. His vision swam, and he began to shake. It was shock, maybe. Sweat ran down his face, and his teeth chattered.

"I'll be careful." Fiona lifted her arms, the way she had during her strange ceremony outside the cave. Her words were unfamiliar except for a few he could pick out. "Grandmother. Brenna. Eva Grace. Mother—"

The names washed over Bailey. He looked up at her, the light in her face, and the waves of energy that pulsed off her body. She was like a warrior goddess. Slender but filled with strength.

She rolled the rock away from his leg. As if it were a beach ball, he thought with a woozy detachment.

How could she do that?

How had she split the side of the ridge in two?

How had she summoned Anna?

His world was tilting on its axis and all because of this petite witch.

Witch?

He groaned, and Fiona said, "Are you okay?"

"I'm great," Bailey muttered. "Just great."

Relieved to feel the pain in his leg ebb a little, he watched through narrowed eyes as Fiona staggered, fell to her knees, then dragged herself to his side.

"I don't fucking understand you." He wrenched the words out. "Who are you? What are you?"

"Your salvation?" Her grin flashed in her grimy face. She pawed through a backpack and pulled out a bottle of water and a candy bar. She offered the first to him and unwrapped the second.

He pushed himself up on one elbow, gulped down some water, and spit it out before drinking it while she inhaled a candy bar.

"What's in the candy?" he asked, remembering the chocolates she had been eating last night before the ghost encounter at the shop. "Pixie dust?"

She rolled her eyes and swallowed, then pushed herself up. "Let's hope it's enough to get us out of here." She nodded toward the large pile of rocks that blocked the entrance. The only opening left was a crack several feet over their heads where the summer sun leaked in. "That looks like a lot of work."

"Maybe you could use the same tactics you used to get in here," he said evenly.

"You saw that?"

"Better special effects than any movie I've seen."

"No special effects," Fiona said as she picked up some of the bigger fragments and threw them behind her. "Magic. Simple enough once I knew I was in the right spot."

He gave a rough laugh. "There's nothing simple about any of this."

Fiona looked at him squarely. "We'll talk about it later. Right now, we have a crisis on our hands. I don't know if you saw much that happened when the cave-in started—"

"I was unconscious."

"Something evil caused all of this, and I'm not interested in hanging around, waiting to see if it comes back."

"So you're saying we need to get out of here sooner rather than later." Bailey sat up. "Let's see if I can stand."

Fiona moved behind him and put her hands under his arms, once more surprising him with her strength as she helped him stand. He could feel his right ankle swelling, and he couldn't put any weight on it. She helped him hobble to a large, flat rock. He grunted in frustration as he sat down. "I don't know how much help I'm going to be in digging us out."

She rolled some of the rocks out of the way. Bailey felt his impatience grow. He didn't like sitting here, doing nothing. But when he started to move, his head spun. He broke out in a cold sweat, and anger rose inside him.

"Why did you bring Anna here?" he demanded.

Fiona turned. "What?"

"My sister was here in the cave when I followed you in, before someone knocked me out. If you are the real deal, a medium or a psychic or whatever you are, why did you bring her to this place? What's she got to do with you?"

Fiona shook her head. "I did not summon your sister. Even if I did, she wouldn't come unless she wanted to, and I didn't feel her here."

"You said you saw her last night."

"But I didn't bring her here." Her voice rose.

"While I went into the tunnel, there were sounds from the front of the cave. Obviously, that was you, following me. But there was no spirit other than my aunt, my spirit guide."

"Your what?"

She made an impatient gesture. "That's not important. What's important is that I didn't feel the presence of any spirits except my aunt until we went into the back cavern." A frown creased her forward.

"I saw her," Bailey snapped. "For the first time since she died, Anna was there in front of me. Do you know how many times I've felt her, but never connected? Why do you think I hate all those fakes who said they'd communicated with her and didn't? Because I could feel her, damn it, always just out of reach."

"Bailey, I'm sorry, but—"

"All day long, I've been thinking about her. Today is her birthday, and she felt so close, like so many times before. You built on that somehow, didn't you?"

"No, I didn't." Fiona glanced around them, shivering. "But I know who might have. We've got to get out of here."

"Who would try to make me think my sister was here? And why?"

She opened her mouth, then stopped as sounds from outside trickled in the opening above them.

Alarmed, Bailey pushed unsteadily to his feet. "What's that?"

The high lilt of female voices brought relief to Fiona's strained features. "They've come."

"Who?"

"My family. They're going to rescue us. Come, on." She ducked under his arm and helped him limp back from the entrance.

"We're here," she called out. "Right here."

Bailey was dizzy. The blow to his head, the injury to his ankle, and the turmoil inside him were just too much. He thought he heard chanting. The earth rumbled. Rocks fell away from the entrance and sunlight poured in.

The air around him became alive and a surge of power chased over his skin.

A group of women stood in the entrance to the cave. Like a tribe.

The one in the lead, with the long gray braid, scowled. His unease spiked. Where had he seen her before?

There was no time to ask before they surrounded him.

Chapter 13

Fiona saw Bailey was in a daze, probably not a bad place for him as her coven took control of the situation. Eva Grace examined his ankle, and used her empathic abilities to ease his pain. He looked around at her family, eyes blinking.

Suspecting he was under a spell, Fiona frowned at her grandmother. "No Remember-Not spells."

Sarah sniffed. "You're the one who put him in danger, bringing him to this place."

"He followed me." Fiona's gaze narrowed. "I don't want his memories tampered with. That spell is dangerous. No telling what you might erase."

"Come on," Brenna interceded. "Let's all get out of here before this place collapses."

With Fiona and Brenna on either side of him, Bailey limped out of the cave.

When everyone was clear, the earth rumbled and shifted and rocks cascaded down to hide the opening again.

Delia turned to Fiona, her expression troubled. "You shouldn't have come here alone."

"What happened?" Brenna demanded. "When I felt you calling for us, you were terrified."

"The demon's back," Fiona said flatly. "And he has help. Albert Connelly."

Sarah swayed and reached for her elder sisters'

hands. "Oh, Fiona, please tell me you didn't let him escape."

"Willow knows Albert is free. She's pissed." Fiona thought she might as well confess all in one fell swoop, like ripping off a bandage.

Murmurs of despair went through the group. Fiona faced them in defiance. "I may have made a mistake, but at least I did something."

"Excuse me," Eva Grace interrupted. "We need to take care of Bailey. I think his ankle is only bruised, but he may need medical attention."

"He was also hit in the back of the head," Fiona said.

Though she looked like she wanted to explode, Sarah agreed they should take him to the Connelly home place. "There'll be a lot of questions if we take him to the inn or the hospital."

Several coven members had driven their vehicles across the desolate landscape beyond the old cemetery and near the cave. Fiona got Bailey into the back seat of Brenna's small SUV where he promptly fell asleep. She climbed in with him. Eva Grace took the passenger seat while Brenna drove.

"Tell me everything," Fiona's older sister commanded as they drove away, her green eyes flashing in the rearview mirror.

Fiona told them about the vision she had seen in the first large room, of the man she thought was Native American being tortured by another man.

Brenna was excited. "That could have something to do with the Woman in White. We're pretty sure she was in love with a Cherokee brave."

"I saw it all in a flash," Fiona said, trying to

remember more details. "Then I could feel a spirit from somewhere deeper in the cave." She told them about the cavern where Albert had been imprisoned. She even produced the photos on her phone that documented the unusual table and the vase.

Eva Grace tucked a strand of long, red hair behind her ear as she studied it. "I can't believe you opened that vase."

"It was like a compulsion," Fiona said, remembering how hard she fought not to touch the vase. "I couldn't resist."

"A compulsion," Brenna repeated, brow wrinkling. "Are you sure it was the demon that came in and took over Albert?"

Shuddering at the memory of the oily, vile entity flowing into Albert, Fiona nodded. "Very sure."

"Then maybe the compulsion came from the demon," Brenna suggested.

Fiona realized Brenna had a point.

"Remember, he showed up at Maggie's door," Brenna added. "He was so convincing she invited him in. She let him into our lives."

"Aunt Celia felt compelled, too," Fiona murmured. "She tried to open the vase, but she wasn't strong enough."

Eva Grace turned to look at her in surprise.

"Aunt Celia?" Brenna's gaze moved from the road to Fiona's again in the mirror. "What does Eva Grace's mother have to do with this?"

"I left out that part." Fiona sent her cousin an uncertain smile. "Your mother came to me after our meeting earlier this afternoon. She said she is going to be my spirit guide."

"What's that?" Brenna said.

"She's determined to help us break the curse." Fiona turned as Bailey moaned in his sleep. *Sarah's spell might be wearing off.* "She led me to the cave, and together, we opened it."

"Where is she now?" Eva Grace said eagerly. "Here?"

"She disappeared after the demon took over Albert." Fiona leaned over the front seat, concerned about her cousin's feelings. "Are you okay with this?"

"I just hope she can help. Seems to me that she led you into trouble today."

"It took a lot of strength for her to be there. Spirits stay away from that cave. That's why I was so intrigued when I felt a spirit in the back cavern." Fiona thought of what Bailey had told her about his sister. Her immediate thought was that the demon had made Bailey imagine he saw Anna's ghost. Perhaps, however, the demon was controlling Anna's spirit. But to what end? What in the world did Bailey have to do with all of this?

She looked at Brenna. "If the demon could make me open that vase, what else could he do?"

Brenna turned her car into the drive at the home place. "Think of everything we believe the demon has been responsible for since the curse started over two hundred years ago. Murders. Suicides. All sorts of other violence. Every time the Woman's tribute is due, he stirs up trouble."

"I guess he could control a haunting, too," Fiona murmured.

Her sister gave her a questioning look as she pulled the car to a stop.

Bailey sat up and looked around, recognition dawning in his ocean blue eyes only when he looked at Fiona. "Where are we?"

"We're going to fix you up," she said and got out of the car.

Marcus and Aiden came down the front steps. Sarah had called to alert them of what had happened. Bailey was groggy, but the men were able to help him into the house and up to Sarah and Marcus's bedroom.

Brenna spread a sheet to protect the bed's moss-green duvet from Bailey's filthy clothes before he lay down. Aiden and Marcus left with Fiona and Bailey's keys, promising to retrieve their vehicles near the old cemetery. Eva Grace brought in a pitcher of water and got Bailey a drink. Brenna fetched a damp towel and washrag from the nearby bath for Bailey to clean the worst of the dirt from his face, neck, and arms.

Finally, he looked up at them and frowned. "I'm sorry, but I don't really know what happened."

Had her grandmother inflicted the dreaded memory-stealing spell? "Do you remember the cave?" Fiona asked. "You were knocked out, then hurt your ankle."

She was relieved when his gaze sharpened. It was important that he recall what had happened today, especially about his sister.

"I saw Anna," he murmured.

"We'll talk about her later," Fiona promised. "Let's make sure you're okay now." She looked at Eva Grace. "Do you think he should go to the hospital? Something or someone hit him in the back of the head when he went in the cave, then he was almost buried."

"Let's see." With efficient motions, Eva Grace

touched his forehead, then ran her hands across his shoulders and along his arms. Bailey only winced when she touched his right ankle.

She eased off his expensive leather loafer. His ankle was swollen and purpling. He groaned at her touch. She placed one hand under the ankle and one on top, then chanted softly.

Bailey's eyes opened wide. "That feels good. Nice and warm."

Eva Grace left her hands in place for a few more moments, then stepped away. "I don't think anything's broken."

"Are you a podiatrist?" Bailey wiggled his right foot. "This feels so much better."

She smiled and turned to Fiona. "We should probably watch him for signs of a concussion. He should stay here—"

"No," he protested. "I'll go back to the inn."

"Nonsense." From the bedroom doorway, Sarah spoke. "You're going to stay here until we're sure you're okay, Mr. Powers." She came forward, her hand outstretched, and introduced herself and the elder aunts at her sides.

Fiona regarded her grandmother and the elders with suspicion. She told Bailey, "You're not going back to the inn. It's almost time for dinner. After that, we'll see how you're doing. I'll stay here with you."

"That's ridiculous," Sarah said. "You're covered in dirt, Fiona. You should go home and clean up. I'm sure Mr. Powers— "

"Call me Bailey, please."

"I'm sure you would like to get a shower, as well," Sarah continued speaking to him smoothly. "You can borrow some clothes from my husband."

Fiona stepped in front of her grandmother. "Don't try to influence him with magic."

The elders clucked in alarm. "Fiona, mind your mouth," Doris warned.

"In the Goddess's name don't be silly," Fiona retorted. "He saw me open the cave. He knows a lot."

Frances lifted a hand. "That's all the more reason to give him a little push."

"Yes," Doris agreed. She lifted her hand, too, and the air crackled.

Bailey's body slumped as he fell abruptly asleep.

"What did you do?" Fiona demanded.

"You're so dramatic," Frances replied. "We just didn't think he needed to hear any more of our conversation. He's asleep, that's all."

"Then just leave him be," Fiona said. "I'll stay here with him, and I'll get him back to his room as soon as he's rested up a bit."

Sarah, Frances, and Doris protested, but this time Brenna hushed them. "For some reason Fiona trusts this man. I'm not sure if I do," she added with a significant look at Fiona. "But let's give her a little credit."

Sarah acquiesced with a grumble. "When he's taken care of, we have to talk about what happened at that cave," she warned Fiona.

Brenna gestured for Sarah to precede her out of the room. "Come on, and I'll fill you in on what she's told me."

Alone with Bailey, Fiona gave in to the weakness in her knees and sat down on the edge of the bed. He was out, his chest rising and falling, his eyes closed naturally in sleep. Without his grin flashing, he seemed younger, she thought. She hoped she wasn't making a mistake thinking she could trust him with family secrets.

The alternative, she realized, would be his leaving New Mourne and never thinking of her again. The elders could even plant a story in his head to replace what really happened. They had done it before, sent hapless strangers back out in the world with only pleasant memories of their visit to the quiet town. They had erased werewolf sightings, fighting among the fae, Druids disappearing into thin air, and much more. They could make Bailey think he met Fiona, decided she wasn't very interesting, and not right for a show produced by his company.

She didn't care that much about the show. However, she cared a great deal about what Bailey thought of her. After knowing him just two days, she cared. She felt a connection with him she had never felt with anyone other than her family.

"Maybe I am just a stupid girl," she whispered, echoing Willow's words earlier that afternoon.

With a sigh, she stood and went into the bathroom to clean herself up a bit. She'd love to take a long, hot shower, but she wasn't leaving Bailey alone that long. Not here in Sarah's house with the elders roaming about.

When she returned to the bedroom, a young girl stood beside the bed. Fiona recognized her right away.

"Hello, Anna."

"You can see me," the girl said, turning with a smile. "Can you hear me?"

Though worried this might be the demon at work once again, Fiona quelled her fear. She was in the home place, and Anna's spirit was the same as it had been last night. "Of course I can hear you," she said.

"Most people can't. He can't." Anna sighed, sat down by her brother, and stroked his cheek. Bailey murmured in his sleep.

"Is he okay?" she asked.

"We think so." Fiona advanced into the room to study Anna.

The young girl wore the same shorts and T-shirt as before. Light pink toenails peeked through the straps of tan sandals. She was slender and tanned, taller than Fiona thought, like a growing colt with long legs. Blonde hair streaked with sun highlights fell around her shoulders. She looked young and carefree, no doubt the same way she'd looked the day she was taken.

"Were you at the cave earlier?" Fiona asked her. "Did you see Bailey then?"

She shook her head, confirming Fiona's suspicion that her cave appearance was a bit of play by the demon. "I didn't get near the cave, even though I wanted to follow Bailey. The spirits told me to stay away."

"What spirits?"

"The ones that live on the road before you get to the dead place." Anna twisted a ring on her finger. "I go a lot of places with Bailey, and I always listen to the ghosts who live there."

"They help you stay safe?"

"Yes. There are monsters among us, even though we're all dead."

"I've heard that before."

"From other ghosts?"

Fiona nodded. Maybe she should warn Anna.

"There's a really bad ghost. His name is Albert—"

"And you set him free," Anna said matter-of-factly.

"So you heard."

"From a woman named Minnie."

"Minnie Doyle?" Fiona said eagerly. "You've met her?"

"She's kind of a protector around here, and she says I should leave. She told me she was going to leave, too, but she hasn't. She's pretty mad at you about letting Alfred out."

Good old Minnie, Fiona thought, trying to protect her town. "Maybe you should listen to Minnie."

"I won't leave him." Anna looked back at Bailey. "I try to stay as close as I can."

"Is there something you need to tell him?"

"I want to talk to him. Could you do that for me?"

Fiona cocked her head to the side. "The problem is that he doesn't believe he can talk to you."

"I know." Anna patted Bailey's shoulder, and Fiona could see that her ring was an old-fashioned setting with an opal surrounded by small diamonds. "I've been trying to talk to him since…it happened, but he—"

"Doesn't want to believe you're here?"

"Yes, and I can't make him hear me. At least not enough for him to pay attention. No one's been able to help."

"Maybe I can," Fiona said. "But you'll have to give me some time."

"Time is all I have," Anna said as she faded away.

Fiona sat down on the bed again and looked around the empty room. She wished she could wake Bailey and tell him about Anna. After all he had seen and experienced today, would he be more open to the idea?

Thinking about those possibilities, Fiona sat back and enjoyed the peculiar intimacy of watching him sleep. He was a virtual stranger, but he had a role to play in their family tragedies. She wanted to know what.

Chapter 14

Bailey woke disoriented in a darkened, unfamiliar room. The soft light of one lamp cast shadows on deep, green walls. A bedroom. He was with Fiona's family, he remembered as he sat up. This was her grandmother's house.

He swung his feet off the bed and onto the floor, testing his right ankle. A little sore, but nothing major. Fiona's cousin had done something to him and the pain had gone away. He was hazy on the details, but he must have fallen asleep after that.

The full events of the day filled his head as he headed to the bathroom. Willow. The snake. Fiona opening the side of a hill. Anna. The cave-in. He switched on a light and faced himself in the mirror over the sink. He looked like one of Fiona's ghost figures. What kind of place had he stumbled upon when he decided to check out Fiona Burns?

He pulled his phone out of his pocket. His email and phone were practically full to capacity with messages from work. His father had texted, wanting to know if there was something wrong. Bailey wasn't sure what he should tell his parents. Even with their very open minds, they were going to think he had lost his when he told them Fiona was some kind of sorceress. And that her family was…witches.

He needed to get out of here.

Bailey went to the sink and used the clean towels to clear the worst of the remaining grime away. He washed his face and combed wet fingers through his short hair. Back in the bedroom, he slipped on his shoes and eased the door open.

Delicious smells filled the short hallway. He could hear voices and laughter from the front of the house. Was there a back way out? He opened a door and came face to face with Fiona's grandmother.

"Bailey," she greeted him with studied cheerfulness. She held out a steaming cup of what looked like tea. "I was just coming to check on you."

"I woke up," he said unnecessarily.

"Yes, and this is to help soothe the aches and pains from your adventure." The older woman's green eyes reminded him of Fiona's. They could draw you in.

"Thank you." He took the cup with automatic politeness. "This looks—"

"Vile. It's vile."

He turned to find Fiona at the opposite end of the hall. She glared at her grandmother. "Bailey doesn't need any of your tea." She came forward and took the cup out of his hands. "Sarah, I told you I would take care of Bailey."

Why was Fiona all of a sudden calling her grandmother by her given name? Bailey sent a puzzled look between the two women.

"Come with me." Fiona led Bailey past Sarah and into a large kitchen where she dumped the tea into a sink. "Never drink Sarah's tea," she told him.

Grateful that Sarah had not followed them, Bailey nodded. He didn't know if he should eat or drink anything this family offered. All of today's events might have been caused by some homemade psychedelic potion.

She took another teacup down from a cupboard. "This is what you need—chamomile and ginger tea. It's one of Eva Grace's staples when you're injured." She filled a tea ball, put it into the cup, and then poured hot water from a kettle.

Remembering her red-haired cousin working on his ankle, he lifted his right leg. "I seem to be almost good as new. Your cousin is amazing."

"She's a healer."

"I thought she ran a shop."

"She also makes potions, teas, and candles, and she can draw pain away with just a touch." Fiona said all of this like Bailey should just accept it. She stirred a spoonful of sugar into the tea and then held it out to him. "Drink this."

Okay, maybe this would all be easier to take if he was high. Bailey took the tea and sipped. Surprisingly, all he felt was relaxed.

"You look better," Fiona commented and gestured to a large pot on the stove. "How about a bowl of stew with cornbread?"

Though his mouth watered, Bailey decided not to risk it. "I think I need to go back to my room and rest."

"But someone needs to check to make sure you don't have a concussion," she protested.

"The amazing Eva Grace's special powers have fixed me up very well."

Fiona smiled. "Even after today, you're trying not to believe any of this, aren't you?"

Deliberately not answering, he patted his pockets. "I seem to remember giving my keys to someone."

"They're in your car, out in the driveway, but I'm not sure you should drive. I'll come with you." Looking purposeful, as she often did, she turned. In the overhead light, red highlights flashed in her dark hair. He was not sure how he knew, but Bailey was confident that fire would be echoed in their lovemaking.

Their lovemaking?

He swallowed hard. What was that absurd thought? Their kiss last night was when his world started to go wonky. He just needed to get away from her.

"I can drive," he protested.

Ignoring him, Fiona pushed through a door and into a large dining room where a group gathered around a table. They all fell silent as he walked in behind Fiona.

He recognized the women as the tribe that had descended on him at the cave, the three gray-haired older ones, several who were around Fiona's mother's age, and younger women including Brenna and Eva Grace. Sarah's husband, the sheriff, Fiona's father, and the Scotsman joined them.

"Bailey is determined to leave," Fiona told them.

A shiver of unease ran through Bailey as members of the group exchanged glances. Would they allow him to leave?

Sarah rose with a smile, making him feel foolish. "You can't go without dinner."

"I couldn't eat," Bailey replied. "I guess I'm a little woozy—"

"But not nauseous?" Eva Grace asked as she stood and came toward him. "I'm still worried about your head."

Bailey fought the urge to back up. "My head's fine.

I'm fine. I just need to leave."

One of the older family members said, "You should at least have a slice of apricot nectar cake. It's one of Sarah's specialties."

"My family can't do anything without food at hand," Fiona explained to Bailey. "You would like the cake."

"No, I'm going." He edged toward the room's arched opening. "Thank you all, for everything."

Not daring look at anyone else, he headed for the door. In a broad, central hallway, he spied what he hoped was the front door.

Fiona trailed him. "We need to talk, Bailey."

He turned to face her. "Frankly, I'm feeling overwhelmed. I need to do some thinking."

"We need to talk so you have all the information you need." Her voice was quiet but firm. "There are things you need to know and things you can never tell anyone."

He studied her closely, looking for signs of a threat. He imagined this group had ways of keeping their secrets, but he was already finding out that wasn't Fiona's style. "I'm not telling anyone anything," he assured her. "It's not as if I'd be believed."

"Exactly," she agreed. "But we have to talk about Anna, too."

He paused. "Are you going to tell me I really did see her in the cave today?"

"No, but—" She blinked, her eyes bright. "I did talk to her today. She wants to connect with you, Bailey. It's what she's always wanted."

Two days ago, Bailey would have laughed at her. He had laughed at her. Now he was…uncertain.

"I can come with you now or come by later," she told him.

He nodded toward the dining room. "I think there are others who want to talk to you first. I will be waiting for you. Room 4A."

He walked away before he could take back his invitation.

Chapter 15

Fiona leaned against a column on the porch long after Bailey's taillights were out of sight.

Right now, he could be making a phone call and telling someone about the Connelly coven, but she knew he wasn't. In her heart, she knew she could trust Bailey Powers. Tonight she would tell him everything, and he would understand that the secret life of New Mourne was worth preserving. Tonight she would place herself in his hands.

Anticipation fluttered in her belly. She was thinking of far more than confession for tonight with Bailey.

Wanting a man the way she wanted Bailey had been a long time coming. There'd never been a special man in her life. Dating wasn't easy when she could be interrupted by a ghost at any moment. There was also the curse to consider. How could she let herself fall in love when she could be the Woman in White's next tribute?

The notion of falling in love rocked Fiona back on heels. She knew her sister and cousins faced this same dilemma. Perhaps she should discuss her feelings with Brenna or Eva Grace.

As she turned, a car pulled into the driveway. It was Willow's Packard, and Fiona rushed to tell the others.

As usual, her grandmother was a step ahead. From the open doorway, she called, "I know she's here, Fiona. Get behind me with the others."

Fiona saw that Sarah held the family wand. According to coven legend, the wand came about after lightning struck a branch from an Irish bog oak. Thunderstorms such as that were not normal in Ireland, even centuries ago. A Connelly witch claimed the severed tree branch before the wood could cool. She worked on it for months, finally producing a finely grained, tapered wand imbued with the power of the rare Irish storm. The wand came to America with the Connellys in the 1700s.

In the broad central hallway of the house, Sarah stood at the head of the coven. The men of the family— her father, Marcus, Jake, and Dr. McGuire—stood behind them. Brenna was to Sarah's right, Eva Grace beside her. Delia was on her left, but Fiona stepped in front of her mother.

"Willow is angry with you," Delia murmured. "Get back."

"I'm not afraid to face the consequences of what I did today," Fiona said.

Just weeks ago she had been terrified of Willow. She was sensible enough to be frightened now, but she wasn't backing down or hiding behind anyone. The days of her being protected were over.

Willow walked into the hall without knocking. In a dark gray dress, her hair white, and skin wrinkled, she looked nothing like the gorgeous winged creature from the cave today, but Fiona wasn't fooled. Willow was old, angry, and powerful. She carried a staff with a gold stag on the end instead of her usual cane.

The stag glowed as Willow faced Sarah. "What are you going to do about your careless young witch?"

"She made a mistake," Sarah replied. "She was seeking answers, and the demon tricked her. He's done it before."

Willow let her staff hit the floor, and the house vibrated with a deep rumble. The staff slapped back into the faerie's hand.

"A mistake?" she sputtered. "That was cursed land. The cave was sealed. The Qing vase sat in the innermost chamber. How many indications of secrecy did she need?"

"She didn't know—"

Again, the staff slammed to the floor and bounced back to Willow. "And whose fault is it that she didn't know? You've been neglectful in training your witches, Sarah Connelly."

Sarah's shoulders straightened. "You have no right to criticize me, you old hag."

Fiona traded a glance with Brenna. Sarah had argued with the old faerie before, but it was still a surprise. Until this summer, they had seen nothing but respect from Sarah for Willow.

Willow slung her staff down. A crack appeared in Sarah's treasured heart pine floor. Everyone gasped.

"You'll fix that," Sarah said through gritted teeth. "I'm tired of you interfering in our business. Just weeks ago you pushed Brenna to confront the demon and the Woman in White, and she was nearly killed. Now you're here, violating all rules of civility."

"What happens in New Mourne isn't just your business."

"Do I have to remind you of all the times your clan

has fought among themselves and you've needed Connelly magic to keep them in line? Did the head of the coven come to you and criticize your leadership or meddle in things that were not our business?"

"This is not the same thing. Albert Connelly broke the rules by killing my sister. He was locked away by mutual agreement with your coven. Now this one..." Willow flicked an icy gaze toward Fiona. "She released him. What are you going to do? Someone who breaks rules deserves punishment."

"I decide punishment here."

Willow cackled. "And what will that be? Some silly spell to get that pretty boy from the outside to forget about her? Taking away someone she fancies is not enough punishment."

Startled, Fiona sucked in a breath. How did Willow know her fears or how she felt about Bailey? This morning, Fiona gave little credence to the old woman's talk that Bailey's destiny was to be here in New Mourne. Now she wondered. What had the old woman seen in the scrying mirror she was purported to use to see the future?

"Forgetting always seems to be the Connelly solution," Willow continued. "You forgot about Albert and now you're in another mess."

Sarah's voice remained firm and calm. "You throwing a tantrum in my home won't get you anywhere, Willow. Your manners have deserted you in your old age."

"You talk to me of manners when your granddaughter has unleashed the demon on our town again?" Willow closed the distance between herself and Sarah. "You know Albert's ghost will be stronger with a demon riding him, and the demon is stronger because Albert has magic."

"We're planning tonight how we'll face this new threat," Sarah told her.

Willow made a mocking sound. "Oh, you can make all the plans you want, but Albert will make you pay for allowing him to be locked up. Then you might want my help."

Dread stabbed through Fiona. From what they had learned about Albert, it was no doubt he would want his revenge.

"We can handle Albert," Sarah stated.

Willow hissed, baring razor sharp teeth.

Sarah thrust the Connelly wand forward, sparks flew, and the faerie retreated to the doorway. The old man who was her driver materialized at her side and hissed his own warning.

Fiona linked her arm through Sarah's and took her mother's hand. The air filled with magic as the coven members formed an unbroken chain.

"How dare you!" Willow sputtered. "You don't want me and mine as enemies. You'll need us soon enough. Believe me, I know." She snapped her fingers, and her staff jumped into her hand. Then she and her driver were gone in a wash of light and heat.

Fiona ran to the front door and saw the Packard already driving away. She whirled back to face the coven. "She's right, of course. Albert will attack us."

"The demon was coming for us any way," Sarah replied, her tone far more even than Fiona expected. "He just has an unexpected ally."

"We have to call him out," Brenna said. "As we did the last time."

"I believe Fiona did that today." Sarah sighed, and Marcus came from the back of the group to stand at her side and slip his arm around her.

"So what do we do?" Fiona asked.

"Strengthen our guards around our persons, our families, and our homes," Sarah replied. "Each of us must be fully alert at all times. Trust no outsiders." She caught Fiona's gaze. "Do you understand me?"

Fiona did, but she did not agree. "So we just go on defense, just wait for the next strike?"

"Of course not," Sarah replied. "I learned something from what happened with Brenna and the demon a few weeks ago. All of you are right. We have to search harder for an understanding of who the Woman in White is. If we know what made her demand such a terrible sacrifice of our family, then maybe we can reach an understanding with her. The family should have done this long ago."

"I like that thinking," Brenna said, stepping forward with eagerness. "Perhaps Aunt Celia's ghost can help Fiona discover more about the Woman's past."

"I haven't seen her since the demon took Albert," Fiona pointed out. "She may not be able to reach me again."

"Keep trying," Sarah ordered her. "Just don't go running off to investigate on your own again. Though I don't care for Willow's manner, she was right to be upset. Albert should never have been set free."

"I'm going to do everything I can to help break this curse," Fiona promised, not quite agreeing to Sarah's demand. In the coven, only she was a medium. Some things she had to do on her own.

"We're going through *The Connelly Book of*

Magic." Delia slipped her hand into Aiden's. "There may be something written in code that we can decipher."

"Or perhaps we can coax the book to speak," Eva Grace said. "The records say it has that power."

Dr. McGuire stepped to her side, his eyes bright with speculation. "I have some experience in that direction. I welcome the opportunity to help you, Eva Grace."

The coven broke out in the usual hubbub of discussion and quickly adjourned to the dining room for more cake and coffee to fuel their planning.

Fiona slipped away as soon as she thought no one would notice she was gone. Despite Sarah's warning, she was going to Bailey.

At the bottom of the staircase in the entry hall, the Granny ghost materialized and gave Fiona a warning look.

"I have to," Fiona told her. "He's waiting for me."

The ghost's eyes glimmered, and then she disappeared.

Fiona went out the door, her heart pounding with eagerness.

Chapter 16

In less than an hour, Fiona stood outside Bailey's room, fighting jangled nerves.

She had gone home, showered, and changed, wishing she had hours to prepare for tonight. But thirty minutes had to do.

Her hair was twisted in a loose bun in back, blunt-cut tendrils falling about her face. She had dug out her seldom-used makeup for a dusting of blush, some mascara, and lipstick. Her one and only little black dress replaced her usual vintage T-shirt and jeans. Scoop-necked and sleeveless, the sheath clung in all the right places. Fiona knew the dress was flattering because Eva Grace had chosen it during a shopping trip to Atlanta in the spring. High-heeled silver sandals were killing her feet, so she supposed they were achieving their goal of making her legs look long and sexy beneath the short shirt.

What would Bailey think? Did she compare to the sophisticated women who were no doubt a part of his life?

"Just see where it goes," she told herself and knocked on the door.

Bailey opened it immediately. His blue-eyed gaze swept from her face to her feet and back again. He grinned, an expression designed to charm women a thousand times more experienced than Fiona. "You look fantastic."

"I had to get rid of the dirt from the cave." Fiona's voice was shaky, and she felt foolish. Did he know her pulse was racing?

They stood awkwardly in the doorway. Fiona ventured, "Can I come in?"

"Excuse me. Of course." Bailey swung the door open and gestured her inside. He had changed into jeans and a white polo shirt. A crumpled dry cleaning bag lay on the floor beside the bed. He snatched it up, along with a towel that was draped on an armchair and hastily stowed them in the bathroom. "Sorry for the mess. I had to pick up my laundry at the front desk, and check in with my office. The time got away from me."

His hair was wet, as if he had just come out of the shower. He gestured toward the small sitting area opposite the bed. "Would you like to sit down? The fridge is stocked with some soft drinks and bottled water if you want something to drink—"

"I'm fine. I hope you took the time to have something to eat." Fiona went toward a comfortable-looking wing-back chair.

"I'm still not hungry," Bailey replied.

"But you feel okay?" She turned to study him with concern. "Your head—"

"Is spinning from everything that happened this afternoon?"

Fiona sat. "I guess you want to know about Anna."

He hesitated, then dragged the armchair from beside the bed and sat to face her. "First I want to return to that question I asked in the cave. What are you?"

"A witch," Fiona said bluntly. She had promised herself she'd be honest with him. "All the women in the

Connelly family are witches. We've always been witches."

Bailey sat back in his chair.

She chuckled. "You thought I'd offer a simple, logical explanation for this afternoon, didn't you?"

"I was hoping." He scrubbed a hand through his hair. "This is a lot to take in."

"There's more." She told him about her ancestors coming from Ireland, their bargain with the Woman in White, and the painful sacrifice made every generation.

"That's what Willow told me."

"I still don't know why she told you so much. We tend to keep our secrets in New Mourne." She continued talking about her family and their history. When she came to the demon, her long-dead ancestor Albert, and his murder of one of the fae ruling family, Bailey held up a hand to stop her.

"Are you taping me?"

"What do you mean?"

"Did that videographer of yours wire you up?"

"Of course not."

"Come on." Bailey reached out to push her hair back. "Are you wearing your hair different in order to hide one of those tiny cameras?"

She pulled away. "Everything I'm telling you is the truth. This is who I am and what I am."

"So you're not a medium?"

"Oh, yes, I'm very much in touch with the dead. As I told you, I talked to Anna today."

"In the cave?"

"That wasn't Anna. That was the demon."

"This demon has my sister?" His look was incredulous. "Are you saying your demon is who killed

Anna?"

"No, no," she assured him. "His kind loves to play evil tricks. He was most likely trying to distract you by giving you something you yearned for. It wasn't really Anna's spirit that you saw."

"I don't yearn to see Anna as a ghost."

"You yearn to see *her*." Fiona tipped her head to the side as his expression darkened. "Don't you?"

He took a moment before he answered. "Even if I buy everything else that you've told me, even if I believe that you're a wizard—"

"A witch. Wizards are very different beings."

"So they exist, too?"

"Of course, just like faeries. As I told you about Willow—"

"She didn't seem much like Tinkerbell."

"No joke," Fiona replied. "That woman could rip out your throat without breaking a sweat. For the most part, fae are fierce, fighting creatures. Now, there are some wee folk sort of like Tinkerbell in the south part of the county, but—"

"Shit." Bailey shoved up out of his chair and paced away from her, then back again. "You believe all of this, don't you?"

"Because it's true."

"But why are you telling me? I'm the guy who wants to put the town on television, remember?"

"That's not going to happen."

"You let me think it would."

"I only talked to you about doing an extension of my webcast for your company," Fiona corrected him. "There's never been any chance that New Mourne would risk exposing its shape shifters or werewolves or

143

any other magical creatures who take refuge here."

"Wolves?" Bailey stopped in front of her, then pointed toward the window. "Last night, outside on the street, I saw a coyote. It was walking along, like it owned the place."

"Did it look human in a way?"

"It looked intelligent, I'll give you that."

"It was a shape shifter. A group of coyotes moved here from North Carolina decades ago. They knew they'd be protected here."

Bailey laced his hands together on top of his head, as if to hold his brains in place.

Fiona felt sorry for him. For a man who couldn't even confront his sister's ghost, the truth about the supernatural was difficult to hear.

"I. Don't. Believe. You." He forced the words out. "I don't know what your game is, but you're not for real. Your family, that crazy Willow, all of it is just fabrications. You're running some huge con game."

"If I'm a fake, then how did I talk to Anna?"

"You didn't." A nerve jumped in his cheek as he stepped closer to her.

Fiona rose. "But I did. She wants to talk to you."

"My sister is dead."

"Her spirit is held here by you."

"Yeah, it's all my fault," he muttered and rubbed the edge of the tattoo on his left bicep.

His words were revealing. Fiona stepped forward. "You blame yourself for her death, don't you? That's why you can't face her."

"That's ridiculous. I was fifteen, and she was abducted by a maniac."

"Yet you believe you should have stopped him."

144

"Let it go." Bailey's voice had gone deep and dangerous. "I told you before that I wouldn't entertain any of this kind of crap."

"It's not crap," Fiona shot back at him. "It's your sister, and she talked to me this afternoon. She was wearing shorts and a Spice Girls T—"

"That was reported on the news," Bailey cut her off. "When we still thought she was alive, everyone knew what she was wearing. That's how you know about her clothes."

"Her ring was beautiful, but it didn't seem to fit her."

His head snapped up. "What ring?"

Fiona described the opal with the diamonds that Anna turned round and round on her finger. "It seemed old-fashioned—"

Bailey's face went white. "How do you know about that ring?"

"She was wearing it."

His fingers gripped her shoulders. "There was nothing in the news about that ring."

"I'm not talking about the news. I saw the ring today."

"But it was never found."

"She must have been wearing it when she died or it was so important to her that it's part of her essence."

Bailey let go of Fiona and dropped back down in the armchair. "The police thought it had been taken, like a trophy, by the murderer." He took a deep breath and held it a moment. "They wanted it kept secret to use the information if they ever got a suspect. No one knew about it but my family and the police."

"Was the ring new?" Fiona stepped closer to

Bailey but stopped short of touching him. He was strung so tightly, she didn't know how he would react.

"Old, actually. Some boyfriend gave it to Grandmom when she was young. She made a big deal about giving it to Anna, acted all mysterious, and said the guy was some kind of star when she dated him."

"She didn't say who it was?"

Bailey was breathing easier, and he looked back up at Fiona. "My dad used to think it might have been James Dean. You know, from the movie 'Rebel Without a Cause.' "

"With Natalie Wood." Thanks to Ryan, Fiona knew plenty about old movies. "Dean died young in a spectacular car crash. Your grandmother knew him?"

"Yeah, she dated a lot of actors when she was young. Dad's named for him," Bailey said, then gave a short laugh. "Man, she would love you and this whole town. She believes in all of this stuff." He stopped and shook his head. "Grandmom's not important now. I still don't know how you could have known about the ring. Do you have a source in the police department?"

She reached out and took his hand. "Anna spirit is attached to you."

He looked around. "Now?"

"That's not how it works," Fiona assured him. "She can't be present every moment. She's part of another dimension."

"That's convenient. So summon her."

Fiona let out a deep breath, hesitant to give him something he might not be ready for. When the light in his eyes dimmed, however, she opened herself to the nether realm. "I can try, but—"

"Don't." Bailey stood and captured her other hand

in his. "I'm sorry, I don't really want you to…"

"Shatter all your illusions?" Fiona cut in. She studied him for a moment. "You want to believe, don't you?"

He shook his head. "Not at all."

"Part of you already knows what I've said is true."

The muscles in his throat worked as he swallowed. "God damn, Fiona. How do you expect me to believe this? I've worked with some strange people in the past. Those guys who work with the snakes are a creepy bunch, but you asking me to believe you and your family and others in this town are a magical group of people with special powers? Or that you really can put me in touch with Anna? I can't—"

"Shh." Fiona lifted fingers to his lips. "Don't say you can't believe. It's all true. There's magic everywhere, Bailey, and according to my grandmother, there's a little bit of magic in everyone. We just express it in different ways."

His gaze was intent on hers, the warmth of his body reaching out, warming her. The connection she felt to this man was electric. Near him, she felt alive in a new way. Her magic was stronger, fuller. She closed her eyes and allowed the sensations to move through her core.

She wanted Bailey to love her.

Now.

Tonight.

His head angled, and his lips moved toward hers, claimed them with brief intensity.

She protested when he moved away.

"I don't do this with people I work with," he said.

"I haven't signed any contracts," Fiona reminded

him. She put her free hand on his other cheek and raised her mouth to his again.

He kissed her the way he had last night before Sarah appeared and ruined the moment. This was how Fiona dreamed of being kissed. Smooth as velvet, but with an unmistakable hunger. His body hardened against hers, and she pressed forward with eagerness.

He stepped back again. "This is not what I intended."

"I did," she murmured. "I came to tell you the truth about me and mine, but most of all I came to learn everything I could about you."

He shuddered as her hands slid up his back, and he pressed his face to her neck. "I guess some mutual discovery is not a bad thing." His fingers freed the knot of hair at her nape, and he drew away to study her.

He skimmed his hands up her bare arms, and Fiona's magic rose along with her heartbeat. A shimmer of light trailed after his touch.

His eyes widened.

"I told you."

Bailey leaned his forehead against hers. "Maybe there's something to your witchcraft after all."

Fiona poured herself into his kiss, letting her lips express what she was feeling.

Then his hands were back at work, fingertips just brushing the sides of her breasts. Her nipples rose against the thin fabric of her dress, and she shifted when his hands cupped her. The tide of need inside her made her gasp.

Bailey's hands slid away, and he tilted her chin up with one fingertip. "Is this okay? Really okay?"

Fiona shivered, and her gaze skipped away from

his. "There's something you should know."

"Full disclosure, remember?"

"I'm...uh...not very experienced," she whispered around a sudden lump in her throat.

"I'm not falling for that." Bailey smiled as he tucked a strand of her hair behind her ear.

"It's true."

This time he didn't argue. His gaze remained locked on hers, and she could see he believed her. "The men around here must be stupid in addition to supernatural."

"In the interest of total honesty, I gave very few of them a chance."

He took a deep breath. "We should slow down."

"No," she protested. "We shouldn't. There's no time to take it slow."

"But Fiona, your first time should be—"

"Of my choosing," she finished. "And I choose now. With you. I'm a Connelly witch. At this point, there's precious little time left for dawdling in my life."

"You have all the time in the world."

"This is our world, and time is measured for my generation on the Woman in White's terms. The curse means the end could come at any time." She gripped his hands again. "I want you."

Something in her words must have convinced him, because he stopped protesting. His arms slipped around her again. "Are you sure?"

"Make love to me," she murmured against his lips.

"I can always claim you bewitched me."

"I will if I have to."

He swept her off her feet, just the sort of grand, romantic gesture Fiona had yearned to experience. With a tenderness she savored, he laid her down on the bed. He went to the door to slip the lock, then turned out lights, leaving only one soft lamp glowing. He came to her side and lightly touched her face. "You are so beautiful. Maybe you are magic."

"That's how I feel." She tugged him down next to her and willed away her nerves to focus solely on his touch and his kiss. Much of her life, spirits had intruded. She often felt she was living too many lives without time for her own. She didn't want that tonight. She needed to feel every moment with Bailey.

He pressed his thumb gently into the wrinkle of worry on her forehead. "Whatever it is you're thinking about doesn't belong here with us. It's just you and me. You and me. Nothing else."

Fiona always placed barriers between herself and others, particularly the few men who had tried to get close. Now those walls evaporated. She gave herself to Bailey. With slow, gentle insistence, he kissed her, touched her, and kindled her desire into a strong, powerful ache.

Instead of the shyness she expected, she felt only growing excitement as he pushed her dress up and over her head. He dipped his head to sample one breast, then the other, each kiss slow and tender. Fiona threaded her fingers through his hair. She savored the movement of his lips against her sensitive nipples, the way his hands encircled her waist, his sigh of pleasure as she arched her body up toward him.

Her magic surged, warming the air around them.

Bailey's grin flashed up at her before he dipped his head and kissed her stomach. Then his mouth went lower, his tongue probing through the black silk and pink lace of her panties.

"Is this okay?" he whispered as his fingers hooked over the delicate scrap of fabric that separated them.

"Completely."

With a deft move, he pulled the panties down her legs. Then his mouth was between them, his tongue inside her.

Fiona rode a cresting wave of heat. The bed shifted. The scent of roses closed around them. She never believed anything would feel more natural than her magic, but this moment with Bailey was perfection.

He could have taken her then. Instead, with infinite patience, he allowed her to slide down from the heights. He took off his clothes. He turned back the covers, settled Fiona in the cool sheets, and cradled her against his muscular body. He allowed her slow exploration of his smooth chest and washboard abs. His iron control held until her fingers curled around the pulsing heat of his erection.

"Okay, witch." One smooth motion brought Fiona beneath him. "You may believe you're supernatural, but I'm only a man."

"A very impressive man," she agreed, smiling. She parted her legs. His rock-hard length nudged against her throbbing center. The spiral of heat built inside her again.

Tiny orbs of light fell around them. Bailey raised eyes filled with wonder. He looked at her. "Is this what always happens with a witch?"

"I wouldn't know," she murmured, opening herself farther. "Let's see what's next."

He smiled into her eyes. "Beautiful Fiona."

His hips rocked forward, shifted, and then pushed

against hers. He slid inside her.

Fiona gasped at this new sensation, but met him with the exhilaration that had overtaken her from the moment they met. Fiona, the good child, the quiet one, wanted to go on any journey Bailey offered.

The magical rainstorm intensified as their cries of fulfillment lifted and fell together.

Moments later, when Fiona's breath slowed and the light show ended, Bailey moved to her side. They faced each other. She laid a hand on his cheek, and he turned to kiss her palm.

His blue eyes were steady on hers as he said, "I believe."

Chapter 17

"What do you believe?" Fiona asked.

Because he did not really have an answer, Bailey nuzzled her neck, his hands in her thick, soft hair. "You smell like a field of wildflowers."

"Eva Grace mixes soaps and fragrances for each of us." She sighed as he trailed his fingers down her side. "Each of us has our own personal scent."

"Your Eva Grace is a genius—a healer as well as a perfumer." Bailey cupped Fiona's cheek with one hand, turning her toward him. Her dark hair fell around her face like a halo. Her smile was slow and sexy. She looked like a wood nymph, at least what he thought a wood nymph would look like. Remembering all she had told him about her hometown, he wondered if there really were wood nymphs.

Instead of asking her about creatures who might be roaming outside right now, he said, "Are you all right? Do you need anything?"

"I'm perfect," she said and smiled at him. "Now, let's go back a step. *What* do you believe?"

He got up, retrieved a bottle of water from the small refrigerator, and opened it before he handed it to her.

Fiona pushed herself up, modestly holding the sheet to her chest as she took the water. She drank, her appreciative gaze on Bailey's body.

He chuckled. "If you keep looking at me like that, I'm going to forget that until moments ago you were a tender virgin."

"First, you have to answer me."

Sighing, he got back into bed, took the bottle of water she offered and polished it off. Then he pulled Fiona gently to his side and settled back against the pillows. "I have to admit that's the first time I've ever made love to a woman who quite literally glowed. I felt like a god."

"A minor or major deity?"

"Major," he assured her with a grin.

She laid her head against his chest. "And?"

Knowing he could not dodge her any longer, Bailey said, "I believe you have some very interesting abilities."

She tipped her head back to look at him. "That sounded reluctant."

"How is someone supposed to sound when they learn the woman they've made love to is a witch and he knows there are werewolves and coyote shape shifters roaming the countryside?"

"I'm talking about Anna." Fiona pushed herself up on one elbow, her gaze intent on his. "What do you believe about her?"

He frowned. "I guess I'm confused. One part of me thinks that if her spirit had the ability to reach out, she should have talked to me a long time ago."

"I told you it's not easy. Some ghosts linger for years and years, never able to express themselves to the people they care most about. I may see them, other people may see the evidence that they exist, but the path between the two realms is not always clear."

"You said a demon made me see her today."

Fiona explained again about her family's curse, the Woman in White, and the demon that came to torture the town and her family each generation.

"Couldn't the demon also be making you see her?" Bailey asked.

She was thoughtful, then shook her head. "Anna came to me at my grandmother's house. So far, neither the Woman in White nor the demon has penetrated what we all consider home."

Although everything he had seen today made it easier to accept that the curse and the demon were real, Bailey was still puzzled. "Why would the demon try to use Anna to distract me today?"

Fiona bit her lower lip. "Willow said you were destined to be here. Perhaps she's right."

"I'll admit being here is strange for me," Bailey murmured. "My parents were insistent I come here to meet you."

"Are either of them clairvoyant?"

"Other than having good instincts about what makes a great TV show, I'd say no," Bailey replied. "If either of them were clairvoyant, they wouldn't have allowed Anna to leave the house the night she was murdered. I seriously doubt my mother would have sent me anywhere near rattlesnakes or caves."

"Magical gifts rarely work in such a simple way." Fiona's fingertips traced the lightning bolt tattoo on his left bicep. "The coven uses a crystal ball sometimes to look into the future, but the direction it gives isn't specific."

"Is that why fortune tellers can safely get away with saying things, like 'a change is coming' or 'a tall, dark stranger will enter your life?' "

Her touch stilled. "You're still caught up in the bad experiences you've had."

"I'm sorry," he said. "I doubt anything can erase how I felt every time someone who promised to reach Anna let us down."

Bailey pulled Fiona back down next to him. "I already told you that I've felt Anna's presence before, and while I was in town today I sensed she was near. Like so many times before, I imagined she was just behind me."

"Are you disappointed or relieved that it wasn't her?"

That question was territory Bailey didn't want to explore. "This town of yours is the strangest place I've ever been. Crows, coyotes, rattlesnakes."

Fiona shivered in his arms. "Nature is being used by dark magic. The crows were a warning, and the snake was supposed to protect those papers hidden in the armoire." She told him they belonged in a family book of spells, history, and potions.

"Who do you think hid the papers?"

"Some misguided member of the family. Between the Woman's tribute visits, my family has difficulty facing the truth about the curse."

"Maybe I understand that," Bailey said. "It's not easy for a family to overcome tragedy. Sometimes they collapse."

"Yours didn't."

"I did my best to make everything more difficult for my parents." He told her about some of his youthful misadventures. "It's to their credit that I came through it all."

"And you joined the family business."

"Dad's idea," Bailey told her. "I was twenty-one, not in school and not doing much of anything other than hanging out at the beach. He told me I had to earn my keep. He was just beginning to add reality TV."

"What did you do at first?"

"Anything I was told to do. Then I got an idea for a show. Dad let me run with it, and it flopped big time, but I was hooked on creating new programming."

Fiona stretched out beside him, completely relaxed. "Tell me about your family."

"I told you about my grandmother," he said. "Grandpop built sets for televisions shows."

"Fascinating."

"My grandparents' connections got Dad and Mom through several doors when they worked on the pilot for their first show."

"You sound more normal than what I've read about other families in the entertainment business."

"What does a witch who grew up in an enchanted town know about normal?"

It was her turn to laugh. "You have a point. Plus, my parents left Brenna and me here while they traveled and studied."

"You must have missed them."

She responded slowly. "I was just always happy to see them when they visited. Brenna resented them for leaving, but I was content with Sarah."

"There appeared to be a little tension between the two of you tonight."

"That's been growing over the past few weeks as we've had to face that the Woman's curse is rearing its head again. I want to be the one who finds the answers, but no one takes me seriously."

"Why?"

"Because I'm younger and different. As far as we know, I'm the first Connelly witch to be a medium. Sarah, Brenna, and Eva Grace have always been protective of me. They're a little frightened of my abilities, but they also don't see me as an equal when it comes to magic."

"Is that why you went to find the cave by yourself?"

She nodded. "Most of the coven is upset about you, too."

"Was your grandmother trying to poison me tonight?"

"Well…"

He sat up. "I knew it."

"No, it would have made you feel better…eventually."

"Great."

Fiona sat up and faced him, expression serious. "I may be able to convince Sarah to allow me to do a show with you about my work as a medium. She would be more receptive if we broke the curse with the Woman in White. But after today, she fears you."

"I'm not a threat," Bailey said.

"Yes, you are. What I've told you about New Mourne and my family is part of centuries-old secrets. You can't share this with anyone. The coven can make sure of that."

"Will they turn me into a toad?"

"Don't joke." Fiona glanced toward the windows, genuine concern in her green eyes. "Don't mock our power."

Realizing she was serious, he leaned against the headboard. "Just what kind of penalty will be required for what happened between us tonight? How does your coven kill mortals who sleep with Connellys?"

"If they did that, my cousin Lauren would have left a trail of bodies," Fiona replied. "Nothing happens if you keep New Mourne's secrets. You have to make a promise and keep it."

Ever since this afternoon, Bailey had been coming to grips with the fact that a show about this town would not happen. Who would believe it wasn't a giant hoax? If the residents were as secretive as Fiona suggested, he doubted he would get cooperation for taping, anyway. His idea about featuring Willow as a recurring character was a pipe dream. He doubted the coyote who had ambled down Main Street last night would grant interviews.

"If you even attempt to tell, your memories of your time here would be wiped out," Fiona continued. "I'm sure Sarah and the elder aunts have cast that spell, even though I stopped them from giving you the tea that would take your memories away."

"So I'm under a spell?"

"That will be set in motion *if* you talk about New Mourne. If you had drunk the tea Sarah made, you would be home and never think of us. You might see someone who looked like me, and you'd have a glimmer of memory." Her expression saddened. "But tonight wouldn't have happened. And if you tell, you will not remember me. Or us."

That hit Bailey like a punch to his gut. Forgetting Fiona seemed impossible when she sat so close in the gentle light, when his body remembered the feel of her, when he thought of the magic that sizzled around them. He wasn't ready to put labels on what he was feeling for her, but he knew she was more important to him than any woman he had ever met.

Still, he resisted. "Your family couldn't do anything like that to me."

"They can and will. They could even make you produce a show called 'The Many and Varied Lives of the Ground Squirrel.' And worst of all, you'd enjoy it." Her laughter held little mirth.

"Then how does anyone ever become part of your circle? How did your father meet your mother?"

"He was her professor at college. He studied and believed in magic. It's the reason they connected."

"And what about your videographer, Ryan?"

"He's my best friend, and Sarah has known him his whole life. She met his grandparents in the Sixties, when the farm was a commune. They settled in town after the commune dissolved."

"Is he a supernatural of some sort?"

"Totally human," Fiona replied. "There are many humans who know our secrets and keep them. They support our community's foundation of peace and acceptance."

"Dr. McGuire is an outsider, and he was with your family tonight. He's very protective of you." Bailey told her about his encounter with the Scotsman.

"Rodric's a renowned expert on the paranormal and is working on ideas to help us end the curse. Besides, he's Jake's friend. Brenna loves Jake, so Dr. McGuire is trusted."

"I suppose Jake is native, too."

"No, but..." Fiona pushed a hand through her hair.

"Jake's a shape shifter. He came here after serving in Afghanistan."

Bailey blinked. "Come again?"

"His other form is a white tiger."

Bailey stared at her, his brain once again reeling.

"Supernaturals have an uncanny way of finding one another," Fiona explained. "New Mourne is a haven for them. We have a pack of werewolves who moved here from Texas. Just as Jake came here, as have others like Willow and the other fae. They become part of what the Connellys protect."

"And you can do this only because you surrender once a generation to this Woman in White?"

"That was the deal our ancestors struck in order to live in peace."

A deal that could claim Fiona's life. The idea seemed outlandish. Yet Bailey couldn't look at her and not trust every word.

He turned away and got out of bed, hoping some distance would give him perspective. At the window, he glanced down at the street. Three crows sat in front of the inn on a bench just below his room. Their eyes glowed. Like the coyote last night, they appeared to be staring directly at him.

He stumbled backward. The crows underscored the stark reality of everything Fiona told him.

"What is it?" Fiona threw back the covers and came to his side just as the crows lifted off the bench and disappeared beyond reach of the streetlight.

Bailey turned to face her. "I promise," he told her. "I won't reveal your secrets."

"So you realize you have something to fear?"

"No." He placed his hands on her shoulders and

savored the softness of her skin, the angular beauty of her face. "I promise because I don't want to forget you."

She stepped into his arms, her smile lighting a corner of his heart he hadn't realized was in shadow until now.

"Let's make the magic again," she suggested as she drew him back to bed.

Chapter 18

Fiona left Bailey's room around nine the next morning. Though he suggested they spend the day in bed, she resisted temptation. Breaking the Woman in White's curse was more important than ever. Her family deserved to live without the threat of death. She had some new ideas in that direction.

Bailey still wanted to expand her webcast into a show that could carefully guard her family's secrets. He planned to stay in New Mourne for a while longer. They would have dinner tonight, and that made Fiona smile as she let herself into her office.

Ryan's voice called out from the studio.

"You're here early." She walked to the studio doorway. Ryan had editing going on over a bank of computers.

"I thought we were going to edit next week's webcast." Ryan turned and looked at her, then whistled. "Look at you, all dressed up." Then his smile faded.

"You act as if I've never worn a dress before."

"You slept with Powers." Ryan shook his head. "I guess I saw that coming."

"It's my life," she said defensively. "And you've got the wrong idea about him."

Sighing, Ryan clicked some computer keys to freeze the action on the screens and stood. "It's not that I don't see the attraction, Fiona. If his interests ran in my direction, I'd be tempted, but I haven't been waiting my whole life for Prince Charming like you. I don't think he's a candidate for your happily ever after."

"That's not what I'm after."

Her friend cocked his head. "Who do you think you're talking to? We've been friends since we were in diapers. I know exactly what you want. I'm not sure some slick outsider with an agenda is going to deliver it."

"I'm not expecting him to deliver anything."

"I hope this is not just another element in your recent rebellions."

She was surprised. Although she usually discussed everything with Ryan, she had not talked about her feelings of frustration.

"I hope you're not just seizing the most convenient way to prove you're going to do what you want."

"So what if I am? If Lauren had slept with Bailey, no one would be surprised."

"Because she's not you. You don't invest yourself casually in anyone." He studied her again. "You're smitten with the guy. You could get hurt if you're not careful."

Irritated because Ryan knew her too well, Fiona turned and went upstairs to shower and dress for the day in her usual jeans and T-shirt. She didn't have time to stand around worrying about being hurt.

To Ryan's credit, he didn't dwell on Bailey or lecture Fiona while they worked on the webcast. The show featured footage shot weeks ago when they investigated the haunting of an old well house in Dalton. The video of Fiona interacting with the ghost featured electronic voice phenomena and a shadow figure. All of it supported a local legend about an unsolved, brutal murder.

Ryan turned from work on the show's pivotal segment. "What's coming after this webcast? The only other thing we have in the can is your session with Minnie."

"That can't be aired. It's too close to the family."

"Of course," Ryan agreed. "But where do we go from here? With what's going on with your family…" Concern darkened his chocolate brown eyes. "Is this really happening?"

She bent to give him a hug. "Yeah, and I have some things to tell you." She filled him in on the rattlesnake, the cave, and Aunt Celia's sudden appearance.

"Has she been back?" he asked.

Fiona shook her head. "No, but I'm going back to the cave this afternoon."

"I'll go with you."

"It's not safe," Fiona insisted.

"You've never said that to me before," Ryan said.

"This is different." After Dagen's run-in with the snake and the way the demon used Anna to distract Bailey, Fiona was worried about the humans in her life. The demon endangered everyone in New Mourne, but she would not knowingly lead anyone into trouble.

She refused to give in to Ryan and went to pick up lunch to take to Siren's Call. Brenna was helping out there on Thursday mornings for the past couple of weeks, and Fiona wanted to talk to her cousin and her sister. They needed to make plans.

The aromas of herbs and incense wafted over Fiona as she walked into the shop. She resisted a new display of crystals and avoided the gemstone-encrusted athame Eva Grace had highlighted on a table near the front. Fiona loved the shop's many treasures, but she couldn't indulge today.

A few browsers lingered in the shop's fragrant, cool air, and Fiona found Brenna and Eva Grace refreshing a display of candles.

"I brought chicken salad from the diner and rolls from Britta's," Fiona greeted them, holding out two bags in her right hand.

"Sounds like a bribe," Brenna murmured without turning around to greet her. "What do you want?"

"Can't a girl simply want to talk to her sister and her best cousin?" Fiona was drawn to the rainbow of candle colors. She picked up a deep red candle symbolizing love, lust, and passion.

Eva Grace took the candle from her, smiling. "I'm not sure you need that."

"Maybe not." Fiona's face flushed under her cousin's study.

"Your aura is so bright. I can tell you slept with him."

Brenna whirled around, nearly upsetting the entire display. "What?"

"She slept with the producer." Eva Grace calmly caught the box of sky-blue candles Brenna dropped.

Brenna drew Fiona to the back of the shop. "You slept with him? Is that what you were planning when Eva Grace and I stuck up for him with Sarah last night?"

"Maybe." Not meeting her sister's gaze, Fiona set their lunch on the counter. She cut off Brenna's soft curse. "There's more to it than sex. Willow said he was destined to be part of the curse."

"Oh, that will go a long way with Sarah. She's still angry at Willow."

"Bailey promised not to tell anyone about us or New Mourne's magical aspects."

Brenna wasn't buying it. "Sarah will send him to the county line on a fireball and maybe give him complete amnesia."

"No, she won't," Fiona said with newfound confidence. "Sarah's just going to have to accept that I can live my life my way, just like she did with Mother and with you. Why not with me?"

"Please say it just like that to Sarah," Brenna said. "And do it so I have time to duck the first fireball."

"Sarah had a one-night stand with a freaking gypsy and ended up the single mother of twins. I don't think she has any room to make judgments about my relationships." Fiona turned to Brenna with sudden anger. "You of all people should understand how I feel. You left for three years to get away from her control."

"And Sarah had me watched the entire time," Brenna said. "After Aunt Celia went away and came home pregnant, Sarah wasn't taking any chances with the three of us."

Sighing in frustration, Fiona turned to Eva Grace. "What do you think of me and Bailey?"

Her red-haired cousin dumped empty candle boxes on the counter. "He might not be the right choice to fall in love with."

Fiona pouted. "I'm not talking about love."

Brenna and Eva Grace looked at each other and laughed. Clearly, they shared Ryan's opinion that Fiona was incapable of a casual relationship with Bailey.

"Oh, shut up." Fiona walked over to the bin of crystals Minnie had disturbed during her visit to the shop. "I need some help with wisdom and perception. Tell me what stones to choose, Eva Grace."

Eva Grace came to her side and pick up a dark green stone. "This is chrysocolla. It aids wisdom and drives off fear. There is a small…ah side effect, I guess you could say."

Fiona had reached for the gem but dropped her hand. "What?"

"It attracts love." Eva Grace gave a merry laugh and pressed the stone into Fiona's hand.

"What about this one?" Fiona pointed to a second, blue-green stone.

"Amazonite. This will help you remain objective and give you insight into both sides of your problem." Eva Grace picked up a white stone with shadows of gray on it. "This will help you stay calm and keep you from doing something without giving it enough thought."

Rubbing the stone with her thumb, Fiona said, "I should have come by here before I went exploring in the cave."

"Please don't do anything like that again on your own," Brenna said.

Fiona bristled. "It's not like I knew what would happen."

Her sister's green eyes were dark with concern. "That's exactly why you need backup."

"Says a witch who has repeatedly challenged the demon and the Woman in White," Fiona pointed out.

"That's why I'm worried," Brenna replied. "The demon sought me out last time. This time it appears you're the target."

"And you don't believe I'm strong enough to fight."

Brenna started a retort, but Eva Grace stopped her. "There's my afternoon clerk." She waved at the young woman who was walking toward them. "She can watch the shop while we talk in my office."

In the small office at the rear of the store, Eva Grace hit the "on" switch to heat hot water in an electric kettle, and then took three china cups out of an antique corner cabinet. Brenna retrieved utensils and napkins from a shelf, and Fiona set out servings of chicken salad and Britta's special yeast rolls. When the kettle boiled, Eva Grace poured the water over three bags of peppermint tea.

The minty aroma soothed Fiona even before she took a sip. Trust Eva Grace to bring harmony to their trio.

Over lunch, they went over everything that happened to Fiona in the cave the day before.

Brenna returned to Fiona's vision of the young Native American being tortured. She was convinced the young man had to do with the Woman in White's story.

"I agree," Fiona said. "I want to go back to the cave and try to see that again. Will you come with me?"

"Sarah will have a fit," Eva Grace said, frowning.

Brenna seemed tempted. "The three of us together are powerful."

Fiona played with the stones in her pocket. "Even though Sarah says she doesn't want anyone near the cave or the cursed land, she did say we needed to be more proactive."

"Delia and Aiden are working with the book

today," Brenna said.

"And Sarah was going to see our cousin Inez this afternoon," Eva Grace added. "She's hoping there's some information about how Albert was vanquished in Inez's family history. She's convinced it wasn't all Willow's doing."

Brenna nodded. "Sarah's also interested in the armoire at Dagen's. She is showing Inez photos to see if she recognizes the piece. The elders think it belonged to their sister who was taken by the Woman, but they're not sure."

"I believe we should do something productive as well." Fiona got to her feet. "Are you coming with me?"

Eva Grace sighed. "I have to call in someone else for the shop and change clothes. I can't wear heels to that cave again."

They took Fiona's van to Eva Grace's small, neat bungalow. Neither Fiona nor Brenna was surprised when Eva Grace came out dressed in crisply ironed jeans, a pastel shirt, and designer boots.

"You really know how to dress for roughing it," Brenna said as Eva Grace clambered into the backseat.

Fiona just laughed and started the van.

They were surprised as they approached the family land on Devil's Creek Road. Green was sprouting everywhere. The field that been gray and brown was now dotted with color and vibrant plants.

"Amazing," Eva Grace said from the back seat. "I wondered if there'd be change since Albert was freed, but this is more than I expected."

Fiona turned to the old cemetery. Crows dotted the landscape, watching them with unblinking eyes and no movement.

"Do you all see the birds?" Fiona asked.

Eva Grace jumped when she turned. "I don't like how they just sit there."

Fiona told them about the crows outside Bailey's room last night.

"Are they warnings or guardians?" Brenna asked, looking thoughtful.

"Interesting observation," Fiona said. "Let's go to the cave."

The three of them headed away from the birds and across the field where grass sprouted beneath their feet and leaves grew on bare, twisted branches.

"Uh-oh," Brenna said as they saw the opening to the cave in the side of the hill.

Fear rippled through Fiona. "Didn't Sarah seal the cave yesterday?"

"Yeah," Eva Grace murmured. "She and the elders thought it was the best option."

"Then why is it open?" Brenna strode to the entrance.

The same foul scent of rot that Fiona smelled yesterday blew out.

Eva Grace hung back. "This could be a very bad idea."

"This is Connelly land." Fiona shook off her unease. "I refuse to be afraid here. Fear has kept our family down for too long. Let's not allow it any longer."

She was rewarded by Brenna's approving look. Her sister put out her hand to Eva Grace, and they followed Fiona inside.

The cave was cool and quiet. Cleared of debris, the

first chamber was wide and open, the ceiling that had fallen yesterday was intact, the passageway leading into the inner chambers now broader by several feet. Fiona pulled out her flashlight and led the way to the first large cavern where she had seen the vision.

Opening herself, Fiona said, "I feel the same presence as yesterday. Not exactly a ghost." She tried to bring the scene of torture into focus again. Nothing came but an increase in the cave's rank smell.

"The demon," Brenna muttered.

Deep laughter boomed around them.

They linked hands, forming a circle of power as natural to them as breathing. Strength surrounded them, glowing with energy and intensity.

The laughter became a voice that exploded from the walls. "That's just what I want, that lusty power that you stupid witches take for granted."

Defiance sounded in Brenna's voice. "The power of a strong coven cannot be easily taken. Didn't we prove that to you before?"

The answer seemed to come from the floor beneath their feet. "But now I have one of your own, a warlock. He stole the powers of a fae, and even imprisonment didn't rob him of all of her skills."

Eva Grace answered, "A warlock is the term given to a liar and one who never keeps his word. The world of magic does not use that term."

"Then it suits us," the voice replied.

A column of fire rose in the pit at the center of the room.

"Albert," Fiona breathed as a man's figure appeared. His tattered black cape billowed in the flames. He laughed, and the fire shot up toward the

Haunting Magic

ceiling.

"Just wait," he shouted, laughing. "You witches will pay double for your freedom this time, and I'll have what I deserve, too."

"*A ligean ar saoire*," Brenna whispered. *Let's leave.*

"Do you think I don't know the language of our homeland?" the voice thundered.

Brenna said, "*Imopar!*"

Fiona gave herself to her sister's power. When she opened her eyes, they were beside her van. Clouds rolled in what had been a clear sky. The crows in the cemetery, so still before, fluttered and fussed.

"I think they want us to go," Fiona murmured.

Eva Grace and Brenna scrambled into the vehicle, and Fiona followed. She turned the key, gunned the engine, and turned toward town.

Even at this distance, she could hear the roar from the cave.

173

Chapter 19

Bailey sat in front of the inn. Though the bench where the crows had perched last night kind of gave him the creeps, it was a good vantage point to observe the town. This afternoon's crowd was substantially smaller than yesterday's. The air was hot and sticky, but he enjoyed being outside after spending most of the day at the computer and on the phone.

He now knew more about paranormal phenomena and supernatural creatures than he ever dreamed. A research assistant at his production company was also looking into the history of this region. If he could turn up any obscure facts about the missionaries who had been the first settlers, that might help Fiona and her family. Bailey was hopeful an outside resource would uncover something they had not discovered on their own.

One side of his brain could not believe he had bought into the entire curse, protective coven, and enchanted town story. If he read this in a tabloid, he would laugh. Fiona, however, was not lying. In all of her strange mix of abilities, he doubted she possessed the skills to lie. No matter how this turned out, Fiona believed every word she said.

His pragmatic, skeptical nature told him there were logical explanations. He had a private investigator doing background checks on everyone involved with the Connellys—including their spouses. Of particular interest to Bailey was anyone who had come to New Mourne from the outside—Fiona's father, Sarah's husband, Jake, and Dr. McGuire. Fiona had explained the relationships last night, but Bailey was curious about these men connected to Connelly witches.

Fiona had occupied Bailey's thoughts to the exclusion of everything else. He never did this with a woman. There had been many fleeting flirtations, but few relationships. He gave women only the time left over after work. He took calls in the middle of romantic dinners and left vacations early. One angry ex had suggested he hire himself a mistress who would be content with the tiny sliver of his life he was prepared to share.

Today, however, he cleared his schedule in order to remain in New Mourne. He called his father and said he was taking some time to get to know Fiona both professionally and personally. His father did not seem surprised and did not press for information. His mother had called almost immediately, of course, demanding all the details. Bailey told her only that Fiona was very special.

What could he tell her that would not trigger the Connelly memory-wiping spell?

Spells. Witches. Curses.

Bailey braced his hands on his knees and sat forward to take a deep breath. *What in the hell was happening to him?*

"Problem, Mr. Powers?"

He looked up. Dr. McGuire and Sheriff Tyler were in front of him on the sidewalk.

"No problems," Bailey lied and stood to extend his

hand.

They eyed him during handshakes—the tall, lean lawman in his crisp, khaki uniform and hat, and the solid academic in rumpled gray trousers and white shirt.

Bailey wondered what Jake would do if asked pointblank to do the shifting thing. Could he become a huge, man-eating white tiger? There was something about him, Bailey admitted, a coiled sense of power.

"We trust you're no worse for the wear after your misadventures?" Rodric's Scottish burr made the question almost musical. He was much friendlier than he had been yesterday when he warned Bailey away from exploiting the Connellys.

"That cave-in could have been much worse," Jake added. "Fiona might have been hurt." It was obvious he didn't much care if Bailey was hurt.

"I'm finding out these Connelly women are quite adaptable," Bailey replied.

Rodric chuckled. "That's one adjective that describes them."

"Do you have a minute?" Bailey asked. "I'd like to talk to both of you."

Jake was blunt. "No one wants you digging around here, Powers. You might as well pack up and head out."

"My plans are to stay awhile," Bailey replied. "At Fiona's invitation."

Maybe Bailey's imagination was working too hard, but Jake's growl was almost feral.

Rodric laid a hand on the sheriff's arm. "Why don't you head on to the appointment you have? I'll stay for a chat with Mr. Powers."

"I wish you'd both drop the 'Mr.' I'm Bailey."

"Sure, Bailey." Still bristling, Jake walked away

and went into the barbershop several doors down Main Street.

"He won't be kind if you hurt Fiona," Rodric said.

Bailey turned back to the rusty-haired professor. "What do you mean?"

"Trust me when I say you never want to know." Rodric sat down and rolled up the sleeves of his shirt. "God, it's hot. The weather in this town has gone to hell. I'm told it's normally cool here in the mountains. Not this summer. Work of the demon."

Bailey looked at him in surprise.

"No need to pretend you don't know what I'm talking about," Rodric added. "I'm sure Fiona's told you most everything by now. She wouldn't become involved with someone unless she could tell him what her family is facing. That's simply the way she is."

"Who said we were involved?"

Rodric laughed again. "I have eyes. The two of you shoot sparks off each other. I decided last night that I could almost like you, seeing how you've been lassoed by another of the Connelly sirens."

Bailey resumed his seat. "Didn't sirens call sailors to their deaths in mythology?"

"Quite right," Rodric observed with a smile. "Their song was said to be so sexually powerful that men could not resist. Just imagine the anticipatory delight of those doomed men. I've never thought it a bad way to die."

Bailey got the impression the professor was a bit of a ladies' man.

"It's quite apt that the beautiful Eva Grace would name her shop after those intoxicating creatures," Rodric continued. "When they call, mere men come running. Even males like Jake, with supernatural resolve, can't help themselves."

"I think you understand the Connelly appeal firsthand." Bailey wondered if the man knew how he looked when he said, "The beautiful Eva Grace."

Rodric laughed again, but did not answer. "You said you want to talk to me?"

Hopeful the man might actually give him some insight, Bailey resumed his seat. "Yesterday, we talked about how you've worked with ghosts and such."

"I study a number of paranormal phenomena."

"So you've seen evidence of it all—the werewolves and fae as well as the witches?"

"These beings exist all over the world."

"Why do you study them?"

A fleeting look of sadness touched Rodric's features. "We all have our personal motivations," he evaded. "As a scholar, I'm fascinated by the truth lying at the root of so many of man's myths and legends."

"But what's your end game?"

"Come again?"

"Are you trying to enlighten mankind about the paranormal? What do you want? Fame? Recognition?"

"I don't care if others don't believe what I uncover. We each have to answer only to ourselves. I just look for answers."

Bailey considered the words for a moment. "That's what I would have said of myself when it comes to anything approaching the paranormal. Every time I looked, however, I found a lie." He gave Rodric an abbreviated version of his family's dealings with psychics and mediums over the years.

"I've always thought of myself as the thinking

person in the family, the one who relied on evidence before just accepting what someone says as truth."

"You had good reason to be a skeptic."

"I thought so. Now…" Bailey shrugged.

Rodric gave him a steady look. "Now you're just trying to resist what you already believe."

"That's exactly what Fiona told me."

"Perhaps you should try trusting your gut," Rodric suggested. "Doubting everything has clearly not proven to be helpful in getting you the answers you want."

The sound of an approaching vehicle on the quiet street made Bailey turn. He stood as he recognized Fiona's van. She stopped in front of the town courthouse, and she, Brenna and Eva Grace got out, talking with great animation.

"What's up?" Bailey called out to the trio.

Fiona greeted him with a wave and came across the street. Bailey watched her with more than appreciation for her slender body and her bright smile. This was someone he wanted to know. Not just sexually, but deeply. Had he ever felt quite this way?

She reached him, looking a little awkward. He gave her a kiss and looped an arm around her shoulders.

Brenna observed them through narrowed eyes. Eva Grace, fanning her crimson face, dropped onto the bench.

"Are you okay?" Rodric asked her with concern.

"We're looking for Jake," Brenna explained. "Our phones are dead or we would have called." She frowned down at the device in her hand. "That's weird. Now the signal's back up."

"Something's wrong," Bailey said. "Where have you been?"

"Back to the cave," Fiona told him.

Before she could say more, "I Shot the Sheriff" erupted from Brenna's phone.

Immediately, a shout rang out from down the street.

Jake pounded down the sidewalk, waving his phone.

"What the hell?" Brenna murmured, running to meet him. Eva Grace leapt to her feet.

"There's been an accident," Jake shouted as he skidded to a stop. "Out at the farm. It's Maggie's father."

Bailey saw the color drain from Fiona's face. "What happened?" she breathed.

"There's no good way to say this," Jake replied. He pulled Brenna into his arms. "He's dead. I'm so sorry, but he's dead. His tractor turned over."

Fiona slumped against Bailey. A sob escaped Eva Grace. Brenna buried her face in Jake's chest.

The women allowed themselves those small expressions of shock. Then they were all action. Brenna went with Jake. Fiona headed to the van, and Bailey automatically followed. "Can I drive?"

She shook her head. "No, I can do it."

"But I'm going with you," he insisted.

Nodding, she turned to look at Eva Grace. "Are you coming?"

Rodric helped her cousin into the van, and climbed in, too. In moments, the wail of a siren sounded from Jake's cruiser as he and Brenna headed out of town. Fiona guided the van after them.

The trip to the Connelly dairy farm was quick. Emergency vehicles were already on scene, an ambulance parked in a field just beyond the big, white farmhouse. Cars were flooding onto the narrow lane. As soon as the van stopped, Eva Grace and Fiona jumped out and darted into the field.

Bailey and Rodric hurried after them.

"Bloody Christ," Rodric muttered, abruptly halting.

Bailey followed his gaze. A tractor was overturned. A white cloth covered a mound nearby. Like a scene from an alien invasion movie, dead cows littered the field, their carcasses gleaming brown and white and red with blood in the hot sun.

A cry cut through Bailey. Up ahead, he saw Fiona, her knees starting to buckle. He ran forward and caught her just before she fell to the ground.

Face tear-streaked, she looked up at him in horror. "I released Albert to the demon and look what he's done. What did I do?"

Bailey held her while she cried.

Chapter 20

Fiona pressed her face to Bailey's shoulder and struggled to contain her sobs. This was her fault. If she had never opened the cave, never freed Albert, Uncle Van would not be dead.

She was grateful Bailey did not try to soothe or reassure her. He just held her and let her cry.

Behind her, she heard more voices and cries of sorrow. The rest of the family was arriving, and she had to face them.

"They'll never forgive me," she said, drawing away from Bailey.

He framed her face with his hands, thumbs gently stroking away tears from her cheeks. "From what you've said, this was all set in motion long before you were born."

She took a deep breath. "We have to end this torture."

Turning, she saw a large group of relatives, neighbors, and sheriff's personnel gathered. Ryan, whose family's farm was nearby, was in the crowd, along with the entire coven. Doris and Frances supported each other. Van had been their brother's only child. Diane, Estelle, and Delia clustered together. Van was their cousin but as close to them as a brother and called uncle by all their children. Van's daughter, Maggie, clutched Lauren while Brenna and Eva Grace looked on, white-faced. Sarah stood alone, grim and silent.

Fiona feared her grandmother's reaction most. Sarah surprised her by opening her arms, and Fiona stepped in.

"I'm so sorry," Fiona said. "I've never been so sorry."

"Hush now." Sarah brushed her hand over Fiona's hair and hugged her close. "This loss is part of our curse."

"We have to end it," Fiona repeated. "We have paid enough."

"Yes, we have." Sarah turned to the family, her arm still around Fiona. "Can someone tell me exactly what happened?"

Maggie's brother, Sully, who ran the farm along with his father, nodded. Broad-shouldered, red-haired, and green-eyed, Sully looked calm despite the blood on his T-shirt and jeans. "We were coming back from mowing in the south pastures when we saw the cattle were down. They were...gutted. You can see the blood."

He pointed toward the barn. "I ran into the field. Dad drove in..." The muscles in his throat worked, and glassy-eyed horror replaced his composure.

Aunt Erin, Van's wife and Sully's mother, took up the story. "I was in the garden near the house. I turned just in time to see the tractor flip. Like a big hand just turned it upside down." She pressed a hand to her mouth, but nothing could muffle her gut-wrenching sobs as her son took her in his arms.

"Black magic," Sarah said. "I can smell it."

The field indeed reeked of sulfur, like rotten eggs

with the underlying coppery odor of blood. A hot, dry wind blew the smell over them, and an uneasy murmur ran through the group.

Jake stepped forward. "Can we clear this area, please?"

A movement above them took Fiona's attention. A single vulture flew overhead, its bright red head almost glowing in the light. Within seconds, the bird landed on a tree limb in a familiar hunched pose. When Fiona looked up again, another vulture circled and settled on another branch.

"Sarah," Fiona said, grasping her grandmother's shoulder. "Look up."

Everyone raised their gazes and stood, transfixed, as a huge flock of the large predators circled just above the area where Sully's body lay.

Jake yelled at the paramedics. "Get moving." He turned to Brenna. "Get the family inside."

Two paramedics and a couple of deputies got Van's body on a stretcher and into the back of the ambulance. When the doors closed, the birds dove and sat like a theater audience on the edge of the land near where the cattle lay bloody and still. They perched in trees, on power lines, the fence, and on the overturned tractor. The black birds were fearsome in their eagerness and silent in their patience.

As the ambulance rolled through the gate and down the drive, Bailey came up beside Fiona and touched her arm. He eyed the birds with alarm. "We should get out of here."

Rodric was beside Eva Grace, urging her forward, as well. Fiona saw her cousin Brian, a sheriff's deputy, help Brenna hurry the elder aunts through the gate.

Marcus and Sarah were beside them, darting anxious gazes over their shoulders. Her mother and father and the rest of the coven scattered like insects on a disturbed anthill.

Fiona resisted Bailey's efforts to move her. She was mesmerized by how the birds held their red and black heads low between their shoulders. They sat in an eerie, unmoving mass as though waiting for a cue.

Jake jogged backward, shouting at Bailey and Fiona. "Come to the house. Now!"

Bailey tugged Fiona's arm. "Let's go."

She stumbled, her eyes still on the birds as the first vulture again rose and circled, its red head standing out against the bright blue of the sky. When the bird settled onto the first cow's body, the others rose en masse, then dove.

And the feast began.

"Dear God in heaven," Bailey said. He took Fiona's hand and pulled her after him. "Let's get out of here." This time, she followed.

The rest of the group was in the house, huddled at windows, watching the carnage outside.

"Get the children away from the windows," Sarah ordered. Sully and his wife swooped up their four-year-old daughter and toddler son and went down the basement stairs. The boy screamed, while the little girl, already showing a Connelly witch's curiosity, tried to come back into the kitchen.

Brenna closed the door behind them. Sarah and the elders drew Maggie and Aunt Erin deeper into the house. The rest of them remained at the kitchen and dining room windows.

"What in the hell kind of birds are those?" Bailey

asked.

"Vultures," Fiona murmured. "But I've never seen them act this way."

Ryan stepped to her side. "Not long ago a flock picked a woman's body clean in less than an hour. They're attracted by the freshly dead cattle."

"This isn't normal," one of the other neighbors said. "I've lived here my whole life and never saw so many vultures at once."

"It's like Thanksgiving at my Nana's house," Ryan said. "They eat a while, and then they fight a while." He lifted his camera and headed back to the door. "I have to record this."

Despite cries of warning, Bailey and Fiona went out onto the back porch behind Ryan. The three of them stopped short of stepping into the yard.

Near the closest dead cow, just beyond the open gate, black birds sat in a tight circle with their wings hunched against their bodies as they tore into the fresh meat. A couple of birds broke away, tussled, and then returned to the meal. The scene repeated across the field.

After nearly thirty minutes, all the vultures rose as if ordered by a commander. They climbed to the sky and flew away.

Fiona tentatively pushed open the porch's screened door and waited. All she heard was silence. No dogs barking or cattle lowing or bees buzzing over Aunt Erin's yellow, orange, and pink zinnias. The busy farm, usually full of life, was as quiet as the cursed land had been just days ago.

"Are you getting all this, Ryan?" Bailey whispered.

"Sure," the younger man said.

Fiona returned her gaze to the field and took a deep breath. "Too bad you guys can't see everything."

"What do you mean?" Bailey asked.

"You're talking to a medium," Ryan reminded him.

Fiona could not even count the number of spirits walking around the field. "I've never seen so many dead people in one place before."

When she headed toward the gate, Bailey grabbed her arm again. "What are you doing?"

She pushed his hand away and smiled in reassurance. "I need to talk to them. Maybe they need guidance to pass over or maybe they have messages."

Fiona approached the first spirit, a young woman who wore an embroidered tunic and faded bell-bottom jeans. Her silver necklace with its bright red, yellow, and blue glass circles reminded Fiona of old jewelry Sarah had allowed her to play with as a child.

"Can you see me?" the girl asked.

"Yes. Can I help you?" Fiona said.

"I'm not sure why we're here." The girl kept looking around, her spirit fading in and out. "I was at my house for such a long time. I liked it there, but they said I had to come."

"Who are they?" Fiona asked.

"The dark ones." The spirit winked out, then glowed again. "I never wanted to leave the house where my mother lives. It's such a happy place. I told Mother I would be ready to go when she was." She waved her arms as if in time to some unheard music, then her arms dropped and she became more transparent. "Something is making me so tired, so tired. I don't think I can make it home."

When the spirit faded, Fiona moved to a man in

weathered overalls and an old work shirt. He looked at her with weary eyes, and she recognized one of her family's oldest neighbors, a sweet man who had died just weeks ago. "Mr. Llewellyn, aren't you ready to pass over?"

"I was waiting for my wife."

Fiona remembered that his elderly spouse was very ill. "Then why are you here?"

"I don't know, little lady."

Fiona smiled at his familiar endearment. "Can you tell me how you got here?"

"Something black brought us." He turned to look over his shoulder, as if startled, but Fiona could not see what distracted him. "They're trying to take us. We have to hide. Bad time's coming, little lady."

The old man disappeared. Fiona looked around. She searched in vain for her Aunt Celia. The spirit that was supposed to be her guide was not here. Neither was Bailey's sister. The remaining spirits vanished as quickly as Mr. Llewellyn did.

Fiona went back to where Ryan and Bailey waited.

Bailey took her hand. "You look like you're about to fall over. What happened?"

"It's bad." A sudden, stabbing headache made Fiona rub her temples. "I think the demon and Albert are stealing the strength of our town's spirits."

"Shit," Ryan said.

"Exactly." Fiona started to sway on her feet, her own energy flagging as quickly as the ghosts' had. "Would either of you happen to have a candy bar handy?"

Chapter 21

The summer sun was slipping toward the horizon as Bailey took a seat on the steps of the farmhouse.

"I want your family on my side if there's ever a war," he told Fiona, who dropped down beside him.

"We are an amazing group," she agreed.

In just a matter of hours, the Connellys had filled a kitchen with food, cleaned the farmhouse from top to bottom, greeted a small army of neighbors and friends, and spread comfort to everyone.

Once her energy was restored with chocolates found in the pantry, Fiona roped Bailey into helping her supervise the children of family and visitors. He sensed she wanted to be away from the rest of the family. Blaming herself for what had happened was crazy, he thought. He supposed he had no business advising anyone about guilt, since he carried a load of his own.

So he kept his mouth shut and helped Fiona with a gaggle of children. For the most part, they kept them occupied and away from the backyard where the sheriff and his deputies processed the scene of the Connelly uncle's death. The rest of the family and some neighbors were using a backhoe, some tractors, and trucks to prepare a large trench to bury the butchered cows. Bailey thought cattle internment might have been easier than lassoing the youngsters.

"Do all children have that much energy?" He

nodded toward a three-foot high tornado of red hair and green eyes chasing a dog and screaming at the top of his lungs.

"I think so." Fiona stood and called out to the four youngsters who were the last of their charges. "Hey kids, want to settle down for a story?"

"Ghost story!" demanded the impish redhead.

Fiona looked at Bailey, rolled her eyes, and laughed. He warmed to her beautiful smile. She was a natural with the children, allowing them to romp and run, then calming them down with stories about brave young men and women who fought evil villains.

The women in her stories were often the heroes, Bailey noticed. He was not surprised. If today was any example, she came from strong stock.

"Cake?"

Turning, Bailey found one of the gray-haired aunts offering him a slice of chocolate cake. She was one of the two that Fiona called "the elder aunts." He stood, but eyed the cake with suspicion, thinking of the tea that Fiona's grandmother tried to force on him last night.

"No need to worry," the white-haired woman assured him. "We've noticed how kind you've been to the children today."

From over heads of her young charges, Fiona nodded her approval, so Bailey took the cake. He had already enjoyed fried chicken, something called summer squash casserole, green beans, and coleslaw, so he was not hungry. He was not even that fond of chocolate cake. He took a bite and his taste buds exploded in reaction to the combination of moist cake and thick fudge frosting loaded with pecans.

"Wow," he muttered around his second bite. "This is amazing."

The elder aunt's green eyes sparkled. "It's called Coca-Cola cake. The carbonation gives the chocolate that rich taste."

Fiona laughed as Bailey polished off the slice and praised the cake as the best he had ever eaten. The old woman bustled off, looking pleased.

The children got up to play again, and Fiona stood beside Bailey. "I'm glad you liked that cake. You'll be eating more."

"I couldn't." Bailey's protest was barely spoken when the other elder aunt came out, also proffering cake. He distinguished her from the previous aunt only because her pantsuit was yellow instead of blue.

"Try this," she said, pressing a plate in his hands. "I use just a smidgen more Coca-Cola." She looked over her shoulder and lowered her voice. "My sister, Doris, has been known to use Pepsi." The last word was spoken as a hiss, like a curse.

"I heard that," the blue-pantsuit woman said from the doorway. "That's not true."

"Eat it," Fiona whispered to Bailey as the elderly twins bickered. "Tell her it's fantastic."

He forced the rich cake down in four bites and pronounced it as good as the first. "I can't imagine either of them being any better," he assured both women. "I need the recipe for my mother."

Sarah and her husband Marcus came out of the house. The two older women went to her side. "How is Erin doing?" the one in yellow asked, referring to Van's widow.

"Eva Grace has put her to bed." Sarah looked

weary, Bailey thought. Some of the power he had seen in her earlier was missing.

"I have to go to Cousin Inez," she told her sisters. "Her daughter told her about Van, and she's taking it hard."

"Our oldest relative," Fiona explained to Bailey. "She was married to a great-great-uncle."

Sarah's eyes filled. "Van visited Inez every week without fail. He even supervised her move from assisted living and into her daughter's home. We all felt she'd be safer there until our current troubles pass."

"Van always reminded Inez of her husband," said the elder aunt in blue. "He loved listening to her read from her journals."

"Do you think Inez is okay?" Fiona asked. "Should Eva Grace go with you?"

"Inez has buried too many loved ones, that's all," Sarah replied. Her husband's arm slipped around her shoulders as she added, "We've all buried too many Connellys."

A chill moved over Bailey. Beneath the bustling activity at the farmhouse, he felt the family's unease. Even when playing with the children, he had seen Fiona's anxiety. She said there were no spirits of any kind around them. That concerned her as much as the dozens she saw earlier. She also searched the sky, as if she expected another flock of vultures to appear at any moment.

There was no doubt in Bailey's mind. The birds were driven by a supernatural force. How else could they descend in such numbers and eat with such ferocity? But why? He was eager to study the footage Ryan had shot during the assault. The videographer had warmed to Bailey a bit before he left the farmhouse, and they were getting together at Fiona's studio tomorrow morning.

No one had an explanation for the cattle's slaughter. It appeared they fell to the ground, dead, and were gutted by an unseen force. The same force had flipped a tractor and killed a man beloved by his extended family and community.

Fiona hugged her grandmother, and Bailey stepped forward. "I'm so sorry for your loss," he told Sarah.

The gaze she swept over him was sharp, but she accepted his condolences with quiet dignity. Marcus shook his hand.

Fiona linked her arm through Bailey's as they watched the couple walk away. "Let's see to these children," she suggested. "It's time for everyone to be going."

They lingered only a while longer, with Fiona making plans around the kitchen table with her sister, parents, and cousins. Van would be buried as soon as the body was released. The sons of another cousin were building a simple pine coffin, which Sarah and the elders would line with homemade quilts to allow for quick decomposition and return to the earth. It was the Wiccan way, Fiona explained. The family would say goodbye during a small ceremony at the Connelly cemetery. A wake was planned for next week at the home place.

Tradition and respect drove the entire process, Bailey thought. Though many emotions were running through the people gathered together, their focus was to honor their dead.

When Bailey and Fiona left just after moonrise, it

spoke to her exhaustion that she allowed him to drive her van. He followed her directions and soon found himself in familiar territory, pulling up to her office and home.

By unspoken agreement, he went in with her. "Are you hungry?" she asked as they started up the stairs to her apartment.

"Not for another week, at least." He gave her a quick grin. "I ate some things today I've never touched, like turnip greens, which I carefully wrapped in a napkin and tossed. But everything else—especially the Coca-Cola cake—you must produce again."

"Neither Brenna nor I inherited the cooking gene. We do bake cookies and breads at Christmas, though. That's our limit." Fiona flipped on lights in a large room that encompassed living room and kitchen.

Bailey was left with the impression of bold colors and green plants before he followed her into a bedroom painted pale blue.

She sank down on the bed. "I can't believe what's happened."

He sat and pulled her close. Ever since those awful moments after they arrived at the farm this afternoon, when he held her while she cried, he had been longing to take her in his arms. There had been no more time for tears or comfort. Like the rest of her clan, she stayed busy every moment.

Now the reality was sinking in. He could see it in her face.

"What if I had waited to open the cave?" she said. "Uncle Van would be alive."

"You don't know that." He knew how she felt, of course. How many times had he faced the same sort of question?

If he had never convinced his parents to let Anna to go out with him and his friends, she would not have been murdered.

"The what-ifs will tear you apart." He silenced her protest with a gentle touch of his fingers to her lips. "Trust me, Fiona. I know what I'm talking about."

She sighed and her slender body sagged against his. "You're wiped out," he said. "You should get some sleep."

"You'll stay, won't you?"

He hesitated, but only for a moment. He wanted to be here when she woke up, when she remembered what had happened. "You get ready for bed," he said, wanting to give her a few moments of privacy. "I'm going to get myself some water."

By the time he came back in the bedroom, Fiona was tucked in. She directed him to towels and a spare toothbrush in her bathroom, but she was asleep when he came back to the bed. He undressed, slipped in beside her, pulled her close, and drifted off.

Deep in the night, Bailey awoke to the scent of flowers and rain.

Fiona.

Her name washed over him like music, even as her lips touched his. The kiss deepened, and she opened to him with a soft moan. He felt her need, urgent and questing. She was naked, her skin heated. Her breasts peaked at his touch, her thighs parted.

Fiona slipped her body over his. "Show me," she whispered in the hot, sweet darkness. "Show me how you want it."

She lifted her hips, and he guided her down.

Shuddering with pleasure, he held fast to his control as he entered her. She was so tight and yet so soft. By instinct she moved. He bucked upward, increasing his speed and the power behind his thrusts until lights spun around them and her cries of pleasure filled his head. They rode fast and clung to each other. Fiona's body clenched and tiny sparks of blue danced through the air. Bailey groaned and followed her.

They lay side by side gasping for breath before Fiona snuggled next to him. The silence between them was easy until Bailey sensed tension in Fiona.

"Something wrong?" he asked.

"I was just thinking about what Willow told you, that you have a part to play in all that's happening here in New Mourne."

Bailey took her hand and held it against his chest. He felt a sudden, urgent anxiety. "Your family is afraid of what's going to happen next."

She shivered. "It doesn't seem real. This is the twenty-first century. Why are we being haunted by this stupid curse?"

"We have to find the answers."

"We?"

"I'm all in," he said. "I have a researcher working to find out more about the missionaries who came here in the 1700s. I got an email from him this afternoon. He says there are some old records about the missionaries stored in a library over in Savannah. An archivist is going to look at them and see if they tell us something new."

"Really?" Fiona sat up. "We all think the key is finding exactly what happened to the Woman in White. That's why we went back to the cave." She told him about her vision of the young Native American being tortured.

"Don't go back there," Bailey said. "It's not safe for you."

"No place is safe until the curse is lifted," Fiona argued. "I can't sit around, waiting on a ghost to come and take one of us. None of us can."

"Have you tried to talk to this spirit?" he asked.

"More times than you can imagine. Sarah and the others told me not to try to summon her, but I have. I can't reach her. Or she's resisting. I keep thinking that when I finally do see her it will be the end."

"Stop it," Bailey said. He reached over to snap on a bedside lamp. He needed to see her clearly, to know that she was listening to him. "Don't try to reach her again."

Her dark hair rumpled, lips swollen from his kisses, Fiona looked vulnerable and tired. His stomach clenched at how many times she had probably placed herself in danger by trying to find this blasted spirit who had cursed her family.

"Promise me," he said again.

She shook her head. "I can't do that. We have to use everything possible to reach her."

Before Bailey could respond, the phone on Fiona's nightstand started to ring. She grabbed it and read the display, frowning. "It's Brenna. What can it be at this time of night?"

She answered, and her face drained of all color. "We'll be right there."

"What's wrong?" Bailey asked as she set the phone down.

"The demon attacked my grandmother. Eva Grace

and Brenna can't get her to wake up," Fiona said. "They need the entire coven to come right away."

Chapter 22

The short drive to the two-story colonial where her elderly relative lived seemed like an epic journey to Fiona.

What could have happened?

Other members were pulling into the drive as Fiona and Bailey were greeted at the front door.

Maeve's graying ginger hair was standing on end, and dark streaks marred her fair complexion. The acrid scent of smoke filled the air.

"What's burning?" Fiona asked.

"They'll tell you about the fire." Maeve's hand shook as she pointed down a short hallway. "They're in the bedroom to the left, where Mother's been since we moved her here last week."

Fiona hurried forward. She found a large room where Brenna, Eva Grace, and Marcus huddled over a bed. Inez sat in a wheelchair near the window. Bailey stayed in the doorway as Fiona crossed to her grandmother.

Sarah lay still as death on a colorful quilt covered in a rose pattern. Marcus sat to the right with his wife's hand in his. Fiona gave him a quick hug, and turned as Brenna stepped to her side. Seeing her sister's eyes swimming with tears, Fiona's panic escalated. "What's wrong with her? Why can't she move?"

"An enchantment," Eva Grace said when Brenna

was unable to respond.

Behind her, the rest of the coven came into the room. Delia, looking ashen, threaded her way through to sit on the bed and take her mother's free hand. Even Maggie who had just lost her father, was here. Fiona could see Maeve with Bailey, Jake, and Aiden just inside the door.

In the sudden silence, Inez's strong voice belied her frail appearance. "It was the demon who did this."

Fiona turned to her. "How do you know?"

"Remember how it came into my room the day you and Brenna visited me?"

Fiona shivered as she recalled being at the assisted living facility. Inez had changed before their very eyes and tried to harm Fiona. Only Brenna's strong magic interceded. That attempt at possession by the demon was one of the reasons the family thought it best for Inez to move back in with her daughter. Though Maeve wasn't a practicing witch, Sarah thought Maeve's home was an environment easier to protect with magical wards. Obviously, she was wrong.

Inez continued speaking, "I was in bed, and Sarah and Marcus were sitting with me, so Maeve could rest a bit. I felt the same evil presence as before. Only this time it was stronger. Darker." Her thin shoulders hunched. "Sarah tried to stop it and now…" Her voice broke on a sob, and the elder aunts swept in to comfort her.

"It went after her journals," Brenna said, regaining her composure as she pointed at a pile of towels near the adjoining bathroom. The wall behind them was black with soot.

"I tried to save all the books," Marcus said. "It's

what Sarah told me to do. But a few of them burned."

"In a flash," Inez interjected. "Like lightning."

"And when the fire was out, Sarah was on the floor." Marcus stroked a finger down his wife's frozen features.

"What did you see?" Fiona asked him.

He frowned. "Just like Inez said, the room was lit up with lightning. Then it was gone, the books were on fire, and I tried to smother it. Maeve came running, and we got Sarah on the bed. I called Brenna. I didn't know what else to do."

"Eva Grace and I thought we could handle it," Brenna said. "But so far Sarah hasn't responded."

"Should we get her to the hospital?" Fiona asked.

Eva Grace shook her head. "This is magic. Very bad magic."

"Albert," Fiona whispered, guilt edging out her confidence. "He's imprisoned Sarah the same way he was trapped for all of those years."

"Stop feeling sorry for yourself," Aunt Doris ordered. "What's done is done."

Frances nodded and looked at Brenna. "We're wasting time. Didn't you call us all here to help?"

The last trace of tears disappeared from Brenna's eyes as she took control. "Marcus, I know you don't want to let go of Sarah, but we need you to step away."

He pressed a kiss to Sarah's forehead before joining the others near the door. Brenna asked Maeve for candles. Like any good Connelly, Maeve had the requisite colors of blue and white she placed around the room.

Jake wheeled Inez away from the bed, and the coven closed ranks around Sarah. Brenna took her grandmother's hand. Eva Grace laid clear quartz crystals above Sarah's head and below her feet, then slipped into her customary place at Brenna's right. Delia still held Sarah's left hand and linked hands with Fiona, who clasped her cousin Lauren's, who took Maggie's. And so it went, the circle forming around the bed, with the elder aunts standing sentinel at the foot.

Brenna raised her arms. The white and light blue candles around the room came to flame.

Fiona closed her eyes as Brenna began to chant.

"To the gods and goddesses we offer our appeal.

A demon has broken our circle and brought us ill will.

Grow our power and elevate our skill to set our leader free.

Banish this enchantment! As we will so mote it be."

They waited in silence. A wind grew in the room, bringing warmth at first and then dying to a chill. Fiona's inner sight fired to life. She opened her eyes just in time to see a small, black orb flying toward her, then through her. The pain was intense but fleeting, and she gasped when the spirit released her.

"By the Goddess," Delia murmured, her grip on Fiona's hand tightening. "What was that?"

Fiona wasn't certain, and it didn't matter anyway. All that mattered was Sarah.

The strong, powerful witch didn't move. The only trace of life was the slight rise and fall of her chest.

Eva Grace was crestfallen. "I don't think our magic even touched her."

Brenna squared her jaw. "Let's try again."

They joined their magic twice more, but Sarah was

unchanged.

Doris began to sway and broke the circle. Bailey and Jake caught her before she fell.

"That's enough for now," Marcus said. He covered the distance to the bed with two, long strides. "I'm taking Sarah home."

"I'm not sure we should move her," Frances said, looking almost as haggard as her twin.

"She needs the home place," Marcus insisted.

Brenna and Eva Grace stepped aside as he bent and gathered Sarah in his arms.

The coven fell back, ceding to his wishes. He carried Sarah out the door, with Aiden and Jake following. Eva Grace and Delia hurried after them.

While her cousins saw to the elder aunts, Fiona leaned over the bed and ran her hand over the quilt, relieved to feel the warmth from Sarah's body lingered. She looked cold.

"What went through you?" Brenna asked her.

"Maybe Albert." Fiona was all too aware of Bailey standing just feet away, studying her with concern.

"Albert and the demon are playing with us," Brenna said with disgust. "We have to make ourselves stronger."

"How?" Fiona asked.

"We have to turn to *The Connelly Book of Magic*. There are clear instructions about what to do if a coven leader falls." Brenna stopped and pressed a hand to her belly. "I can't believe we're talking about this. Nothing can happen to Sarah." She hurried from the room without another word.

Fiona's gut twisted.

Bailey stepped to her side. "What do you need me

to do?"

"We're going to be working at Sarah's. You don't have to come."

He shook his head. "There's not a chance I'm leaving you right now."

"This is coven business," she replied.

"Which you made my business as soon as you told me the truth about your family." His features were steely with resolve. "Come on, we'll stop to get you some fuel before we go to your grandmother's house."

When they were back in her van, Bailey asked, "What was in your cousin's journals?"

"Maybe some answers about the curse. Inez recorded her entire life in those books, including history of the missionaries who settled here before our family. The problem is that there are dozens of books, and Inez can't remember where she wrote everything. We've been going through them one by one, looking for information."

"Which may have been destroyed tonight." Bailey's expression hardened. "I'm going to get that information on the missionaries from Savannah as soon as possible."

"That could help," Fiona said as she lay back against the headrest. She felt drained since the spirit had passed through her. Dawn was breaking on another hot, summer day. Who knew when she might get to sleep again?

Bailey pulled into the parking lot of a convenience store just up the street. "What do you need beside candy bars?"

"Trail mix," she said. "And nuts covered with Greek yogurt. A few energy drinks."

"Okay. Just give me a few minutes."

As soon as he was gone, Fiona closed her eyes and relaxed, giving into fatigue.

Scratching on the window roused her seconds later. "Bailey?" She could see him still inside the store, so she let her eyes drift shut once more.

Scratching began again, this time from the rear of the van. Fiona jerked around but saw only a young man fueling his truck at the pumps.

The scratching, in front of her, filled her with dread. She turned and came face to face with the largest black crow she had ever seen. Her blood froze.

The crow spread its wings to span the dashboard.

Then it did not move.

Fiona tried not to breath. She carefully undid her seatbelt and opened the door. She scooted out in the smallest opening possible. The crow remained, watching her with steady eyes. Fiona edged away, ready to slam the door.

A movement in her peripheral vision made her turn. The black orb from earlier swooped toward her. Fiona braced herself, but nothing could have prepared her body to be thrown to the other side of the parking lot. Pain shot through her right side, and gravel dug into her arm as she began to fight her unseen tormentor.

The man at the gas pumps yelled as Fiona was lifted and slammed to the pavement.

Chapter 23

Noise erupted outside. Bailey ran out just in time to see Fiona smash to the ground.

A young man at the pumps was pressed up against his truck. Two dogs barked and snarled from cages in the back. "Something's got her," he shouted at Bailey.

But what? Though Fiona was fighting and kicking, she was caught by an unseen force.

Bailey ran toward her, but a few feet away he slammed into a wall that wasn't there. He hit it hard enough to bounce back and land on his backside, his breath pushed back into his lungs. His head spun, but he struggled to his feet and started forward. Again, an invisible barrier held him back.

"Get help," Fiona shouted at him. "There's nothing you can do. Call Brenna."

She wrenched away from her captor and flung herself against the wall only to be dragged back and shoved to the ground. She looked up at Bailey, her eyes dazed. He rushed forward once more, trying to reach her. A strange wind kicked up, and in the thin morning light, Bailey saw a black funnel descending behind Fiona. Like a tornado from hell.

Knowing his efforts to break through the wall were futile, he wheeled back to the parking lot. The young man at the pump was in the bed of his truck, unlocking the doors to the cages of his snarling, barking dogs.

"Stand back," he shouted to Bailey.

Freed at last, two large gray dogs streaked past Bailey. Sharp teeth bared, foam dripping off their jaws, they broke through the barrier and leapt toward the black storm with ferocious growls. Debris flew from the tornado, but the wind weakened.

As suddenly as it had erupted, the storm was gone.

Bailey barreled forward and slid to a halt at Fiona's side. "Are you hurt? What's broken?" His hands shook as he ran them over her. She stared up at him, and his heart pounded. Was she caught like her grandmother in some sort of spell?

From behind him came a shout, "Watch out."

"What?" Bailey looked up and saw the dog's owner gesturing in panic.

"Stay still," the young man shouted. He whistled. "Heel, boys. Heel."

Only then did Bailey realize the two dogs were on either side of him and Fiona. Eyes glinting, gray hides with black dots bristling, the dogs stood with ears laid flat to their heads. He could smell their breath, and they had been eating something more than dog bones.

"Heel!" the young man shouted again.

Bailey swallowed hard, thinking of the vultures that had descended on the cattle yesterday. Nature had gone wild in this bedeviled town. Were he and Fiona about to become a meal?

The dog on his left sniffed. Bailey tried not to react. The other dog leaned down to smell Fiona. His mouth opened, and Bailey almost shouted. The dog washed a big, pink tongue over her face. She gasped and the pall over her features was gone.

The young man began to laugh, and the dogs ran to

him like puppies, barking and yapping.

Bailey sagged in relief and turned to Fiona. "What the hell happened?"

"They ran off a bad spirit," the dog's owner said, looking delighted. "My granddaddy told me there's nothing like a blue tick hound for chasing the devil. He was damned right!"

Bailey focused on Fiona. "Where are you hurting?"

"I'm fine," she said, although she grimaced as she sat up. Scrapes on her arms were bleeding, and a bruise was blooming on her left cheek.

"You need a doctor."

"I need to get to Sarah's. Eva Grace will take care of me."

"But what happened?" Bailey carefully helped her to her feet.

"Didn't you hear him?" she asked, nodding at the young man who was still praising his dogs and feeding them treats. "Those hounds chased away the devil."

"And he backed off." Bailey felt a glimmer of hope. "If the demon backs away from these dogs then..."

"It wasn't our demon," Fiona explained. "Just an aggressive spirit spurred into action by black magic."

"How does that happen?"

"We have our share of malcontents here in New Mourne, but it's not the usual."

"It threw you around."

"Because I wasn't ready," Fiona replied. "The crow was warning me, but I wasn't really paying attention." She looked to the brightening morning sky. "There'll be more. Let's get out of here."

They paused long enough for Fiona to thank her

canine rescuers properly.

"Keep them close," she told the owner. "Bad times are coming to New Mourne."

Bailey got Fiona in the van and drove away. She sat with her head back, eyes closed. "That's my first experience with anything that rough." Her voice was low and weary. "And I kind of hope it's my last."

"Did you know that ghost?"

"Yes, we've met. He was a miserable child and hellacious teenager. He ran away and was killed in Atlanta. His mother brought him back here to be buried, and his ghost tagged along. He does stuff in his parents' home, breaking dishes, throwing books."

"Why would he attack you?" Bailey asked as he slowed to make the turn leading to Sarah's house.

"I've tried several times to help him pass over, to get him to stop haunting his parents. He refuses. No doubt the demon has given him some extra power."

"Shit," Bailey said and paused. "Shit. What does all this mean?"

Fiona turned to face him. "I'm not sure. We need to put all the pieces together and figure out how the demon is tied to the Woman in White. Then we have to get rid of Albert again. And all without Sarah." Her last word caught on a sob she barely repressed.

Bailey pulled into her grandmother's drive way, drew to a stop, and put his hand out for hers. "She'll probably be fine. With all of you working to help her..."

"But you saw how we failed earlier." Fiona's fingers curled in his. She was pale, shadows under her eyes, and fatigue dripping from every pore. "Brenna's strong, and she will be a great leader, but she's frightened now. I haven't seen my sister afraid very often. It's hard to look at."

Reaching across the seat, Bailey gently pulled her into his arms. "I thought you were dead," he whispered against her hair. "When I saw you fly across that parking lot, I couldn't breathe. I've never felt so helpless in my life, trying to beat down that barrier."

"I know." Fiona lifted his hand and kissed his bruised and scraped knuckles.

Bailey's adrenalin had been pumping so hard, he hadn't noticed the injury until now. He could just imagine how strange he had looked, punching the air. He wondered if the convenience store's security cameras had caught any of the action. When this was all over, and Fiona was safe, that footage would be incredible on her show.

What would any of that matter if Fiona had really been hurt? If she was right, if more of that was coming, he just needed to protect her. They all did.

"Let's get inside," he suggested, looking around with unease.

"You seem a little worried."

"Something about seeing you fly through the air has me jittery. I think you need your family."

"And you," Fiona said. "You came to the rescue."

"And let two dogs upstage me."

Her smile was weak. "Well, you haven't been properly trained in chasing devils."

"But that's what we're going to do, isn't it?"

"You don't have to stay."

"Yeah, I do." He let his hand drift down her hair. Anger quickened as his fingertips grazed the bruise on her face. "I can take care of you."

He remembered the last time he had said that and believed it was possible—the night Anna was murdered. The memory sent a chill through him, but his resolve stiffened. Whatever came for Fiona would have to go through him.

Chapter 24

Once she crossed the threshold of the family home place, Fiona felt stronger. Sarah's protections and wards washed away some of the residual effects of her battle with the angry and violent ghost.

Brenna sat alone at the dining room table, studying *The Connelly Book of Magic.* One eyebrow lifted as she looked at Bailey. Then her gaze sharpened on Fiona and she arose, alarmed. "What happened to you?"

"I'm okay," Fiona assured her, but winced as she took a chair. Her face was swelling, and the cuts on her forearms stung. The beating from the ghost had jarred every bone in her body. She explained her bruises and cuts to Brenna.

"Eva Grace is with Sarah," Brenna said. "I'll get her."

"No, please don't," Fiona spoke at the same time Bailey said, "That's a good idea."

Fiona frowned. "Sarah needs her."

"You do, too," Bailey insisted. "You can't help your family if you're hurting like this."

"I almost hate to say this," Brenna said. "But Mr. Hollywood is correct." She hurried out of the room.

"You're hurt worse than you said." Bailey knelt beside her chair, his blue eyes clouded. "We should have gone to the hospital."

His genuine worry touched Fiona. He really cared,

she realized. Too much had happened for her to spend much time analyzing the emotions going on between them, but his concern filled her with warmth.

Brenna and Eva Grace rushed back into the room, her cousin carrying her leather medicinal pouch. The moment she touched Fiona, the pain lessened. Soft, healing magic flowed through Fiona's body, easing every throb and twinge. Brenna left and brought back a basin of warm water and a washcloth, and Eva Grace began to clean the abrasions on Fiona's arms.

"Make her some ginger tea," Eva Grace told Brenna.

"And get me some chocolate," Fiona requested. "Bailey left everything he bought me at the convenience store."

"I was a little busy dealing with invisible shields and devil-chasing dogs."

Eva Grace demanded that Bailey tell her everything as she applied a cool salve to her cuts. "There's comfrey in this," she explained as she brushed some over the bruise on Fiona's cheek. "It promotes healing."

"Good," Bailey said, spectacular grin replacing his grim expression. "We can't have any permanent damage to this beautiful face."

Fiona lost herself in his smile. He thought she was beautiful. No one had ever called her that. Eva Grace was beautiful. Lauren was glamorous. Maggie was pretty. Brenna was a voluptuous force of nature. Fiona had always felt ordinary beside her fellow witches. Until now. Until Bailey.

Eva Grace cleared her throat in the silence. "My, my," she murmured with a knowing look at Fiona. "So that's the way of it."

Shaking her head to clear it of fanciful dreams, Fiona flushed. She was grateful that Brenna appeared with a cup of tea, a bowl of broth, and a large slice of Coca-Cola cake. Fiona attacked the chocolate first, while Brenna disappeared into the kitchen again. She brought out the same meal for Bailey.

"Eat it," Fiona ordered at Bailey's protest. "You'll feel better."

"Marcus got the broth out of the freezer," Brenna explained to Fiona. "Sarah keeps it on hand, infused with magic to deal with headaches and other small ailments."

"Is she taking food?" Fiona asked, hope quickening inside her.

Eva Grace shook her head, looking worried. "Marcus and I poured a bit into her. It's important to keep nourishing liquids going in to keep up her strength. As a last resort, we'll have an IV set up. I may have Dr. Hargrave come out and see her." She referred to a surgeon in town who was the grandson of a Cherokee healer and understood their ways.

"Where's everyone else?" Fiona asked.

"Delia and Aiden are resting so they can sit with Sarah later," Brenna replied. "I sent the others off to rest and get ready for the remainder of the day. Uncle Van should be buried before moonrise."

Fiona protested. "Not until Sarah wakes up. She will want to see his body."

Brenna was firm. "She would want us to follow tradition. The county medical examiner released Van's body. The coffin was taken to the funeral home, and we'll be ready at sunset today."

"So we just go on without Sarah?" Fiona's voice shook. Bailey laid a comforting hand on her shoulder.

Brows drawn, Brenna flicked a glance between him and Fiona. "We're trying to find answers, Fiona. None of us have ever dealt with an enchantment like this."

"Have you found anything to help in the *Book of Magic*?"

"No, I just started looking through it."

Eva Grace put the container of salve back in her kit. "Rodric is coming over soon. He has some ideas about getting the book to speak. For now, I'm going back up to Sarah. Maybe I can get Marcus to rest for a bit."

After she exited, Bailey said, "Did she say the book would speak?"

Brenna scowled. "That's none of your concern."

"He knows everything," Fiona said defensively. She turned to Bailey. "There are family legends that say the book can talk. We wonder if there are secrets it might reveal that could help us break the curse."

Though Brenna gave Bailey another glare, she said, "It's past time for the book to give up something to help us. We may be the first generation to actively battle this curse, and some assistance would be appreciated."

A puff of wind blew out of the fireplace and ruffled the pages of the large, open book on the table.

"Granny Ghost," Fiona observed. "She's unsettled."

"I am trying to help." Bailey told Brenna about the missionary papers his researcher had located in Savannah.

"We need anything we can find," Brenna said with

grudging gratitude. "I've also got Lauren searching Coven Glan for a way to help Sarah."

At Bailey's questioning look, Fiona explained, "Coven Glan is a secret internet for practitioners of the craft. You have to know special access codes and possess magic to use it."

Brenna gave her sister another stern look.

"Please stop worrying," Fiona exclaimed. "He's sworn to secrecy."

"I have nothing to gain by revealing your secrets," Bailey said. "Other than possibly being institutionalized for delusions."

"It's happened to visitors before." Brenna stood with her hands on her hips, her eyes betraying her distrust as she studied Bailey.

Another breeze blew through the room. Fiona stood up so fast she knocked her chair over.

"What is it?" Bailey asked.

Brenna looked around in alarm. "Who's here? I doubled Sarah's wards."

Recognizing the essence of the spirit who wavered in the air, Fiona said, "Aunt Celia. Where have you been?"

Sarcasm bubbled out of Brenna. "Good question. Are you two going to go let another ancient ghost go free?"

Celia's shimmering form disappeared, and guilt climbed through Fiona. "I'm sorry, Brenna. Celia and I thought we were helping. We were just looking for answers like everyone else."

"You're not helping Fiona." Anger snapped in Bailey's gaze as he faced Brenna. "She's beating herself up about what's happened. She doesn't need your blame, too."

Brenna's body sagged, and she scrubbed a hand through her thick auburn hair. "I'm sorry, Fiona. No one blames you or Celia. I just want you to be careful."

"What has being careful done for us so far?" Fiona asked with weariness. She stepped forward and reached out with her special sight. "Celia? Come back. Tell me what's wrong."

The figure that was so like Fiona and Brenna's mother formed in front of Fiona. She put out her hand.

"There's trouble," she told Fiona. "Most of the spirits in town are in hiding away from Albert. The demon has him and together they are spurring the more restless spirits to misbehave. And anyone who hadn't passed over now can't."

"Uncle Van?"

Celia shook her head sadly. "He's caught."

In addition to her uncle, Fiona thought of Mr. Llewellyn, whom she had seen at the farm yesterday and of Bailey's sister.

"Is Anna hiding?"

At the name, Bailey stepped forward. "What about her?"

Celia said, "I don't know where the girl has gone. Some others are gathering at the old cemetery."

"Why?"

"I'm not sure." Celia's form began to fade. "Please come, Fiona. You may be able to help."

Fiona expelled a deep breath. Brenna and Bailey were on either side of her, puzzled looks centered on the empty space where Celia had been.

"What did she say?" Brenna demanded.

"I have to go to the cemetery."

"No," Bailey and Brenna said together.

Fiona almost smiled at this rare moment of agreement between the two. "You can waste time arguing with me or I can get over there and find out what's happening."

"Not alone," Brenna protested.

"I'll be with her," Bailey said.

"Oh, that's reassuring."

"Bailey will go with me," Fiona told her sister. "You need to stay here and keep researching what to do to help Sarah."

Brenna acquiesced with a troubled sigh, and Fiona hugged her. "You and Eva Grace should also grab a nap or at least a beauty spell this morning. You look like hell."

Fiona left her sister huffing and went with Bailey to the van. Her cousin's healing, the magic broth, and the rich chocolate cake had restored her energy, but she still allowed him to drive.

"What was that about Anna?" he asked.

She told him what Celia said.

"What do you feel about Anna? You said she's usually near me."

"She's not here," Fiona said and tried not to be concerned. She had not seen Anna since she appeared at the home place the day before yesterday. "Remember how she mentioned Minnie? I'm sure Minnie is helping her." She hoped she sounded convincing.

Bailey frowned. "I don't understand any of this."

"Maybe we'll find some answers at the cemetery." Fiona turned to look out the window to hide her worry. Outside, the day that had dawned clear was now overcast and dark. Clouds boiled over the mountains when the van turned onto Devil's Creek Road.

Bailey brought the vehicle to a stop at the cemetery, and they stepped out into heavy, moist air.

They saw no crows assembled on the graves today, just a black, swirling mist. Fiona distinguished some shapes, and a low keening joined the thunder that rumbled overhead. Even Bailey said he could hear the noise.

"Maybe you should stay here," Fiona warned him.

"Save your breath. Where you go, I go." He gestured toward the cemetery. His expression sobered as they once again faced the simmering cauldron of unrest in front of them. He held up his phone. "My video is working right now. I'm going to record this so we can look at it later."

He took her hand and they stepped forward. The mist closed around them like doors, filtering the daylight and blocking the sky.

Fiona stopped and Bailey immediately stepped in front of her. "What is it?"

"Do you hear a baby crying?"

He listened a moment but shook his head. "Just that moaning sound."

"It's the baby," Celia said, appearing beside Fiona.

"Whose baby?" Fiona asked.

Celia moved forward, disappearing in the gloom.

"Stay close to me," Fiona told Bailey. "Celia's here, and she'll help me."

"Let me know if you see your visitor from this morning," he said. "He's not going to throw you around again."

Fiona stopped and looked at him. "How will we stop him?"

"Run?"

Bailey's expression almost made Fiona laugh. The high, thin wail of a baby captured her attention again, however, and she led Bailey through the crumbling gravestones.

Shapes formed in the mist. Hands reached for Fiona, and she reached back. "What is it? What's wrong?"

A half dozen ghosts responded to her, each more insistent than the other.

"Find the baby."

"The baby wants its mother."

"Help the baby."

"Only its mother can quiet the child."

"She never comes for him."

"He needs her."

As each spirit spoke, it disappeared until only one ghost stood in front of Fiona. It was a man dressed in the clothes of a farmer. He looked directly into Fiona's eyes and said, "Get the baby to his mother and then you must help us."

That said, he too disappeared.

Celia drifted into view. "Come with me."

"What's going on?" Bailey whispered.

Fiona held tight to his hand and followed her guide. Her shirt and jeans were damp from the dense, wet air, and water ran down her back. Bailey's face glistened with moisture. The atmosphere was like a giant sponge. Fiona found it hard to breathe.

"This is not good." Bailey's breathing was heavy, as well.

Overgrown weeds covered the back of cemetery. In the deepening gloom, Fiona stumbled over a stump.

Bailey grabbed her arm, pulling her up before she hit the ground. "Are you sure we should go on?"

The baby's screams filled Fiona's head. She had to help this child. She plunged forward.

The grave markers in the back of the cemetery were the oldest ones. Some of them were so weathered it was impossible to read the names and dates on them. When they reached the back corner, Celia stopped and pointed to a pile of stones, moss, and snarling weeds.

Fiona knelt. All she could hear was the baby's cry.

She dug through the weeds and scruff, ignoring the sting of thorns on her hands. Bailey dug with her, and soon she touched the cool stone of a broken grave marker. They pushed the weeds, dirt and twisted vine away, and letters became legible on the marker.

Fiona scrubbed off the dirt. "Baby MacCuindliss" was carved in uneven letters deep in the stone.

"It's her baby," Celia said.

"Are you sure?"

The spirit nodded.

Bailey drew in a deep breath beside her. "What does this mean?"

"This is the Woman in White's baby." Fiona dropped to her knees and traced the name on the marker with tender fingers. "Please don't cry," she whispered. "I'll try to find your mother, I promise."

The baby's cry faded to a whimper. Celia disappeared. The mist blew away, leaving Fiona and Bailey under a canopy of threatening clouds.

"MacCuindliss," Fiona breathed. "The Woman's name."

Lightning streaked over the mountains, and the ominous stink of sulfur infused the air.

Chapter 25

"How do you know it's the Woman in White's baby?" Brenna asked. She was looking at the photos Bailey had taken with his phone.

Fiona bit into a thick ham sandwich she had fixed when they returned to Sarah's. She nodded to Bailey to answer her sister.

He clicked his phone to an email from his researcher that came while they were in the cemetery. He opened an attachment and zoomed in. "Look at these papers. See those names?"

Brenna peered at the small screen. "MacCuindliss."

"This is a photo of an old document at the library in Savannah," Bailey explained. "It's a list of the first missionaries who supposedly came to this area. The name MacCuindliss appears three times with three different initials. F, C, and something I can't make out. It could be an M or an N."

"The Woman, her father, and the baby?" Brenna asked.

Fiona did not think so. "The Woman and her father are two of those names. Not the baby. Remember, the legend said she had a child with the brave she married."

Brenna frowned. "Would her father let them put his family name on that grave?"

"Perhaps there were more charitable souls among the missionary families," Fiona suggested. "The baby was an innocent, and obviously someone thought he deserved a decent grave."

"At any rate, I believe you have a name for the Woman." Bailey tucked into a salad piled high with ham and Marcus's homemade Russian dressing. "What's next?"

From the end of the table, Fiona's cousin Lauren looked up from her laptop. "I'm running the name in Google and Coven Glan. Maybe we will turn up something interesting."

"My researcher is looking as well," Bailey said.

Fiona turned to Brenna. "Is Eva Grace still with Sarah?"

"She's upstairs, asleep." Brenna stifled a yawn. "Delia and Aiden are sitting with Sarah. Marcus hasn't left her side, either."

"Any more ideas to help her?" Fiona nodded at the *Book of Magic*.

"I've pulled a few things from the Internet," Lauren told them.

"We'll try them once Uncle Van is buried." Brenna stood.

Fiona summoned the courage to make a suggestion she knew her sister would not like. "Perhaps we should call in Willow?"

Brenna's green eyes went stormy. "Never."

"But she has power."

"Which she may well have used against Sarah."

"How do you know that?" Lauren asked.

"It would be just like that damned old faerie to try to punish Sarah this way," Brenna retorted. "We're not calling her." She headed for the hallway. "I'm going to get a little rest before the coven starts gathering for the ceremony."

"I'm staying here," Lauren said to Fiona and Bailey. The striking auburn-haired witch gave them a disapproving look. "You two might want to get some rest and clean up."

"A polite way of saying we're grungy."

"Yes." Lauren turned her attention to the computer. "You don't want to be covered in dirt with your hair standing on end for Uncle Van's ceremony."

Fiona swiped at her hair. "I guess not."

"You look fine," Bailey assured her.

She laughed. "Well, you don't." She leaned over to wipe a smudge from his cheek. "Perhaps we should make ourselves more presentable."

Bailey said he was not leaving Fiona alone, so they stopped at his room to pick up his clothes and toiletries.

At her place, Ryan was in the studio running video of the vulture attack. When they told him what happened this morning, he left to go talk to the convenience store about security tapes in their parking lot, hoping they caught the attack on Fiona.

After taking a shower, Fiona agreed to nap. Bailey cleaned up and tucked himself in beside her, solid and strong. She drifted off, feeling safe in his arms.

She slept hard, but dreamed of crying babies, of her Uncle Van's anguished face, and of sweet Mr. Llewellyn running away in fear. Finally, Minnie stood ringing her hands in the center of the coven's sacred clearing. Oily black tentacles bubbled at her feet. Just beyond the kind and familiar ghost, the Woman in White drifted through the trees.

The Woman turned, and her fathomless eyes were deeply, darkly sad as she looked at Fiona. "You think you can help me, silly witch? I dare you to try."

Fiona woke with a sudden jerk.

Bailey's arms tightened around her. "You were moaning in your sleep."

"Just a dream," she said as she allowed her eyes to adjust to her dim bedroom.

"You said, 'Let me try.' " Bailey turned on his side, his hand on the side of her face. "What are you planning?"

Instead of answering, Fiona asked, "What time is it?"

Bailey squinted down at his watch. "Nearly six."

"We have to go soon." She sighed.

"Okay." Bailey leaned down to kiss her. "Whatever you say."

She gave herself over to his caress. It felt so natural for him to touch her, to bring her body to soaring, swift passion with his hands and his mouth. Even more right for him to bury himself inside her, for them to cling together in shuddering release.

"I could spend my life with you like this," he murmured against her throat.

Fiona closed her eyes, savoring the weight of him, the intimate entwining of their bodies and minds. She could drift away on a daydream of more afternoons like this with Bailey.

Except for the echo of the Woman's voice from her dream.

"*I dare you to try.*"

Bailey seemed to feel the change in her. "What's wrong?"

"Just thinking of laying Uncle Van to rest," she lied.

He seemed uncertain, but Bailey nodded. They got up. Fiona chose a soft summer dress of white, fixed her hair, and used a touch of makeup. She left Bailey shaving in the bathroom and went downstairs. In her backpack she made certain she still had candles, her ceremonial athame, and her hooded cloak of crimson satin.

Unfortunately, she had more to do tonight than bury a beloved uncle.

The ceremony was held in the family cemetery, at the edge of the original Connelly land. Though the extended family would gather later for a wake, only blood kin and Van's wife attended the burial.

Bailey was convinced to stay at the home place. Marcus was with Sarah, whose white, still features haunted Fiona as she filed with the rest of the coven to their places under tall pines and ancient oaks.

True to centuries-old custom, men of Connelly blood dug the grave earlier in the day. Women decked the pine casket with flowers. The four males of Fiona's generation carried the casket to the graveside. The other men stepped forward to help them ease it onto a system of rope pulleys.

Holding her grandson, Aunt Erin stood with her two granddaughters—the two youngest Connelly females—as the casket lowered into the ground. The men stepped away.

Brenna in her royal blue cloak, led the coven around the grave. Candles sparked to life, and they formed their magical circle. Together they chanted, "Back to the earth, where we begin, we send our dear and beloved kin. May his soul soar beyond our sight, forever after filled with light. A man of truth, set truly free. As we will, so mote it be."

Birdsong filled the air as the family said their last goodbyes.

Fiona wondered that no one could feel the agitation around them, the stirring in the trees. She thought of her dream, and her uncle's deep sadness and how Aunt Celia said he was caught in his world by the demon's mischief. Was he here in the breeze? That kind, decent sweet man deserved to pass to his reward. She had to find a way.

The entire family covered the grave, and evening shadows crept through the trees by the time they finished.

Filled with impatience, Fiona walked back to the home place with the others. She lingered with family, sharing their sorrow, touched by the love among them. What she wanted to do, however, was follow the path her dream had opened.

She was afraid for Bailey to go with her, but Fiona knew he'd never let her slip away alone. "We have to go," she told him as the last of the family drifted away.

"Where?" Bailey asked as they walked down the porch steps.

"I'm going to see if I can summon the Woman in White."

Bailey turned her to face him. "That can't be safe."

"But I have to do it."

He seemed uncertain, glancing back toward the lighted windows of the house. "Shouldn't we get Brenna or Eva Grace?"

"I have to do this myself." Even though Fiona knew the Woman's power, she was not in fear for her life. She felt certain the Woman was not going to take her. Not yet.

"I'll go without you," Fiona said as Bailey hesitated.

He squared his shoulders and turned toward his car. "All right. Let's go. Where to?"

As they drove several twisting back roads, Fiona explained to Bailey about the coven's clearing and its importance to them.

"It's sacred ground to us, blessed hundreds of years ago by the first Sarah Connelly," Fiona said. "It's where we perform all our coven rituals and rites. It's also where Eva Grace's fiancé was killed a few weeks ago."

"That's Jake's friend, Garth, right?"

"Yes. We thought he was killed by the Woman in White, but it was the demon impersonating her."

"So what's to keep the demon away tonight? Or one of the ghosts he's empowering?"

Fiona paused. "You're right. You shouldn't be with me. Something could happen."

"Not a chance," Bailey said, his face setting. "I'm not letting you out of my sight."

She directed him to the heavily forested back entrance of the coven's clearing. He parked his Mustang beside the road, and they got out.

Fiona hefted her backpack and started into the woods.

"Can I point out that you're not exactly dressed for hiking?" He took the backpack from her.

"I know these paths by heart," Fiona said, but she took a flashlight from the pack to pierce the dusk gathering fast under the trees.

As they entered the clearing, the sound of rushing

water filled the air.

"Mulligan Falls," she explained to Bailey. "The creek runs to here, and then drops down onto the dairy farm in the valley below."

"I'm beginning to get my bearings." Bailey looked around intently. "I feel something."

"What is it?" Fiona asked, looking around for unexpected visitors.

"The air's different here."

"Not surprising," Fiona said. "This is a magical place, and I'm sure the residual magic can be felt by anyone who is sensitive."

"I'm not sensitive."

"After everything that's been happening, I don't believe you can continue to claim that."

He suddenly turned again.

"What is it?" she asked.

He darted a look over his shoulder. "For a minute, I felt Anna. Just a glimmer of her, same as always."

"Perhaps she's here." Fiona took her supplies out of her backpack and put on her red cloak. She took her athame and drew a circle around Bailey. When she had finished, she poured salt around him and said, "Do not try to leave this circle. It is your safety."

"But—"

"Trust me," she said, and he nodded.

She then set the candles at the five points and brought out a small incense holder in the shape of a three-headed dragon. She lifted her hands and said, "*Solas.*" The candles and incense began to burn.

She turned to face Bailey. "Once I begin, you have to stay. No matter what happens, just remember I'm in control, and I'm safe."

"That's a little hard to accept remembering this morning."

"That's not going to happen here. I'm ready now and on guard."

Fiona moved into the circle and closed her eyes to increase her focus. When she felt centered, she lifted her arms and chanted, "Souls trapped within space and light, bring me closer to the realm of sight, allow me to summon the Woman in White. In the midst of nature, I come in peace; as I will so mote it be."

The silence in the clearing was resolute, broken by the occasional scurry of an animal in the woods and the rustle of leaves. Fiona waited with her head down, her body alert to any change in atmosphere.

When nothing happened, she raised her head and said, "Your name is MacCuindliss, and you had a baby." She paused. "A baby that died."

A chill grew around her. She turned and faced the rocks where the waterfall dropped off the cliff, hoping she would finally meet the one spirit that had always eluded her.

Instead of the Woman in White, however, three circles of light drifted down. They came slowly, swinging around Bailey, who seemed unaware of their presence.

"She won't come to you."

Fiona recognized the voice. "Uncle Van?"

"Yes, I'm here." His spirit materialized beside her, as sturdy and red-haired as he had been in life. "The demon won't let me pass."

"Aunt Celia said as much," Fiona replied. "But how are you being stopped?"

"He waits near the light and tries to take our souls,"

Van explained. "It gives him power. He's taken several already."

She shivered. "Is Mr. Llewellyn with you?"

Her elderly neighbor appeared beside her uncle. "I have not surrendered to the demon yet."

"If he takes our souls, he'll own us," Van said. "She does nothing to stop him, and I don't know why."

"Are you talking about the Woman?"

"She drifts among us," Van explained. "Only she laughs at the demon. She has more power than him."

"Does she speak of the tribute?" Fiona asked.

Van shook his head. "Not to us."

Minnie appeared behind Van, just as she had in Fiona's dream. "I told you there are too many portals. They've upset the balance of the spirit world in New Mourne. There aren't many more places to hide." There was a soft pop as Minnie disappeared.

Mr. Llewellyn looked fearful and vanished, as well.

Only Uncle Van remained, though he was fading. "Find the answers, Fiona. Help her if you can."

"The Woman?"

"She suffers," he said with sadness. "But she's the only one who can stop him. If he's not stopped, we'll be here for eternity."

"Wait a minute, Uncle Van, have you seen a young girl? Is she with Minnie?"

There was no answer as Van faded. The candles blew out. Fiona dropped to the ground, her head in her hands.

Bailey waited with clear impatience and finally asked, "Are you okay?"

Looking up, Fiona was surprised to see Anna

standing behind Bailey. She smiled at Fiona but winked out of sight in a hurry. By the Goddess's grace, the demon had not claimed her soul.

Bailey glanced behind him. "Is she here?"

"She's gone, but she's okay."

Fiona stepped into his arms and told him what she had learned.

"So the Woman has the power to stop the demon," he repeated. "What does that mean?"

"That we have to reach her. My uncle says she's suffering. Maybe if we can bring her to her baby, she'll release the curse."

"If he's part of the spirit world, why can't she reach him now?"

"I wish I knew," Fiona said as the questions and the fear inside her rose like a tide. She turned to Bailey. "I want to go back to the home place, to see Sarah again. Can we go?"

"Of course." He stayed close at her side as they walked back through the woods. Fiona's phone rang when they neared the car. It was Eva Grace.

"What's wrong?" Fiona asked anxiously.

"Everything's the same," Eva Grace replied. "I was wondering if you could go by Siren's Call and pick up my crystal ball. We're going to try a session to find some answers about Sarah. I need to leave the ball in the moonlight tonight."

"Of course," Fiona said.

"Where are you?" Eva Grace asked, her tone suddenly suspicious.

"With Bailey and headed for the shop. See you soon." Fiona clicked off the phone. She would tell everyone about the ghosts in the clearing when they were together.

As they drove through the darkness, Bailey said, "If this was a script I was writing, I'd have you put the baby in the Woman's arms and the demon would explode."

"Great idea." She glanced at him. "Do you write scripts?"

He shrugged. "I've tried my hand at it, but I don't have a lot of time."

"But if you did?"

"Sure," he admitted. "I'd give it a whirl."

"And would your parents support that move?"

"I'm not sure my father would be too happy to lose me from reality development, but if it were something I wanted, I'm sure he would listen."

"You should do it." She smiled at him. "Most people enjoy a good ghost story."

"Are you offering yourself as a subject matter expert?"

"Once this nightmare is over for my family, yes, I would."

Bailey gave her a long, considering look. "Maybe I'll take you up on that."

"When it's over." Fiona stared out at the night, eager for that day to come. She wondered how many Connelly witches had thought the same thing.

Chapter 26

As events unfolded, Bailey was glad he and Fiona managed a little sleep before the funeral. They delivered the crystal ball to Eva Grace. Then Fiona's phone rang with a New Mourne resident needing help with an out-of-control ghost, and so it began.

In the middle of the night, Fiona convinced a newly-dead grandfather there was no need to be banging barn doors, setting hay bales on fire, and stampeding cattle at his family's farm. She assured him he would be able to cross to the other side soon, and she summoned Minnie to help the ghost hide.

Bailey and Fiona were headed to her place when Ryan called. The rampaging ghosts of two former students had set off the fire alarm and bolted the doors to the library at the county high school. When Fiona and Bailey arrived, the two were ripping pages out of books and turning the sprinkler system on and off.

These hoodlums, who had spent decades haunting the school, did not respond to Fiona's invitation to hide with the other ghosts. They were eager to use power from the demon and Albert to raise hell. Fiona finally evoked a binding spell that sealed them both in the 1950s bomb shelter behind the school.

"They should stay put until we get this under control," she told Ryan and Bailey.

Only when would that be? The town's most

restless spirits were rebelling in the only way they knew how—by upsetting the humans near them. Bailey spent the entire day running from the scene of one haunting crisis to another with Fiona. Ryan stayed with them, recording most of the incidents.

Nearly twenty-four hours without rest had Bailey punch drunk as he sat in the van and studied video of Fiona trying to reason with a ghost at the big discount store on the highway south of town. All the computers had malfunctioned, adding charges to every transaction. The TV sets in the electronics section ran an endless loop of blood-filled gore, while female shoppers were touched and chased from the dressing rooms.

Thankfully, the ghost was an unhappy teenager Fiona intimidated with her witchcraft. Now she and her family were busy doing cleanup at the busy store with the Remember-Not spell.

Bailey never saw the ghosts, but he could see the toll they were taking on Fiona.

From the van's dashboard, Fiona's phone played the tune, "I Shot the Sheriff." Having heard this ringtone a lot today, Bailey knew it was Sheriff Tyler and answered.

"I need Fiona now," Jake told him.

"She's still busy."

"I need her more over at Fred Williams' church. I've got trouble with some kids and a ghost."

Bailey retrieved Fiona from the store, and they drove to a section of town he had never seen. They swept past security guards watching sturdy, electronic gates. Behind brick walls, he glimpsed McMansions with lush lawns and swimming pools.

"Who lives here?" he asked.

"It's called The Enclave, and it's mainly people who moved up from Atlanta. Their kids go to this church school." Fiona turned into the parking lot of a sprawling church and school campus. Unlike the outdated public high school, this building was a modern glass and stone paradise.

A group of children and a few adults stood at one end of the parking lot, near an old oak tree. Fiona swung in beside two sheriff's cruisers. She and Bailey got out of the van and headed toward Jake. He had his hands full with a trio of angry-looking women and about two dozen children, most of them crying.

"We don't need the sheriff's department," one woman shouted at Jake.

"We got a call," Jake told her. "Someone heard the kids screaming and thought there was a problem."

Another woman pointed toward a little girl standing under the oak tree, crying. "This child is clearly disturbed. She stirred up the whole group before choir practice. We've called her mother."

"We'll stay until the mother's here," Jake said, though the women continued to protest.

Fiona's cousin Brian, the sheriff's deputy, was trying to reason with the child, but she was inconsolable. Bailey could not see what was upsetting her.

But it must not have been pleasant, as Fiona turned pale.

"What does she see?"

"A woman under the tree. She's been beaten and shot. Her dress is covered in blood."

Bailey saw nothing, but after this day, he did not doubt Fiona. She headed straight for the child while

Bailey stepped up beside Brian.

Fiona crouched beside the sobbing little girl. "It's okay, honey. I can see her, too."

Instead of being comforted, the child's storm of tears intensified.

"It's okay to be frightened." Fiona gently turned the girl away from the tree. "She's scary."

"Nobody else sees her," the child cried. "Why do I have to see her?"

"Do you know she's a ghost?"

The little girl drew in a trembling breath and shot a look over her shoulder. "A ghost?"

"She died a long time ago," Fiona said. "Have you seen other people like her?"

"My mom says I'm making it up."

"Your mom just doesn't understand. She can't see ghosts like you and I can."

"I...don't...want...to." The little girl's gulping sobs tore at Bailey's heart.

"Oh, honey, I know." Fiona drew the child into her arms. "I know it's really hard. I could help you if you want, if your parents would let me."

As if sensing she were truly with someone who understood, the girl leaned into Fiona.

"This is something you can do that most people cannot," Fiona told her. "When you're older, it won't be as scary."

"Can you help that woman? She's bleeding, and she's really sad."

"I'll try." Fiona asked the girl to go to Brian. When the young deputy had the child, Fiona turned back to the tree. "Why are you here?" she asked the spirit.

Wishing he could hear the other side of the

conversation, Bailey came to Fiona's side. He wanted to be close if she needed help.

Fiona listened and replied, "That was a long time ago. Why would you come here now to frighten a child?" She paused, and then shook her head. "You don't have to do anything the demon says."

After another moment, Fiona told Bailey, "After decades as a wandering spirit, she wants to cross over. She's haunted her husband, who got away with killing her, but what's happened since Albert and the demon appeared has upset her."

"Does she know the demon could steal her soul if she tries to pass?"

"That's why she came to the church. She was a member of this congregation thirty years ago, when she died. She believes she can avoid the demon here."

Bailey looked up at the soaring church steeple topped with a cross. "What's your opinion?"

"That I respect her beliefs, and I want to help her." Fiona moved forward, her hands outstretched.

A few days ago, Bailey would not have believed Fiona was holding the hands of a troubled spirit. Now, he could almost imagine the tragic figure in the bloody dress. He felt something electric emanate from Fiona and grow. A bright white light appeared near the tree and dimmed slowly until it disappeared.

Gasps ran through the crowd, and a woman's voice rang out, "Witch! She has performed Satan's magic right here on the church grounds!"

Bailey turned to see a well-dressed, slender middle-aged woman step through the crowd. "You are a witch, Fiona Burns," the woman proclaimed. "You have blasphemed God and his holy church."

She was the pastor's wife, Bailey realized, the icy blonde woman he met Wednesday morning on Main Street. He started toward Fiona, ready to defend her, but Brian stopped him.

"Fiona can handle Ginny Williams," the deputy said.

"You are a spawn of Satan, an evil presence in our good town," the pastor's wife shouted.

"You're frightening everyone, Ginny." Fiona turned to Brian. "Get the child out of here, will you?"

Ginny kept moving toward Fiona. "Something should be done about you and your family. I've always known what you are. We should return to the day when stoning witches was accepted."

Jake turned from trying to herd the women and children toward the church. "That's enough. You need to stop right where you are, Ginny."

She whirled on him. "I know all about you, Sheriff. You're sleeping with a witch too. The Connellys have bewitched you, the same as so many other men. What we need is someone who will get rid of them once and for all."

Jake's voice had a growl in it. "I said that's enough."

"Don't you dare tell me what to do," Ginny screamed, her face crimson with rage.

The women and children fell silent, and a man Bailey recognized as the pastor strode through the group. "What's all of this?" he asked as he looked at his wife.

She tossed her head. "That strange little girl pretended to see something again, and Sheriff Tyler got this Connelly witch involved."

The man turned to the sheriff. "Is that true?"

"It's okay now," Jake told the pastor. "Fiona calmed down the little girl and her mother is on the way. But your wife is very upset, and she needs to go somewhere and cool off."

"I'm not going anywhere," Ginny said. "This is our church and you're the one desecrating sacred ground. Get this witch and her wicked spells out of here."

Bailey had been silent long enough. "You don't know what you're talking about, lady. Fiona just helped one of your church's members pass to the other side."

"What heresy." Aghast, Ginny's eyes went wide. "But I expect no less from another witch's consort."

The pastor took his wife's arm. "Let's go into the church. We'll pray with the children and calm them down."

"Good idea." Jake went back to motioning for all the women and children to go to the church. "It's time for everyone to calm down."

Ginny tried to face Fiona again, but her husband held her tightly. "Let's go. Now." He looked at Jake. "We'll talk later, Tyler." Then he half-dragged the fuming woman into the church.

Just as the doors closed behind them, an SUV drove up and the little girl ran to her mother. Brian followed.

"That Ginny is a nasty woman," Bailey commented.

"I think she's starting to lose it." Jake looked at Fiona. "Your family needs to steer clear of her."

"Ginny Williams is not going to intimidate any of us," Fiona replied. "You know how Brenna feels about her."

"Yes, but when tempers run as high as Ginny's, there's cause for concern." Jake nodded toward the little girl and her parent. "Is there something you want to say to this child's mother?"

Fiona headed over to them.

Jake's gaze followed her. "She's running on fumes."

"We all are," Bailey agreed. "Are you going to call Brenna over here for the Remember-Not Spell? We left her and Lauren at the store."

"No need. I imagine Fred and Ginny will convince them all that they saw nothing, and that this was just in the imagination of a child."

Bailey saw the child's mother turn away from Fiona and march toward her vehicle. She loaded her daughter in the back seat, got behind the steering wheel and sped off.

Fiona's shoulders drooped as she and Brian walked back. "I imagine you'll be hearing from that mother, Jake. She told me to get away and stay away when I tried to suggest what her daughter had seen. I feel so sorry for that kid."

"You did what you could. Now you need to get some rest," Jake advised her. "Let Powers drive you home."

That was as close to a vote of confidence from the sheriff as he was going to get, Bailey supposed. He did convince Fiona to go home, and the two them were able to eat and sleep. Fiona was still asleep when Bailey woke in the darkness. She did not stir as he tucked covers around her and gently smoothed hair away from her face. She needed every bit of rest. No doubt, tonight would be another long night of ghost hunting.

He got up, dressed, and went in the other room to make some coffee. Checking the time, he decided to call his parents.

His father's face came onscreen. "Son, I've been wondering about you today. How are you?"

Bailey did not want to go into everything that was happening until he had proper time to process it himself. The easiest thing to say was, "I'm working with Fiona."

"Still?" His father looked interested. "I have to admit I was expecting you to have debunked her abilities and be headed home by now."

"No debunking," Bailey said. "She's for real. In many ways."

"Is that so?" A grin played about Dean Powers' mouth. "Is her show still a possibility or has all of that been replaced by something personal?"

"I honestly don't know. I'm working it out."

"Do you need anything?"

"I'm fine. How are things going there?"

"Smoothly," Dean replied and gave him an update on several projects.

"Sounds like I am not missed."

The picture onscreen shifted, and his mother came into view. "I miss you. What's up?"

Bailey laughed. "Dad will fill you in."

"You look tired," his mother added. "Are you eating well?"

"Sure. Have you ever heard of Coca-Cola cake?"

"Sounds like a lot of white sugar."

"It's amazing, trust me. Everything you ever heard about Southern cooking and Southern cooks is true."

Beth looked concerned, but Bailey just smiled. He

heard stirring in the bedroom. "Hey, I need to run. Fiona's waking up."

His mother cocked an eyebrow. "Waking up?"

"We'll probably be out all night," Bailey said. "Gotta go." He cut off the phone, and Fiona came toward him looking rumpled and tired in her pajama pants and tank top. He pulled her against him and guided her to sit on the loveseat.

"I was hoping you'd sleep awhile longer," he said, giving her a kiss and tasting the mint of her toothpaste.

"I woke up and missed you." She laid her head on his shoulder and closed her eyes. "Everything okay?"

"Yeah. I just felt like it was time to call my parents," Baileys said.

"All's well out there?"

"They're fine."

She nodded absently. "I've been thinking…"

"Which I'm learning can be dangerous."

"The woman at the church was able to pass over. Maybe all the spirits that need to pass should go there."

"Do you think it was the place or her faith?"

"You're right." Fiona sagged against him, looking disappointed. "I just want to find a way out for those who want to go."

Her phone chirped before Bailey could reply. He put both arms around her. "Let it ring. They'll leave a message. Just stay here with me a few minutes."

Fiona sat still for only a few seconds. "Gotta get it. What if someone's life is in danger?"

As she answered, Bailey laid his head on the back of the loveseat. He could hear the frantic voice on the other end and knew their interlude of rest was over. Giving a heavy sigh, he rose and went to grab some juice, fruit, and protein bars for Fiona to eat on the way to wherever they were going.

About a half hour later, he pulled into a lane leading to a farmhouse. A sheriff's cruiser was parked out front. Fiona's cousin Brian came to the van to meet them. Bailey got the video camera. Ryan, who was crashing on a cot in the studio, had decided not to come with them.

"Still on duty?" Fiona said to Brian.

He nodded. "The last few hours have been kind of calm. Almost too calm, if you know what I mean."

"I do," Fiona agreed. "Makes me wonder what will be next." She turned as a crash sounded from inside the house. "What going on here? Annalee just called me."

"We got a call from the girlfriend of one of the pack members," Brian said.

"Pack?" Bailey looked up from the camera.

"Werewolves," Fiona said as casually as she might say, "Plumbers." She turned back to Brian. "Go on."

"Anyway, the woman who called this in was worried after she stopped by here earlier and Annalee wouldn't let her in. She's human, and a new girlfriend to Rob's brother, so she instinctively called the law."

"Rob's great-uncle took up residence in the attic three months ago after he died," Fiona explained. "He went suddenly, and he just wasn't ready to pass. I knew he was here and was afraid he'd be trouble."

"Now he is," Brian said. "I sent Annalee over to her mother's house. Getting humans out of the way seemed prudent. Rob's in there, trying to get his great-uncle to calm down." Another crash sounded from the house. "Between Rob in wolf form and the ghost, they're tearing the place apart. Annalee is really pissed, and trust me, Rob does not want her pissed. I've known her a long time."

"What do we do?" Bailey asked. So he was about to meet one of the other creatures who lived here in New Mourne. Was it geeky of him to be excited?

A blood-curdling howl split the night air, and his excitement abated. He looked at Fiona in concern. "What can you do with a werewolf?"

"I'll help," a voice said from the darkness.

A tall man with chiseled features and hair graying at the temples stepped into view.

Brian straightened his shoulders. "Alpha."

As in head of a werewolf pack? Bailey thought his head might explode, but he managed to stand still.

Fiona greeted the man, her voice respectful.

"I hear you've been very busy, Fiona."

"Yes, sir." She introduced Bailey.

The alpha greeted him politely enough, but he gave the camera a pointed glance. In the moonlight, his eyes were flat and feral, menacing. Bailey set the camera on the hood of the van.

"I'll get Rob out of there, and perhaps you can deal with his great-uncle," the alpha said. "It's near the full moon, and Rob's having trouble with control."

"Rob." Though said quietly, the words reverberated throughout the yard. "Come to me."

In answer, a chair flew through the front window. Brian stepped back. Bailey moved to protect Fiona from flying glass.

The alpha didn't even flinch. "Come, Rob."

A wolf, larger than any Bailey had ever seen, jumped through the broken window. It landed and stood at least four feet tall with gray fur tipped in black, growling low in its throat and sniffing the air. Bailey fought the urge to drag Fiona away.

The wolf trotted to the alpha, who laid a hand on the creature's head. The wolf showed long, sharp teeth, but sat down obediently.

To Fiona, the alpha said, "Rob thinks you should give it a few minutes before you go in. Great uncle's spirit is disturbed tonight. It's the evil in the air."

"No doubt," Fiona agreed.

"It's stirring the dead and the living," the alpha added. "This is the third member of the pack I've had to visit tonight. I hope the Connellys will rid us of it soon. Give my best to Sarah."

The alpha and wolf strode away, Bailey heard a flurry in the underbrush, and then two howls lifted through the night.

He shivered though the air was warm and humid. "Jeez, those were werewolves."

"And they don't know about Sarah." Brian looked in question to Fiona.

"Brenna doesn't think we should let the other supernaturals know yet." Sighing, Fiona turned back to the house just in time for a wooden table to fly out through the window.

Fiona pulled out of Bailey's hold and headed toward the house.

"You sure you want to go in there?" Brian asked.

Bailey stepped up beside her. "She won't be alone."

"Well, shit." Brian joined him. "You leave a guy no choice but to be brave."

So they went inside, and Fiona talked down a ghost who was able to upend a sleeper sofa in the den and turn over a china cabinet. Fiona convinced him to shift out of wolf form and go back to his attic. Though Bailey couldn't see him, of course, Fiona said he was upset about the demon coming close to his nephew's home. Like the alpha, he wanted the Connellys to do something.

Fiona was so weak she could barely focus on unwrapping a Snickers bar in the van as they pulled away from the house. Her phone sounded again. She answered it without hesitation and listened for a moment, then said, "We're on our way."

Bailey slammed his palm into the steering wheel. "You're dead on your feet, and if you don't get something to eat besides candy and protein bars, you're going to collapse."

"It's the hospital calling," Fiona protested. "We have to go there."

Knowing arguments would be futile, Bailey headed for the hospital. This time, he left the camera behind. His only mission was to support Fiona.

They walked through the quiet, deserted hospital lobby and took an elevator down.

"What's the problem here?" he asked.

"Shades."

Thinking of blinds on windows, Bailey frowned. The elevator doors slid open, and he caught a glimpse of something to his right. Then it was gone. "Did you see that?" he asked Fiona.

She nodded. "That was a shade. You only catch a little look at them in your peripheral vision. They're very distracting."

As he followed her down a hall, several more shades rippled in and out of sight. The effect was dizzying. "Whoa," he said, putting a hand on the wall to steady himself. "That's really strange. Why can I see them when I can't see ghosts?"

"Shades are spirits that a lot of people can see." Fiona stopped in front of double doors marked with a small, black placard.

"Morgue," Bailey read aloud. He swallowed hard. "We're going in the morgue?"

"The nurse who called said shades seem to be gathered down here," Fiona explained.

"Then why can't we leave them here? Seems like a good place." A pale apparition darted in front of Bailey. He stumbled, and he thought he heard malicious laughter.

"See?" Fiona pushed Bailey back against the wall of the cool, dimly lit room. "These shades are working themselves up. We can't have them in the rest of the hospital. There are sick people here, and not all of them need encouragement in dying. That's what the shades could do."

While Bailey watched, Fiona took off her backpack, drew a circle in salt, and set her candles at the five points. Her words were in Gaelic this time, so he didn't understand. The shades that had dipped and darted about the room disappeared in a whirl of light.

Bailey helped Fiona pack her tools and clean the floor. She was so tired he was almost carrying her by the time they reached the van. When they got to her place, he walked her upstairs and straight toward the bed.

Her phone rang, and she reached for it, but he took it first and sent the call to voice mail.

"You can't do that," she insisted, gathering some

hidden spark of energy to defy him. "I have to help them if they need me."

"You can listen to the message later."

"Make me some tea while I go get a shower. That will make me feel better."

He grumbled as he went to her kitchen to comply. Bailey wasn't sure he'd ever seen anyone so devoted to what she saw as her duty. He felt more tenderness toward her than he had anyone other than his family. Somehow, he had to get her to rest.

When the tea was ready, he took it to the bedroom and found Fiona asleep propped up against the headboard. She clutched her phone. She slapped at him when he tried to take it away.

"Okay, enough of this." He picked her up and laid her down on the bed. She stirred and mumbled but fell into slumber. Now he had to guarantee she would stay that way, and he knew who could probably help.

He eased her phone from her and scrolled to find the name he sought.

Eva Grace answered on the first ring.

"It's Bailey. I think I understand the value of an empath now, and I was wondering if you might help me."

Chapter 27

Fiona awoke to bright sunlight warming her face. She stretched and realized she felt better than she had in days. Seeing the clock dial read after eleven, her eyes widened, and she threw back the covers.

Several thumps sounded on the floor. Upon investigation, she found celestite, lapis lazuli, and howlite, all crystals that promote deep, restful sleep. Sprigs of lavender were under her pillow. Someone had been working to ensure she slept longer than she should.

She started to go downstairs, but decided it might be a good idea to shower and brush her teeth first.

She put on the first pair of clean jeans she could find, and bolstered her mood with her favorite vintage T-shirt nipped from Sarah's collection.

Downstairs, Bailey was working on his laptop at her desk, looking as rested as she felt. She dumped the crystals and herbs beside his computer and gave him a stern look.

"Who told you about all this stuff?"

"Good morning, sunshine," he said with a grin. "Feeling better?"

"How did you know about the crystals and lavender?"

Bailey closed his computer and leaned back in the chair, clasping his hands across his stomach. "Eva

Grace came over and helped me set everything up so you could get some healing sleep."

Five days ago, Bailey had said he didn't believe in anything magical. "So now you're in league with an empath?"

He shrugged. "I've seen her in action. You were too tired to do anything more last night, but I knew you would keep trying and never slow down. Eva Grace put everything out, chanted some very pretty-sounding words, and you did not move again until now."

He leaned forward on his elbows, his gaze steady and firm. "You can't save the world or even this town if you're so exhausted you can't function. It was time for you to get some rest. And guess what? The town is still standing this morning."

Fiona walked over to look out the front window. People were walking on the sidewalk, shopping in the stores, and generally doing what they did every day. She wanted to hang on to her anger, but she couldn't find a reason why. Bailey was right. She barely remembered leaving the hospital and knew nothing about what happened after they got here.

He came up behind her and put his hands on her shoulders. "It's okay to let someone else take care of you."

She rested back against him. "I've been trying really hard to stand on my own two feet lately."

"You don't have to try so hard with me around," he murmured as his arms slipped around her.

A bubble of happiness rose in Fiona. How nice it would be if she could just stand here with this man, her lover, and not worry. Despite his warm, strong presence, despite the sunshine outside, her family and all those connected to them were still in trouble.

Sighing, she turned back to him. "Did Eva Grace say anything about Sarah?"

His eyes clouded. "She's the same. I shut off your phone, but I made Eva Grace promise to call me or get someone over here if anything changed with your grandmother or if there was a real emergency."

"My phone." Fiona jerked around. "It wasn't upstairs. Do you have it?"

He pointed to the desk.

She took her phone off the charger. "What if something awful happened while I was playing sleeping beauty?"

The only message she had was from Eva Grace telling her the younger witches were meeting at Sarah's tonight to work with the crystal ball. The trouble with ghosts had delayed that attempt until now.

"Any Armageddon occur during the night?" Bailey asked at her side.

"No."

He grinned. "So will you admit that I was right to call in the empathic backup to help you sleep?"

Her agreement was grudging. His kiss, however, left her unable to maintain irritation with him at all. It deepened and quickened her pulse. She thought longingly of the rumpled sheets on her bed, of Bailey taking off the clothes she had just donned. Of an entire afternoon of the two of them together.

Her stomach rumbled, and he laughed.

"Come on." He pulled her toward the stairs. "Ryan came by earlier and brought the stuff to fix killer omelets. Let's go up and eat."

He made omelets with ham, spinach, and cheese,

and they ate at her small, round table at a long window overlooking Main Street. Fiona wondered if the whole town was taking a break. Her phone did not ring.

"You'll have to see what Ryan has edited on the ghosts at the high school and the store," Bailey told her as he stacked their plates and put them in the sink. "The guy's a genius. Whether you do a show or not, I'm hiring him."

"You can't take Ryan away from me," she protested.

"Then perhaps you should think about expanding." Bailey nodded to the window and the quiet street below as he refilled their coffee and sat down. "Let's face it. Aside from your current troubles, there are only so many hauntings the two of you can investigate here."

"I can't make plans now," Fiona said.

Bailey took her hand. "All of you are going to figure this out," he said with the confidence Fiona realized came as naturally to him as his brilliant smile. "No one's going to die this time. Then you'll be free. All of you."

That idea caught Fiona's imagination as she glanced out the window. She could see the front of the antique store. She'd heard yesterday that Dagen was recovering well and would be back at work soon. Delicious aromas drifted up from Bitta's Bakery, all filled with her teasing, tempting kitchen magic. Families and couples strolled in and out of the diner, the usual heavy traffic for Sunday after church.

This was Fiona's home, and she had never thought about leaving. Bailey, however, was filled with ideas. "I was thinking we could go to Europe and to do some filming. I thought we could ask your parents and Rodric for some ideas."

"We?"

"I think this is a show that will need my constant executive production," he explained with a roguish grin. "There are so many places we could go and see. It would be fun."

Only in that moment did Fiona realize how much she wanted what Bailey was offering. She had never felt limited until now.

"I thought you were going to be holed up somewhere writing screenplays," she said, taking his other hand.

"No reason I can't do it all, is there?" He infused Fiona with his enthusiasm. "I'm sure what you find will give me a lot of ideas."

"You may find the ghosts I attract a bit difficult to live with," she said. "They don't operate on schedule, as you may have noticed the last couple of days."

Bailey sobered. "Through everything that happened yesterday, you didn't mention Anna. Have you seen her?"

"Not since Friday night in the clearing." Fiona pushed her sight out, looking, but Anna did not answer. She fought not to show her unease and tightened her grip on Bailey's hands. She had summoned ghosts since the cradle. She would find Bailey's sister.

"If I summon Anna now, she'll be able to tell you what she's wanted you to know all these years. She'll be at peace. The woman who passed yesterday was finally ready to leave. If Anna delivers her message, she may be able to slip through, too."

Bailey considered her offer, his expression serious. "I'm still not sure about that," he said at last. "Even after what I've seen the last few days I don't know if I'm ready."

"Can you tell me about Anna?" Fiona asked. "I'd like to understand why you feel this way. I know the guilt I feel about releasing the demon and Uncle Van's death will stay with me for a long time, too, but communicating with his spirit the other night helped. Perhaps if you and Anna finally connect..."

"Maybe you're right." Releasing her hands, Bailey sat back. "Anna and I were only eleven months apart, and we fought practically from day one. She won most of the time because, let's face it, girls are cuter than boys, and Anna was a cutie."

Fiona pictured two California blond children. "I bet you were a hellion," she commented. "I can imagine your parents had a hard time saying no to you when you gave them that smile of yours."

"Yeah, I was a brat," he admitted. "Anna was the good kid. I was the chief cause of most of the trouble she got into." His expression saddened. "That was true to the end."

For a moment, he looked away, and then continued, "Anyway, we grew up in a great neighborhood in Brentwood. By the time we were in middle school, my parents had several giant hit shows in primetime, and we probably could have moved into a mansion quadruple the size of the home we lived in. Actually, we had a weekend place at Malibu."

"Tough life."

"Yeah, but Mom and Dad wanted us to be normal. They grew up next door to each other, and they wanted the same kind of lifestyle for us. We had friends up and down the street. We were in and out of each other's pools. Anna could swim like a fish. She was on the school swim team, and we never missed a meet. I played baseball and football and had dreams of UCLA."

Knowing he needed to get it all out, Fiona said, "Tell me about the night Anna died."

He focused at a point over her head. "A bunch of us were going to the amusement park for one last night before school started. Anna was begging to go with us, and I convinced my parents I could watch out for her. What I was actually planning to do was get to second base with my latest girlfriend. In fact, I was hoping to score."

"Sounds pretty normal for a fifteen-year-old boy. Especially one with your charm and amazing blue eyes. I bet the girls at your school had crazy cat fights over you."

He almost smiled. "Yeah, they were epic, all right. Later on, I was on the 'do-not-date' list of bad boys."

But it was that hint of danger that made him more appealing, Fiona thought.

He continued, "The point is that I wasn't really watching out for Anna that night. She was off with her gaggle of friends. I saw her a few times, having a great time. I mean, there were kids everywhere, just like always. It was a fun place. She was fine. I wasn't worried until it stormed. This freakish thunderstorm blew in off the ocean." Bailey frowned.

Fiona shivered. "Evil enjoys a good storm. Do you think it was supernatural?"

"After what I've seen this week?" Bailey rubbed the jagged edge of his tattoo on his left arm. "Maybe it was."

"What happened?"

"Lightning, wind, rain, thunder—it was a mess. When my girlfriend and I took shelter with some others in a pavilion, I saw Anna's friends. She wasn't with them." He swallowed hard, his gaze suddenly intense on hers. "The lightning was like a constant stream, and you know amusement parks, there's metal everywhere. One bolt struck the motor of the Ferris wheel, and I felt it all over my body. I knew, just like that, that Anna was in trouble."

Bailey stood and crossed his arms on his chest. Fiona said nothing, feeling he needed the quiet to order his thoughts.

"I grabbed some of my friends and headed out. We looked everywhere, went from one end of the park to the other twice. No one had seen Anna since just before the storm began."

Fiona could hear the pain in his voice as he talked about calling his parents and the arrival of the police. Although the park had closed and many people were gone, the police questioned everyone who remained and searched every corner.

"It must have been four in the morning before my parents and I went home, and all we did was sit in the living room waiting to hear from the police. My mom rocked back and forth, trying not to cry in front of me. My dad couldn't talk. Grandmom got there as soon as she could, and she looked so bad. I remember it was the first time I thought of her as old.

"I kept waiting for one of them to tell me how bad I had screwed up. I mean, that's usually what happened. I did something stupid, and my dad would say, 'What were you thinking?' Then it would be okay. This time no one said a word. They didn't have to. I knew what I had done."

Bailey's hands dropped to his sides, and he sighed deeply. "They found her body the next day. It was worse than we could ever imagine."

Fiona's stomach clutched at the loss in his voice.

"She had been beaten so badly her face was unrecognizable. The police thought she was still alive when he left her on the beach not far from the park, but she wasn't found in time."

Bailey sat down again, his body falling heavily into the chair as if he couldn't stand any longer. He rubbed his tattoo. "I got this a few years later to remind me of the storm the night Anna died. I never wanted to forget. As if I could."

"Anyone can understand why you blame yourself," Fiona said.

"It's my fault," Bailey said with dull finality. "Nothing will ever change that. Worst of all, I could feel Anna hovering around me. I told my parents. They needed to believe me, so we went from psychic to psychic. I hoped somebody could help me tell her how sorry I was and ask for her forgiveness."

"What was going on with your parents?"

"They were out of their minds with grief. Grandmom believed in psychics, mediums, the whole ball of wax, so she encouraged them. Mom wanted me to reach Anna. It became an obsession. One day one of the psychics started saying stuff that was true, that we did not think anyone else could know. She convinced Mom that Anna was at peace. She said Anna did not blame me."

Bailey slammed his fist into his other hand.

"Damn, but I wanted to believe her!"

"Why couldn't you?"

"Because I didn't feel satisfied. I felt Anna, still, that same pushing I had felt from the moment I realized she was missing."

"I don't think Anna was blaming you—"

"You weren't there." His voice was deep with its passion. "You don't know what I felt or how it was to know she was with me everywhere, accusing me, making me feel like shit. And there was something else with that fake psychic. I saw my father give her a fat envelope full of cash."

"Maybe he was grateful."

With a mirthless laugh, Bailey shook his head. "I confronted Dad, and he confessed that he just wanted it to end; he had paid the psychic to tell Mom and me what we wanted hear. He gave the psychic everything she used to convince us she was communicating with Anna."

"How could he do that to you?" Fiona said, aghast. Because Bailey always spoke of his father with such respect, she was surprised.

"Oh, I punished him," Bailey replied. "For years, I was in one mess after another. I barely graduated high school, flunked out of college, and became a useless human being."

"Until?"

"I asked Anna or what I thought was Anna's spirit to leave me alone. I was strung out, drinking, partying and trying drugs. I was at rock bottom, and I begged her to leave me alone."

"But just days ago you said you could sense her sometimes."

"She was always stubborn," he said. "A few years after she left me, when I had put my life on the right path and mended fences with my parents, I started feeling her again. I knew she was there, but she wasn't trying to get to me. I didn't try to reach out to her, either. I could not go through that again. That feeling of hope and then that awful disappointment. It was easier to say that ghosts don't exist and all psychics or mediums are fakes. I convinced myself, and I tolerated those little moments of awareness."

"What does your mother know?" Fiona asked.

"The whole truth. Dad finally told her."

"Yet she's maintained hope of connecting with her daughter?"

"Mom will never be truly at peace with any of it, but she was strong enough to move forward and not let the loss dominate her life. She accepted my wishes about letting Anna go. I forgave Dad for tricking us, and let them settle that issue privately. She still worries about me, about the effect this had on me."

Fiona was puzzled. "You're very successful, and you work with them. I'm sure she's proud—"

"I'm alone, and she doesn't like that." Bailey hesitated, and put out his hand to Fiona. "At least I *was* alone."

She stepped into his arms.

"I can't explain it," Bailey said. "I've only known you for days, but you've touched me in a way I've never experienced before. Could it be magic?"

"Sarah has always told me love is the most potent magic." Fiona raised her lips to his.

He kissed her, then drew away. Bailey looked deep into Fiona's eyes. "Could you reach Anna now? Maybe

I am ready."

Heart pounding, Fiona went for candles and her ritual supplies. This had to work.

Moments later, from the middle of her circle, she said, "Anna, it's time. Bailey is ready to talk to you. You can tell him whatever you like. He's ready to hear."

Bailey watched her, unmoving. She could see the hope in his gaze.

"This is a safe place, a quiet place, where you can speak to Bailey and tell him whatever you like."

Panic raised perspiration on Fiona's forehead. She could feel nothing. Not Anna. Not Celia, Minnie, or Uncle Van. Not a glimmer of response from the next realm. She pressed outward with her power. Even the ghosts locked away at the high school were missing. The barrier she and Bailey encountered Friday morning at the convenience store was now keeping Fiona from reaching what had always come so easily to her.

The candles went out, and she slumped into her chair. "I'm sorry, so sorry."

The disappointment in Bailey's eyes was difficult to face. Worse was the sudden anger that followed. She felt it like a slap.

Bailey walked to the door. He opened it, turned back to Fiona, and said, "Isn't it funny that the two ghosts you really want to talk to won't come to your call?"

Chapter 28

Depression enveloped Fiona as she stood beside her grandmother's bed. Sarah was still and quiet.

Marcus sat in a chair on Sarah's right side, his voice rough as he read aloud from his wife's favorite poet, Irishwoman, Katharine Tynan. The stirring words of "Any Woman" were a tribute to female strength and courage.

Fiona waited in vain for Sarah to respond.

Soon, she fled the room and went downstairs. The poem's words were shards of glass piercing her heart, each one reminding her she was the reason Sarah was lying in that bed, lost to Marcus and her beloved coven.

At the bottom of the stairs, Fiona took deep cleansing breaths. Keeping her eyes closed, she focused on her energy and magic, wiping away the depression and sadness that had plagued her since Bailey walked out earlier today.

He had not returned.

His car was not at the inn.

Fiona could not bring herself to go in and ask if he had checked out. She was too afraid. Instead, she had tried again and again to summon Anna and the spirits of New Mourne. Their silence sent her to the home place. Here, her strength and magic usually found fuel. Still, she could not find peace. Even the Granny ghost was missing from the house.

Maybe trying the crystal ball would help. She went to the dining room where the younger witches were gathered. The crystal ball had absorbed moonlight for two nights, gaining strength and illumination for this session.

The elder aunts were in a weakened state, depleted by Sarah's continued enchantment. Delia and the others of her generation were working on spells, trying to draw power from Connelly stone and dirt in order to help Sarah.

Only the five youngest members of the coven gathered around the ball. The five who were in line to die, Fiona thought. She could not help wondering if that would break the grip of evil on Sarah's life. If the Woman had her tribute, surely the demon would be silenced. Without him, Albert's power was moderate at best.

Eva Grace sat at the end of the table with the ball in front of her. Brenna and Fiona were on her right; Maggie and Lauren sat on her left. Curtains covered the windows. Candles were lit—white for calm and peace, light blue to help clear the mind, and yellow for divination. In addition, a crystal lay in front of each of Eva Grace's four companions.

A distinct, violet aura surrounded Eva Grace. As the priestess for this session, she had prepared with intense meditation. She was the seeker of truth tonight, something they all needed.

"Each of these crystals has a special purpose." Her voice was hushed but steady. "Brenna has the moonstone, which will give her the wisdom to lead our small coven group. Fiona's stone is a carnelian, to help alleviate her sorrow and strengthen her focus on what is ahead for her. For Lauren, I chose a rose quartz for insight in difficult situations."

She turned to Maggie, who was shivering. "We know these troubled times have brought you great anxiety, dear cousin. You are the only one among us who is a mother. You take that responsibility very seriously, and it leaves you constantly on guard. I chose selenite for you. It will enhance your powers and aid you in making decisions."

Folding her hands in front of the crystal ball, Eva Grace looked from one to the other of them. "Let's all take three deep breaths and clear our minds. The focus needs to be on the ball. You know what to do. Stare deeply into its core and look for the truth. We are searching for the past of the Woman in White, the story of who she is."

The women breathed in unison and then focused on the glass orb in front of Eva Grace. Fiona could see the ball stirring with wisps of color and light.

"Now picture yourself in the midst of the magic you see."

The lilting melody of an Irish ballad drifted through the air. Fiona pushed herself until she could feel the color and light surrounding her.

"Think about the Woman in White and expand your space."

Fiona could picture the spirit, her long, white dress with its old-fashioned collar and sleeves, her golden curls lifted by the breeze, and her translucent complexion, stained by anger.

No matter how hard she pictured the ghost, however, nothing appeared in the magic space to aid their quest.

Eva Grace told them to take another deep breath and back away from the magic space in the ball. The glow in the center faded. When the ball went dark, the music ended, as well. Fiona felt the familiar heaviness return. They had reached another dead end, and time was running out.

"That was futile," Brenna said bluntly.

"I could see the Woman," Maggie said, her voice tentative.

"She was angry," Fiona added.

"What did we Connellys do to make her so furious? We have to find out."

Brenna sighed. "I got a call from that college in Savannah that Bailey told us about."

"And?" Fiona prompted.

"Bailey's family made a sizable donation to the school. In exchange we get full access to those papers about the first missionaries in the area."

"Rodric and Aiden left this morning to study them," Eva Grace added. "They called just a little while ago. There's evidence that our Woman's father was not very popular among his fellow missionaries."

"Too much fire-and-brimstone," Brenna explained. "The leaders were concerned about sending him so far into the wilderness and away from supervision."

Thinking of her vision in the cave, Fiona nodded. This new information fit what they suspected.

"Rodric said the records show his wife died before they left Savannah." Eva Grace stared into the empty crystal ball. "This MacCuindliss headed west with a few followers just days after her death. His trip was not altogether sanctioned."

"So he took off on his own." Brenna picked up the

moonstone in front of her.

"With his daughter," Fiona murmured. "Can you imagine her riding off alone with just her father and few other men?"

"There were most likely some soldiers with them at first," Maggie suggested.

"Probably not for long," Eva Grace said. "They knew she had to help the men carve out a settlement, and they were alone."

"Except the Cherokee people," Brenna said.

"At first, she was probably waiting for savages to set upon her at any moment." A cold draft made Fiona shiver. She looked up, hoping to see Granny Ghost. There was nothing but a feeling of desolation and fear.

"I found out something more about MacCuindliss," Lauren said, leaning forward. "On Coven Glan, there's some discussion about an ancient family of evil sorcerers by that name."

"Could the Woman in White have had magic before she died?" Brenna looked concerned.

"I have put questions out online about that family," Lauren said. "I'll keep looking."

"I need to go to my mother's," Maggie said. "She's babysitting Rose, but she's missing Dad so much, we don't leave her alone much."

As Lauren and Maggie left, Brenna went up to check in on Sarah.

Eva Grace and Fiona remained at the table, still looking at the large, darkened crystal.

Eva Grace's head tilted to the side. "I feel as if the whole truth about the Woman is just beyond our reach."

"But what if she was a black witch?" Fiona said. "If so, there could be no reasoning with her, even if we learn why she cursed us. Even if she finally comes when we call."

"Maybe." Eva Grace shifted her gaze to Fiona. "You're really down. Where's Bailey?"

Fiona told her cousin about Anna. She began to cry as she relayed how Bailey had finally asked her to use her medium abilities to reach his sister.

Eva Grace moved closer and wrapped an arm around Fiona's shoulders. "He has to understand that we're dealing with strange circumstances with Albert and the demon on the loose. You've told him that most of the spirits are in hiding."

Wiping tears from her cheeks, Fiona said, "I failed him. Just as I failed the family by setting the demon free. My gifts are not making a difference to any of the people I love. The awful part is I have no idea what to do about it."

Soothing warmth moved from Eva Grace and into Fiona. "You shouldn't waste your energy on me," Fiona said.

"It's never a waste when it's someone you love." Eva Grace pulled her close, as she had done so often when they were younger and Fiona was upset or frightened. Though Brenna had been Fiona's hero, Eva Grace was the constant who anchored Fiona when the dead who needed her were overwhelming.

"Take this." The redhead pushed the carnelian into Fiona's palm, and then closed Fiona's fingers with her own, holding the dark red crystal in place.

Irish music filled the room once more, and colors danced in the magic ball. Fiona could feel strength moving into her body and spirit.

"Thank you," she whispered to her cousin.

"You've made it better, just like you always do."

"This is your time in the cycle," Eva Grace said with sudden calm. "I can feel it. Can't you?"

"For weeks now, I've known. Even before Bailey came, I knew. But something about him being here helped me understand. It's like Willow told him, he's part of our fate."

Eva Grace looked uncertain. "I'm not sure what all of this means, Fiona. I wish we could talk to Sarah."

"And maybe we will soon." Fiona hugged her cousin. "Soon."

****

Half an hour later, Fiona stood in the quiet of the coven's sacred clearing. She slipped on her cape and used magic to light her candles. With a turn of her hand, the flame jumped to a bundle of sage for purification. Her mind fixed on the Woman in White with determination.

Fiona knew she was in danger of death, but she did not offer herself to the Woman. Instead, she wanted a confrontation. After two-and-half centuries the Woman owed her family answers.

Fiona stood in the circle with her hands upraised and felt the atmosphere change.

"I, Fiona Connelly Burns, call to the Woman in White. I summon you to come to me and help me with my quest. I am here to be your conduit, your voice, your vessel." She opened herself to the spirit world.

When she opened her eyes, however, she looked into the smiling, evil face of Albert Connelly.

"Hello, niece," he said. "We've been waiting for you. We're so glad you've come to us willingly."

Fiona worked hard to tamp down her panic and

fear. "You flatter yourself," she said evenly to the squat and ugly ghost. "I'm here for someone else."

"Yes, I know." His laugh echoed through the trees. "Your Woman in White, yet she is strangely absent, isn't she? This is your second attempt, and you've failed again."

"There's always a chance you won't find what you're looking for when you begin your search." Fiona hoped she sounded confident and unafraid of the evil she was facing alone. She recalled Eva Grace's words about it being her time in the cycle of things. Fiona's cousin had been more correct than she'd known.

Albert walked around Fiona's circle like an animal marking his space. "It seems we've solved another of your problems, niece."

Fiona turned so he wasn't at her back. "What do you mean?"

"We have the other spirit you seek," he said, indicating an area behind her.

She jerked around and stifled her scream. A black aura encased Anna's small spirit.

Once again, Albert's shrill laughter rang through the clearing, and Fiona felt lost. How could her plan to help her family go so wrong again?

Chapter 29

Anna's entrapment chilled Fiona to the bone. She didn't know if it was safe to leave her circle or if the circle was providing protection from Albert. He watched her with glee, his eyes glowing red from the demon inside him. The candle's flames wavered but didn't falter.

"We do have a deal for you," Albert said. "We think you'll find it accommodating because it will let you help the sweet Anna."

Looking back at Anna's ghost, Fiona could see she wasn't fading but growing brighter. Albert and his demon meant to use Anna. Fiona thought of Maggie and the way the demon had taken her will and made her fight to take Brenna's power.

Now it was Fiona's turn. Were her power and control strong enough? She had to play this right because it was all a game to the demon. A horrible game meant to entrap her just as they had Anna.

"What makes you think any bargain you have would interest to me?" Hopefully she sounded bolder than she felt. "Real Connellys don't make deals with demons."

This time Albert's laugh was a low, dark chuckle. "You're just like all the other Connelly females. You're selfish and far too pleased about being the holders of power."

Fiona heard the envy in his voice. No wonder the demon took control of Albert. He craved power that could never be his, and opened him to the darkness.

"Before you decide, maybe you should hear our bargain." His wide, black grin made Fiona shudder. "In exchange for releasing young Anna's spirit, all we ask is the gift of your power."

Though she had expected the request, she was surprised at the panic she felt. She should have told someone she was coming here. She reached out with her magic, hoping to call the coven as she had the day in the cave.

"No, no, no," Albert said as he wagged his finger at her. "You're not getting help this time. We've learned a few things about your kind's trickery."

Fiona forced her whirling thoughts to coalesce. Marcus had taught her to play poker, and this looked like a good time to call a bluff. "You fool. Help is already on the way."

"I think not," Albert purred. "Your coven is scattered and torn."

"You can't believe I'd just turn my powers over to you so easily. I'm not that gullible."

Albert said, "That's too bad!"

The demon jumped out of Albert and crossed the clearing so fast Fiona saw nothing but a black blur. He jumped into Anna and transformed her. Her eyes glowed bright red. Her teeth sharpened to tiny points. She snarled and growled, mouth drooling and snapping like a rabid dog.

Seeing Anna in this state was agony for Fiona. Bailey's sister could spend eternity as a monster feasting on the souls of the innocent. Unless Fiona complied, she destroyed Bailey's last chance to know Anna's forgiveness.

"Oh, yes." Albert rubbed his hands together. "The thought of his pain hurts you, doesn't it? Does seeing his sister like this change your mind about making a deal?"

The howling of Anna's ghost increased, and Fiona turned away. Bailey had trusted her to help him talk to Anna. Now he would never know what Anna wanted to tell him. He would never believe in the wonder and magic of Fiona's world. His heart would harden against Fiona's memory while the wild, angry beast that Anna was now would bring havoc to that world.

"What's it going to be, Miss Connelly Witch?" Albert screamed.

Fiona closed her eyes and took a deep breath. Even as a child, she helped the dead move forward and find peace. She would not turn her back on Bailey's sister. Fiona loved Bailey too much for that. He might have loved her, too. If there had been time, they might have been happy. Instead, she was a Connelly witch, and with or without the Woman in White, her legacy was heartache.

She pulled her fraying power closer. Surrendering would be difficult. She would fight against this evil with everything she had.

"Come on, Fiona." Albert's nasty voice filled the clearing. "If you give yourself freely, that will increase our power tenfold. We will conquer the supernaturals in New Mourne and make it the kind of place it should be." He paused and gave her a leering grin. "But really, what choice do you have?"

Closing her eyes, Fiona brought calm into herself

and found the power to resist his cajoling voice. "You'll have to take me."

"All right, we'll do this the hard way." Albert raised his arms.

"No!" Bailey's voice brought Fiona's head up, and her heart sang with hope.

"Tell him no!" Bailey ran toward Fiona and straight for the circle.

Instead of igniting an explosion, his entry made the circle open and close around them both. The candles fired to bright spears of flame, and Fiona felt her power rise.

Bailey pulled her into his arms and kissed her. White orbs rained down on them like a cleansing rain. Here was love and a strong push of magic.

When they separated, Albert's face was a mask of evil fury. He beat against the edge of her circle in frantic frustration.

"She's mine, you stinking human, mine! You can't change that!"

"They have Anna," Fiona told Bailey.

"I know," he said. "I can see them. I can see her."

"Then you know you have to let me go, or they have her forever."

There was a flash and Albert held a wand that glowed red with fire at the end. He pointed in toward Anna, who writhed and howled.

Fiona started toward her angry, evil relative. "Stop it. Let Anna go."

Bailey pulled her tighter against him. "Look at me, Fiona, look at me." He turned her face, so that she saw only him. "Here, here is where life is. Please, don't even consider giving this creature what he wants."

"Bailey," she said, clutching his shirt in her hand and burying her face against his chest. "You need to know what Anna has to tell you."

"Anna is dead, Fiona. No matter what I learn, she won't live again." His blue eyes compelled her to see the truth. "I know what I feel is real because I've never felt anything so powerful and wonderful in my life. I love you, Fiona Burns, with everything in me."

"Goddess, help me," she said as her tears wet his shirt. "I love you too. I can't imagine my life without you." She looked up at him. "Which is why I can't surrender Anna yet. Not without a fight."

"Come on, human," Albert said and danced a little jig. "Let her do what's right. She's a good little Connelly witch." He hammered against the circle, and Fiona feared he would break through.

She gasped in surprise as new magic flooded her body. She felt her family—Brenna, Eva Grace, her cousins, the elders, even Sarah.

Sarah had broken the enchantment, Goddess be praised.

As Fiona identified each bit of power, she grew stronger, the magic radiating from her center.

"Hold onto me, Bailey. Whatever happens, do not let go and do not step out of this circle. You and I have a little job to do."

She turned, Bailey put his arms around her, and she raised her hands. The candles flared again, surrounding them with fire.

"Candles bright and love inspired, bring me spirits led by my guide; banish evil and free us three. As I will so mote it be."

Celia floated into the clearing, her face fierce with

anger, and her arms wide. Other spirits arrived in groups of twos and threes, surrounding Albert. They pulled him away from Fiona and Bailey's circle. With the demon still inside Anna, Albert was not strong enough to fight them.

He screamed in pain and fear, calling to the demon, "Come to me. Save me."

Fiona turned to the monstrosity who held Bailey's sister. She called to the powers of earth, wind, sky, and water. "Your playtime is over, demon."

The demon jumped free of Anna. His form puddled on the ground like oil and struggled to solidify. The black aura around Anna snapped, and she ran toward the other spirits, and Minnie took her hand.

Bailey gasped. He could see his sister as the girl she had been, Fiona realized.

The colorful capes of the coven appeared among the trees, and Albert's ghost writhed. He struggled against the spirits who held him fast.

A flash of red lit the sky. Willow, in full fairy form, descended in front of Albert. The ghosts hurtled him forward like a sack of sand. He began to weep and plead.

Willow's red gown glowed. Her ruby crown sparkled. Her nails glittered with fire. In one hand, she waved a tiny, green bottle. With her staff in the other hand, she pelted Albert with light. "Albert Jonas Connelly, mine you were and mine you are. Now get yourself into my tiny jar."

Albert's form thinned to a single stream and poured through the container's neck. Willow pushed a cork into it and waved her staff again. With a flash, the jar was covered with stone, and the stone was covered with a beautifully decorated steel box.

Clutching the package to her chest, Willow rose into the air. She hissed in the direction of the coven, and said, "Damn fool witches. Keep your nosey selves out of my business from now on." Her wings unfurled, and she shot high in the air and out of sight.

As if one, the ghosts went toward the demon that struggled to pull itself out of the ground. The spirit mass parted before reaching the oily puddle and suddenly ceased motion.

Fiona's hands fell to her side. The Woman in White walked toward her.

Chapter 30

Fiona doused the candles and stepped out of her circle.

Bailey followed. "I can see her, you know."

"We don't believe she's shy when she wants to be seen. Stay close to me."

The Woman moved across the clearing in an elegant glide, walking through the other spirits as though they weren't there. When she stood within a few feet of Fiona, her smile brought the frost of winter to the summer air.

Fiona set herself. "I'm glad to talk with you."

Again, the Woman's chill enveloped Fiona. "You should be afraid."

Fighting the urge to retreat, Fiona went on. "I want to help you. I'm a medium—"

"I know what you do!" The voice of the ghost rang through the clearing and the other spirits moved back. "Who are you to think you can help me?"

"I can help you cross over," Fiona said, taking a step forward. "You can reunite with your loved ones. You could put this curse to rest, be at peace, and leave the Connelly family in harmony."

The Woman turned to look at the demon, her skirt swirling in the soft grass. "You want to know about my happy family? Take a look."

Mist appeared like a veil in front of Fiona and

277

Bailey. In its center was the Woman, her long blonde hair in a smooth braid down her back. With a face much softer than the spirit she was now, the Woman bent over a wooden cradle and tucked a blanket around a sleeping baby. Just beyond, a young man with black hair and copper skin poured water into the black pot hanging above the fire. The young parents smiled at each other as the vision faded.

The Woman spoke, "I had what every woman wanted until it was taken from me." She pointed to the demon. "He took it because of his hatred and ignorance. He thought himself superior to the savages he came here to save. In truth, he wanted to dominate them, and he craved me for himself."

The Woman turned to the demon, cold eyes glittering with hatred. The demon shrank farther into the ground.

"He thought he would stop me from getting away," the Woman said. "Even in death he wants to conquer me. That is why he disrupts the lives of those with magic. He yearns to destroy me as he did before."

Glowing with anger, the Woman moved closer to the demon. At the clap of her hands, the black, oozing mass took form again, with legs, arms, and head. The noxious odor of sulfur filled the air as its body started to bubble and boil with heat.

Fiona felt another chill of fear. Was the Woman about to set it loose again?

The spirit looked at the demon as though it were a bug she was about to squash with her shoe. "Your demon form is as repulsive as your human body," she said. "The hate that consumed you has made you even uglier."

"Someday I will gain my power, and I will defeat you." The demon's voice was graveled and forced, painful to Fiona's ears. "You will submit to me again."

"Never," the Women yelled. "You are here at my behest, only because I allow you to exist. You will suffer forever, just as I will."

The demon writhed as if in pain. Then he rose to a monstrous height, and yelled, "Catriona!" before the Woman's power slung him to the ground again.

Her name was Catriona, Fiona thought. At last, they had her full name, a connection to the person she had been. Fiona took another step toward the ghost.

Bailey grabbed her arm. "Don't."

"I'll be all right."

"Damn it, you don't know that," Bailey said. "She can take you whenever she wants."

"He's right," the Woman said. "Any time." A lightning bolt crashed behind her. "I want." The boom of thunder pealed through the air.

Still Fiona faced her. "What separates you from the demon, Catriona?"

Fury stained the spirit red. "What do you mean?"

"You claim his hatred makes him ugly, that he took everything from you. Why do you do the same to us? Why not leave and destroy him, too? You suffered so much in life. I can help you cross over. I can help your baby. You could be with him forever."

The spirit flinched, as if in pain. "Don't speak of my child."

"Please," Fiona said. "Release us from our bargain. Set us and yourself free."

The Woman turned, and a sudden cold wind almost knocked Fiona to her knees. "The world treated me with cruelty," she shouted. "Why should it be easy for you?"

With a wicked laugh, she began to disappear. "You can't help me, Connelly witch. The first of you who walked this land could not help. It remains the same, and I will continue to take from you as long as I want. Survive my father, if you will, but I will come again."

A bright streak of lightning filled the night and the Woman in White was gone.

The demon roared behind Fiona, and she jerked around. For a brief time he appeared in a more familiar form with a bright red body, black horns, cloven hooves, and a pointed tail. Then just as quickly, he looked human, with the face of the old man Fiona had seen on the rattlesnake's head.

"I will take your power," he said and moved toward Fiona.

Fiona raised her hands and picked up a Gaelic chant from the coven behind her. She opened herself to her full sisterhood of magic. Focused on her, the demon missed the spirits who were close on his back and powered by fierce menace of their own.

"You will be mine," the demon roared.

He couldn't move as the first ghosts pushed him to the ground.

Fiona pushed more magical power through herself, strengthening the ghosts as they attacked the demon.

They pounded at him until he shrank and slithered among the stones. He disappeared into a hole like a long, black snake.

Chapter 31

As the last vestige of the demon disappeared, Fiona took Bailey's hand. "Come with me." In her red cloak, she moved like a beacon among the ghosts in the clearing. Many were waiting to pass over. Others simply wanted to return to their haunts. All of them parted as Fiona pulled Bailey toward the edge of the clearing.

"Come talk to Anna," she invited him.

Though he had seen his sister when the demon released her, Bailey found it hard to face the flickering, small spirit who looked at him with Anna's eyes and smiled with Anna's smile.

He stepped toward her. "Oh, my God. It's you, Anna."

Her form wavered, but held steady. "Hello, Bailey."

He dashed away the tears that welled in his eyes. He could barely believe he was seeing her or hearing her voice. "I'm so sorry, Anna. I wish I had—"

She held up a hand to stop him. "Please don't, Bailey. I'm not angry with you. I've never been angry or blamed you. I've always just wanted to tell you that I'm okay."

"If you were okay, you'd be alive."

"That wasn't meant to be."

"If I had done as I promised and looked after you,

you would be alive."

"You always thought you could run my world." Anna looked at him with the same sort of derision she often displayed when they were young. "If not that night, I could have been taken later. He was waiting for me."

Bailey's heart quickened. "Did you know him? Who was it?"

She shook her head. "I never knew his name. When the storm started, I ran. My friends went to a pavilion, but this guy kind of swept me into the video arcade. He looked like a college guy. I thought he was cute, and I didn't get scared until he led me through a door at the back of the arcade. I screamed, and he hit me. The storm was so loud no one could hear me. He dragged me down the beach."

"How do you know he had been waiting for you?"

"He told me," she whispered. Her eyes were deep pools of pain. "He knew my school, my name, and our address. He knew who Mom and Dad were. He knew your name."

"He found you in our perfect little community," Bailey murmured. "Mom and Dad would have been better off living in a mansion with guards."

"Sometimes evil just finds a way." Anna turned to Fiona. "You have to realize that, too, and stop blaming yourself for what's happened in your family. The demon and his daughter—they're waiting for one of you, the same as the man who murdered me was waiting."

"I want to believe I didn't make any of this worse," Fiona replied. "I'm not sure I can."

"Don't waste any time on regrets," Anna advised.

"That's one thing I've found on this side. There's never enough time."

Bailey said, "I should have tried harder when I first felt you near me, Anna. Maybe we could have caught your murderer. You could have moved on."

"Sometimes there are good reasons to wait. Maybe you needed to wait for Fiona." Anna looked at Fiona and smiled. The light around her began to glimmer. "I want to go now," she told Fiona. "Can you help me?"

"Of course." Fiona's glance at Bailey was uncertain. "Are you okay?"

"Mom and Dad..." he said to Anna. "Don't you want—?"

"They let me go long ago," she murmured.

He nodded, emotion clogging his throat. He would never again feel Anna waiting for him to turn around and see her.

"I'll still be watching," Anna told him. "Be happy. Or I'll see if I can come back and haunt you again. I won't be nice this time."

His laugh was half sob. "I love you, kiddo. I always will."

"Love you, too." Anna said and reached up to touch his cheek.

Bailey felt a tingle on his cheek. Then Anna was gone. Really gone.

Fiona gripped his hand. "She's at peace."

"Thank you." He pulled her hand to his lips. "I'll never be able to thank you enough."

He wanted to sweep Fiona away, but first she had to greet her grandmother. "I'm so glad you're okay. Should you be out of bed?"

"It was nothing serious," Sarah assured them. "Just

a little enchantment helped along a bit by Willow."

At her side, Brenna gasped. "What did I tell everyone about that sneaky faerie?"

Sarah explained she had come out of the enchantment while the demon and Albert were focused on Fiona. "I knew something was wrong. I woke up and told Brenna to gather the coven." An impish smile crossed her face. "I'm afraid there'll be reports of UFOs on the radar tonight over Mourne County."

"So you can fly," Bailey said. "I figured as much."

Sarah glared at him.

"Before you say anything, I want you to know I love Fiona," Bailey said, "and I will do nothing to hurt her or her family."

"We can ensure that you don't," Sarah warned.

Bailey put up his hands. "I don't need amnesia."

"Just so you know it's always on the table." Sarah's burgundy cape swirled as she stepped away.

Brenna laughed.

"I really don't believe any of you could make me forget loving Fiona," Bailey told her.

Brenna patted him on the arm. "I still don't trust you, Hollywood, but you came through when it mattered tonight. How did you know Fiona was in trouble?"

"That's the strange part of the story," Bailey admitted. "I was in my room at the inn, sulking and thinking about leaving town. As soon as I packed my bag, I knew I couldn't leave. I had to find Fiona. I felt compelled to find her." He slipped an arm around Fiona and pressed a kiss to her temple. "I wasn't sure how I would find this place again in the dark, but I knew if I headed east, I'd find you."

"Thank the Goddess you did." Fiona smiled at him. "Now I have some unfinished business."

She moved to the ghosts who still waited for her help. With infinite care, she helped several cross into the light. To her Uncle Van, she gave a sad smile. "I'm so sorry for what you've been through."

He looked at the gathered coven, gaze lingering on Maggie. "Break this curse," he told them. "I know you can."

Fiona held out her hands to him, and his essence drifted into the stars.

The ghosts were gone, and the witches were headed for the home place as Fiona wrapped her arms around Bailey's waist and laid her head on his chest. "Are you sure you want to stay around for more of this?"

"Are you kidding? I'm thinking I'll take six months off from the production company, follow you around, and write an incredibly scary ghost story. It'll start when a mild-mannered Hollywood producer arrives in a small town in the Georgia mountains. I see the Oscars in our future."

"Sounds good." Fiona snapped her fingers, and a lit candle appeared in her hand.

As they walked away, he said, "Do you think Sarah would ever agree to fly on television?"

"You're just determined to be turned into some kind of animal, aren't you?"

"Maybe a crow," Bailey suggested.

"Absolutely not," Fiona said as she pulled him to the path toward home. "After these last few days I could never kiss a crow."

Epilogue

The soft laughter of the couple in the clearing floated through the trees. Catriona scowled after them. For spite, she called the wind and rain. Yet still she heard the young witch and her lover laughing.

White dress billowing, she walked after them, thinking of another couple, a young woman and her Cherokee brave. They had been so happy in their little cabin with their baby before her father ripped their lives apart.

Now Catriona brought lightning with every step. This was her woods, her place, and her altar for tribute.

Thinking of taking a Connelly, of causing them pain, should make her smile. So why was she weeping?

She only knew she hurt, she yearned, and she would have her due. Which Connelly would be taken and how hard would the others grieve? This generation was fighting hard, and she would punish them well.

She let go of the storm abruptly. Then she sobbed. She sent the sound echoing through the hills. Animals stirred in unease. Humans locked their doors. The Connelly witches stopped their pointless celebrating in the house beyond the woods. They should all heed her message.

Hear me weep, and be ready to die.

A word about the author...

Neely Powell is the pseudonym for co-writers Leigh Neely and Jan Hamilton Powell. Long-time friends, they're the authors of "The Witches of New Mourne" a paranormal series about a family coven, a centuries-old curse, and an enchanted town. *AWAKENING MAGIC* is available from The Wild Rose Press, Inc. *HAUNTING MAGIC* continues the story in 2017. Their first paranormal novel, *TRUE NATURE*, is also available from The Wild Rose Press.

Writing as Celeste Hamilton, Jan published 24 bestselling romance novels. Her day job is in corporate communications in Tennessee.

Leigh has a long resume as an editor and freelance writer and is managing editor of a regional magazine group in Florida.

Neely Powell writes about shifters, witches, werewolves, faeries, and ghosts, mixing in shades of mystery, romance, and thrillers—the kinds of books they both enjoy reading.

Web presences:
www.neelypowellauthor.com
www.facebook.com/NeelyPowellAuthor
https://www.twitter.com/@NeelyPowell3
www.pinterest.com/leigh2132
https://www.goodreads.com/author/Neely_Powell

Thank you for purchasing
this publication of The Wild Rose Press, Inc.

If you enjoyed the story, we would appreciate your
letting others know by leaving a review.

For other wonderful stories,
please visit our on-line bookstore at
www.thewildrosepress.com.

For questions or more information
contact us at
info@thewildrosepress.com.

The Wild Rose Press, Inc.
www.thewildrosepress.com

Stay current with The Wild Rose Press, Inc.

Like us on Facebook

https://www.facebook.com/TheWildRosePress

And Follow us on Twitter
https://twitter.com/WildRosePress